THE SPEED OF SOULS

THE SPEED OF SOULS

A NOVEL FOR DOG LOVERS

NICK PIROG

DECIQUIN

Published by Deciquin Books

Cover designed by Nick Venebles

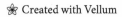 Created with Vellum

For Potter and Penny.
My forever dogs.

1

"LOSS"

Cassie

Life is fleeting.

Take the tadpole for example. Well, not one, but the many swimming in the small blue pool in the backyard. Amidst the layer of pollen on top (which keeps making me sneeze) and the dirt residing at the bottom (from my paws, I'm a digger) are hundreds of little tadpoles. They are at different stages. Some resemble nothing more than little floating worms, others have a bit more heft to them, corkscrewing their way through the water.

I know from previous summers that only a few tadpoles, the Chosen, will survive the long journey to Frogdom.

On the edge of the pool, a tiny frog sits quietly. He is green and shiny. I wonder if he's one of the tadpoles from last year.

I lean down until my nose is nearly touching him. I give him a sniff. He smells *froggy*. Startled by my apparent intrusion, the frog leaps off the rim of the plastic pool and jumps into the grass. The grass is long; it's been weeks since the men with the noisy machines have come. I sniff the frog out, sending him (all frogs are *hims* to me for some reason) jumping. We play this game for a long minute until he finds his way to the sanctuary of the wild mint that grows near the deck.

I bark twice.

Come back.

I want to play.

After a long minute, I return to the small pool and again find myself lost in the dance of the tadpoles. So much life. *Enjoy it while it lasts,* I want to tell them. You never know when your time will come. You never know when a dog—who is just trying to be friendly and wants to play—will accidentally, without malice, trample you to death.

Sorry, Greenie.

I do a lap of the yard, try to do some digging (but my heart's not in it), then head inside. My food bowl is in the kitchen. It's empty. It should have been full hours ago. Just a light film of water is left in my silver water bowl. I lie down next to it, licking up the last dredges.

I walk into the bedroom. Jerry is on his stomach, one arm draped over the side of the bed. All he's been doing for the past two months, since *it* happened, is sleeping. I lift my front paw and scratch the bed near his head.

Once, twice, three times.

Finally, he stirs, opening one eye. Jerry's eyes are blue. I remember the first time I saw them. It was the day he rescued me.

* * *

The Shelter wasn't all bad; in fact, compared to First Home and the Street, it was cushy living. No one screamed at you and hit you with a newspaper. No one made you wear a choke chain. You didn't have to dig through trash for food. Your water was always clean. I didn't know life got any better. I thought the Shelter was the jackpot. Then I saw those blue eyes.

He leaned down next to my cage. His knee hit the cage, making a loud rattle, and I hunkered in the corner.

"I'm sorry, girl," he said softly. As far as humans went, he was nothing special. But his eyes; I was mesmerized by his blue eyes. They sparkled with kindness. He slinked a few of his fingers through the cage and said, "It's okay, it's okay."

I was still hesitant. First Home said, "It's okay, it's okay," a lot. But it was never okay.

"What's her name?" the man asked a woman who filled my food bowl earlier.

"Cassie."

"Is she a golden retriever?"

"Border Collie, Golden Retriever *mix*. See those white markings on her face and feet? That's all collie.

"How old is she?"

"We think she's around four."

The man turned his attention back to me and said, "Hi, Cassie." His eyes crinkled and he added, "I just want to say, hi. That's all. I just want to say, hi."

Well, I can say hi, I remember thinking. And what could he do to me through the cage?

I slowly unfurled and took a half-step.

"Thatta girl," he said. "Come on, just a little closer."

I took two more half-steps.

The man wiggled his fingers through the cage. I leaned forward and gave a few light sniffs. His fingers smelled like pickles. I took another step forward until his fingers gently brushed the fur above my nose.

"Do you want to come home with me, girl?" he asked.

I did.

So badly.

I gave his fingers a lick and did a twirl.

"I'll take that as a yes," he said, his blue eyes beginning to water.

* * *

Now six years later, Jerry's second eye opens. Just as quickly, it closes.

I bark.

"Go back to bed," Jerry mumbles, turning over on his back and scratching at the patchy brown fur on his face.

No.

I will not let you sleep your life away.

And I'm hungry!

I jump on the bed, stick my nose in his ear, and lick his face.

"Cassie! C'mon!"

Get up! Get up! Get up!

"Just let me sleep a little longer," he says.

I hop off the bed and go grab my water bowl. I jump on the bed and drop the bowl on Jerry's chest.

"What the he—"

His eyes open, then close. "Ten minutes!"

I bite the blanket by his feet.

"Ouch! Cassie! Stop!"

I bite again and again.

"Fine, I'm up!"

With eyes half open, Jerry fills my water bowl, then he goes to the storage closet and fills a big cup with food and dumps it in my bowl. He goes back to the storage closet and I hear him refilling the cup.

Not again.

He comes out of the closet, takes two steps in my direction, then his half-open eyes spring open.

There is only one bowl to fill.

Not two.

Like I said.

Life is fleeting.

Jerry

This is the third time I've done this in the last two months. It had become such a routine, so autonomous to fill up *two* bowls with kibble.

It takes me a few breaths to compose, another breath to will the moisture back into my tear ducts, then I head back to the storage closet and dump the kibble and the large measuring cup into the plastic dog food container.

Cassie is lying next to her dog bowl. I'm not sure if it's my current state, or simply the morning rays shining through the window highlighting her golden and white coat, but I'm once again struck by her beauty. Her ears curl forward, resting near her large amber eyes.

I get down on my haunches and say, "I'm sorry, girl."

It's an all-encompassing sorry. I'm sorry I haven't walked you lately, played with you, that I haven't taken you to the lake in two months, that I let your water bowl get empty, that I didn't feed you on time, that I keep forgetting there is only one of you now.

She gives my hand a couple of soft licks.

"I'll try to do better," I tell her.

I open the refrigerator and pop open a clamshell of blueberries. They are Cassie's favorite. Hugo was all cheese and bacon, but not Cassie. She likes carrots, apples, and especially blueberries. I imagine if she were human, she would have been one of those yogis.

I hand-feed her a few berries, watching her savor each one as though it is an immeasurable delicacy. That was another difference between her and Hugo. Hugo would devour his food, or treat, with force, with animosity, *how dare you not have been eaten already*. But Cassie was a nibbler, a savorer. One bite of kibble at a time, chew, chew, chew, swallow. Then gingerly pick up another.

I hold out a blueberry and tell her to sit.

She does.

We go through the rest of the routine.

Lie down.

Shake.

Twirl.

Play dead.

But she won't.

Not since *it* happened.

My heart would rip in half, but there's nothing left to tear. Like when you rip a piece of paper in half, then rip those pieces in half. It's easy the first couple times, but when you get to the fifth or sixth rip, the pieces are so small, the callus of paper so thick, it becomes nearly impossible.

I let out a sigh, give Cassie a head rub, then find my way to my desk and laptop. I flip it open and check my email. I have a backlog of emails, mostly from fans, plus an email from my agent, Chuck. I open his email. It's two words: *Call me!!!*

I find my phone, turn it on, and see I have twenty-five missed text messages. All but a handful are from Chuck. They date back nearly eight weeks. The others are from my mom or Alex. I disregard the texts from Alex—I'm sure they're just pictures of girls from whatever dating app he's currently using—then skim over my mother's texts. Mostly it's her asking if I'm okay. Her last text is from a few days earlier, informing me that they will be here mid-June and are staying for most of the summer.

Here is South Lake Tahoe.

I've been living in my parents' vacation home for the past three years. I don't want them living with me for the summer, but my piddly royalty checks hardly cover my monthly living expenses, and my parents have been letting me live rent-free for the past six months. I would just have to put up with them. Not that they're bad, in fact, they're great, but no thirty-five-year-old man should be forced to cohabitate with his parents for three months. But on the bright side, it will be good for Cassie. Two more people to lather her in love. And maybe take her for a walk.

I skim through Chuck's text thread, which is redundant and can be summed up by "Where is the book?"

I hit the call button and the phone rings.

Chuck picks up on the second ring. "Jerry!"

"Hey, Chuck."

"Long time."

"Yeah, sorry."

"How you doing?"

I take a deep breath. "Better."

"I went through it with my cat a few years back. It's tough."

I want to say, "Your cat was fifteen, Chuck, and she couldn't hear and she could barely see. She had a long, full life. Hugo didn't reach his *third* birthday. He had an entire life ahead of him." I don't. That cat could have been Chuck's whole life for all I know. Though with a wife and three kids, I doubt it. Still, if I'd learned anything in the past couple months, it was not to judge someone's capacity for love. *Or* their grieving process.

"Yeah, it is," I say.

There's a small pause, then Chuck says, "So, the book?"

"Yeah, the book."

"How's it progressing?"

I tilt my head back and gaze at the skylight set in the stained wood high above. "It's going great. I've really thrown myself into it. Helps keep my mind off things."

It's a lie. I haven't written a word since Hugo died.

"Really? That's great to hear. Can you send me what you got? Alison has been hounding me for a draft."

Alison is my editor at HarperCollins. They signed me to a five-book deal after *Pluto Three* climbed to #6 on the *New York Times* bestseller list.

"You know how I am with drafts," I say.

I don't like letting people read first drafts. First drafts notoriously suck—at least mine do—and the story is still fluid. There's nothing worse than hearing a bunch of opinions, good or bad, while the story still has an active heartbeat.

"I know," Chuck says, "it's just, they're a little worried over there."

Tell me something I don't know.

Pluto Immersion, my follow-up to *Pluto Three*, had been, in a word, a flop. It made the publishing house money, but it was widely considered a miscarriage of words. A rush project for the money that didn't deliver. It currently carried a 2.7 customer review rating on Amazon. And my follow-up, follow-up, *Pluto Destiny* was so bad HarperCollins almost decided not to publish. And in hindsight, they shouldn't have. They did a 150,000 copy first run and only sold 40,000. It had a 1.9 rating on Amazon and the last review I read, maybe three months back, simply said, "I hate Jerry Ryman for having made me read this crap."

I feel a lick on my ankle and glance under my desk. Cassie is curled near my feet. I smile at her, then turn my attention back to the call. "Give me three months," I say.

"Three months?"

I know this is a stretch. I'm already four months past my deadline. "Yeah, three months. It will be worth it."

"I'll see what I can do, but they're not gonna be happy."

There isn't much they can do. They already paid me the advance.

"Tell them I said that I promise it will sell more copies than *Pluto Three*."

Chuck must be stunned because he doesn't say anything for a long second. I've never said anything like this before. In fact, I hardly ever brought up *Pluto Three*.

"Wow, well, then, shit, okay," he stammers.

I laugh.

"Okay then, I'm stoked buddy," he says. "I guess I'll leave you to it."

We hang up.

I look down at Cassie and shake my head. "Why did I say that? Better than *Pluto Three*? What was I thinking?"

She glances up with her amber eyes and pants. She doesn't know either.

I click on Google Drive and open the folder for my new book. It's called *Citizen Three*. I'd nearly driven the *Pluto* series into the ground with the second and third installments, but I thought a prequel would appeal to an audience.

I click open the manuscript document and scroll down. I have twelve chapters written, which is half done. Could I whip out the second half in three months?

Sure, I could.

Summer season in South Lake Tahoe was getting ready to explode. There would be fifty thousand new tourists each weekend from the end of June until the beginning of September. While all those people were splashing around in the lake, gambling at the casinos, and altogether having a great time, I would be hunkered over my laptop at Starbucks, guzzling Passion Tango iced tea by the gallon.

And if I threw myself back into the book—like I told Chuck I had—it would take my mind off Hugo. Maybe give me a reprieve from the hundreds of small things that reminded me of him. The tile floor in the bathroom where he would sprawl out when it was hot. The big Nylabone that he would drop in my lap and want me to hold while he chewed on it. The broken molding on the bedroom door frame he smashed into when chasing after Cassie. Yelling at him to get his enormous head out of the toilet when there was perfectly good water in his bowl.

I type the words: *Chapter 13.*

I stare at them for a long minute. Then another. I open a new tab and go on Facebook. I shouldn't do what I'm about to do, but I can't stop. I click on *Photos* and scroll to a picture of Hugo.

He's coming out of the lake. He has two balls in his mouth. His orange tennis ball and another ball—a regular yellow tennis ball—

that a different dog was playing with. The other dog, a petite black lab, is behind Hugo, staring at him, uncomprehending: *why did you take my ball?*

But there is little the lab can do.

Hugo is, well, huge. Even by Bernese Mountain Dog standards. Most Bernese top out at one hundred pounds. Hugo went to the vet a few weeks before the photo was taken. He was one hundred and eight pounds.

Cassie was the one to pick him out.

* * *

Cassie and I had recently relocated to South Lake Tahoe after living in downtown San Francisco for the previous four years. *Pluto Immersion* had come out three months earlier and was in the process of flopping. I was hard at work on *Pluto Destiny*, not to mention nursing a broken heart after a girl I was engaged to left me for another guy. Cassie had a bunch of dog friends where we lived in San Francisco, but at our commiserative refuge in Tahoe, there was nobody to play with.

After a few lonely months, I decided Cassie needed a playmate. Two hours later, we were at a breeder on the outskirts of Sacramento called Bernese Mountain Bliss.

The owner, Bonnie, a woman in her early fifties who had been breeding Bernese Mountain Dogs for going on twenty years, led Cassie and me around to the back of the property where four adult Bernese and a litter of twelve puppies roamed the freshly cut three acres. Immediately, Cassie and I were under attack by a vicious pack of black, tan, and white, balls of fluff. They were small, no more than fifteen pounds, but they had these amazingly massive paws, like little kids running around with boxing gloves on.

The nine-week-old puppies each wore a different colored

piece of yarn around their necks to distinguish them. There was one puppy who I was immediately drawn to: Green.

Green quickly took a liking to my shoes and within a short minute, he'd untied both my shoelaces and pulled my left shoe off my foot. He was so rambunctious. I was already in love with him.

But Cassie had other ideas.

She was rolling around in the grass a few feet from me, four or five of the puppies pouncing on her, nibbling at her ears, and sniffing every inch of her. While I was busy playing with Green, Cassie picked up one of the puppies by the scruff of its neck and *literally* dropped the puppy in my lap.

Red.

He looked up at me with his light brown eyes and floppy ears and wiggled his little butt. He was adorable, but I'd already made my choice; Green was coming home with us.

"Sorry, girl," I said to Cassie.

I pushed myself up from the ground and made my way over to where Bonnie was sitting in a chair, drinking iced tea.

"I'm gonna go with Green," I told her.

She flashed a knowing smile and said, "He's going to be a handful," then went into the house to grab the paperwork.

I felt a soft nuzzle on my hand and turned.

It was Cassie.

There was something in her mouth.

Red.

I couldn't help but laugh.

Cassie dropped Red at my feet and then she did something I still haven't heard since. She barked five times. (Cassie rarely barked and never more than three times in a row.)

Bonnie returned with the paperwork and with a scrunch of her forehead, said, "I thought you were going to take Green?"

I glanced down at Cassie, then Red—who was on his back sniffing his little wiener—and said, "Change of plans."

* * *

The little puppy was an instant influx of energy and love. My flopping book, Avery's dumping me, having to move into my parents' house, none of these things mattered. All that mattered was the uncoordinated, flailing ball of love that had come into our lives.

I didn't have a name for him for the first two days, but on the third day, he was chasing Cassie around and he bumped into my dresser and knocked over my Hugo plaque—an award given to the best sci-fi book each year—which I'd won for *Pluto Three*.

I remember picking up the plaque, then looking at the big, lumbering puppy and it clicked.

Hugo.

* * *

I scroll through photos for half an hour, then I grab my phone and pull up my videos. I find the most recent video and push play.

We're in the backyard. It's late February and we'd just gotten a crazy snow storm. There is easily three feet of powder and Hugo and Cassie are going nuts jumping, diving, and rolling in the snow.

I watch the video several times. It's the last video of Hugo I will take. He will be dead less than forty-eight hours later.

I turn the phone off and flip the lid down on my laptop. A minute later, I'm back in bed. Cassie is next to me, licking the tears from my eye

2

"REBIRTH"

Hugo

I'm awake.

At least, I think I'm awake.

But if I'm awake, I should be able to see. But I can't see. I'm surrounded by darkness. I've been trying to open my eyes for the past few hours, but they won't work. Why won't my eyes work?

I can't hear either.

Or smell.

But I can feel. I can feel things moving all around me. Squirming against me. I want to yell at them, "Stop touching me!" But I can't speak either.

What is going on?

My brain is all swirly. Like when Jerry picked me up from the vet *after*. After they took my balls. Not my orange tennis balls. Not the ones that Jerry would throw and I would fetch. No, *my* balls— the ones between my legs.

I remember the drive back from the vet. My head was all swirly. And I had this stupid thing wrapped around my neck so I couldn't see very well. And when I got home, I just wanted to sleep. That's how I feel now.

Swirly.

And tired.

And hungry.

Luckily, there's food a couple of inches away. I don't know where it comes from, this magical food, but it's there. It tastes, well, like nothing. But all I want to do is eat it. All I want is this magical elixir.

I wonder where Jerry is.

Is he the one feeding me this magical elixir?

Jerry?

Jerry?

Oh, right, I can't bark.

What is going on?

* * *

It's been days now.

I still can't see.

I still can't smell.

But I can hear. A little bit. Sounds are dull, but they're there.

And my head. My head is less swirly.

Things are starting to come back to me. Images. A rabbit. Something about a rabbit.

Something is still touching me. Not something, *somethings*. Stay still you somethings!

And what is licking me?

Is that Cassie?

Cassie?

Cassie?

Ugh, I still can't bark.

But I can eat. Thank God for the never-ending supply of

magical elixir. It's always there. And it tastes now. It's sweet, like those shakes Jerry is always eating.

Where is Jerry?

Jerry?

Cassie?

What is going on?

* * *

Okay, it has to have been like a week by now.

The swirls are gone.

I still can't smell. Why can't I smell? Smelling was my thing. I miss smelling. The lake, grass, the wild mint in the backyard, cheese, bacon, Jerry, Jerry's shirts, Jerry's feet, Cassie, I loved smelling Cassie, mailboxes, those silver metal thingies, squirrels, rabbits.

The rabbit.

I remember now.

He jumped out right in front of me. What nerve. Going on a walk and he jumps out right there, right from the snow. He looked at me, right in the eye, then he took off. We were on the street by the place that smells like pancakes.

Jerry yelled, "No, Hugo! NO!"

But the rabbit, Jerry. The rabbit.

I pulled, pulled, pulled.

"Stop pulling, Hugo!" Jerry screamed.

I pulled harder. There was a snap. I could feel my collar come off. I was free.

The rabbit was in the street. I'd been trying to catch a rabbit for a while now, but I could never get one. Today, that would end. Today, I would get a rabbit.

I ran into the street.

"HUGO!" Jerry screamed. "HUGO!"

I was a couple of feet behind the rabbit.

Then darkness.

Then sleep.

Long sleep.

Then I woke up with the swirls.

But, like I said, the swirls are gone.

I try to open my eyes. I've been trying this for a week now. My eyelids, they are so heavy. Hold on, I think something happened.

Light.

Was that light?

I try again. Try to hold my eyes open for a few seconds.

Yes.

Light.

I can see.

* * *

I can keep my eyes open for a few hours at a time now. That's the good news. The bad news is that although I can see, I can't *really* see. All I see are blobs. The somethings that have been touching me are blobs of gray with little blobs of blue in the middle. There are five or six of these blobs, then one big blob. The big blob is connected to the magical elixir. I'm not sure how all this blob stuff works.

* * *

I open my eyes.

It takes me a moment.

I can't see perfectly, but I can see much better than when I fell asleep.

I turn my head and look at the somethings—the blobs—that have been touching me for all these days.

No.

It can't be.

The blobs.

The somethings.

They are tiny, little—

Cats!

I am surrounded by a bunch of little cats!

What is going on?

I glance up.

The big blob, the one connected to the magical elixir, is—

Oh, no.

Oh, no.

It's a big cat.

I've only met a few cats, but I don't like them. There was a big orange cat that lived in the house across the street. All it ever did was sit in the big window and do nothing. I would bark at him and nothing. I was fifty times bigger than him, but he didn't seem to care. Another cat would climb on our back fence every once in a while. I would bark at him and scratch at the fence and the cat would just sit there licking its paw and ignoring me. Then it would hiss at me, then run off.

Those cats were small. But the cat here, now, is huge.

Why do I feel like the magical elixir cat is bigger than me?

Why am I so small?

Why am I so small and why am I surrounded by a bunch of little cats and one big cat?

I turn and look around.

All I see is brown.

Tall brown walls on every side.

Where is Jerry?

Where is Cassie?

What is going on?

I try to bark.

Nothing comes out.

I squirm away from the little cats. My legs are all wobbly. I take a couple of steps, fall, take a couple more. I look up at the giant wall of brown. It soars high above me. But at some point, it stops and gives way to a white sky.

Why am I in this little brown house with no roof, surrounded by a bunch of little cats and one big cat that is connected to a magical elixir machine?

What is going on?

Jerry?

Cassie?

I'm scared.

I hear a voice.

I look up.

High in the sky. Is that? A human? Some sort of giant?

The giant reaches down and picks me up.

It brings me close to its face.

It's a human.

A she-human.

A *giant* she-human.

"Hi there, little guy," she says.

She rubs her finger on my head.

From up high, I look down at where the giant pulled me from. It isn't a giant brown house. It's a box. A cardboard box with a yellow blanket inside. The cardboard box is on the ground inside a house. An *actual* house. But the house isn't mine. It isn't where I live. It isn't Jerry's, Cassie's, and my house.

The she-human holds me in one hand.

Why do I fit in a she-human's hand? How big is this giant? Had I stumbled into a land of giant humans and giant cats?

The giant she-human says, "Say hi to the world."

I turn around.

The giant is holding something in her hand. It's like Jerry's, only it seems bigger. I know it's called a "phone."

Sometimes when Cassie and I were lying next to Jerry on the couch, he would take out his phone and hold it up like how the giant she-human was doing now. Then I would see myself on the phone. I'm not sure how it worked. But there I was on his phone and then this little light would flash. Then I would be living on his phone. Jerry would say, "That's a good one," or, "You guys are such dorks," or, "I look kind of fat in this one."

I look at the phone the giant she-human is holding. I see her face in the phone. Her hand. There is something in her hand.

Wait.

I cock my head to the side. The something on the phone cocks its head to the side.

I open my mouth. The something on the phone opens its mouth.

Ah, barf.

I'm a cat.

3

"GROWING UP KITTEN"

Hugo

I'm a cat.

I used to be a dog. Now I'm a cat. And not just a cat. A little cat. A *baby* cat.

How could I be a dog one minute and then a baby cat the next?

Is this all a dream?

It seems too real to be a dream: the five other baby cats surrounding me; the Big Cat that all the baby cats are snuggled against; the brown walls of the cardboard box; the giant she-human who comes and goes.

If it is a dream, it's a nightmare. But if it's a nightmare, then Jerry would have woken me up by now. I'd seen him do it with Cassie before. When she would be asleep on the bed and her legs would be twitching and she would be making these weird huffing noises. Jerry would rub her face and her ears and tell her she was just having a bad dream—"a nightmare"—and that everything would be okay.

I want Jerry to wake me up. I want Jerry to rub my face and my ears and to tell me everything will be okay. But he can't. Because this isn't a dream. This is real.

But if this is real, then how did it happen? How does one go about being a dog one minute and then a baby cat the next?

I have so many questions: How did this happen? Why did this happen? Where are Jerry and Cassie? Where am I? Where is my house? Where is the Lake? Where are the Mountains? Why are my nails so small and pointy?

I think maybe the Big Cat might have answers, but I can't talk. I can open my mouth, but nothing comes out. The Big Cat stares at me when I do this, when I try to ask her a question. She'll stare at me, then lick me, then she'll nudge me toward one of the magical elixir faucets hidden in her light gray fur.

That's what I'm doing now. Drinking from one of her faucets.

I'm smashed between five other baby cats who are all drinking from other faucets. After a long drink, I feel a poke on my back and turn. It's one of the other baby cats. He pokes at me with his paw.

He's white and light gray with a few darker gray stripes on his head. He has a tiny little black nose surrounded by white whiskers. He has small triangular ears and big blue eyes. I only saw myself on the giant she-human's phone for a quick second, but I know I look pretty much the same. This can be said for all the baby cats, except one, who is all-gray like the Big Cat.

The baby cat pokes me again with his paw.

Oh, no, you don't.

I lift one of my tiny pathetic little paws and push him backward. He rears back on his hind legs, then falls over. He rights himself, then he pounces on me. I fall backward. I bite him on the shoulder. He doesn't yelp and I remember that I don't have any teeth.

Two more baby cats join in, pouncing and tumbling. I try to inflict as much damage as I can, but the baby cats don't seem to understand. They think I'm playing.

Finally, after a couple more minutes, the wrestling match ends. The other baby cats slink back to the Big Cat and squirm their way between the others.

I don't.

I pad across the yellow blanket to the far corner of the box, as far away from the Big Cat and the baby cats as I can get, and curl up in a tight ball.

* * *

I'm starving.

I don't know how long it's been since my last drink from the magical faucet. I've stayed in my corner. Stayed curled up in a ball. The giant she-human picked me up and put me back next to the Big Cat a few times, but each time I would crawl back to my corner.

A few of the baby cats had come over. A few poked me, but I didn't react. I was protesting. Protesting being a cat.

I almost give up a few times.

I'm so hungry.

All I can think about is the magical elixir.

I close my eyes and try to think about anything else. Anything besides food. I think about Jerry and Cassie. I think about how much I miss them. How I miss Jerry's smelly feet. Cassie licking my ears. My orange tennis ball. Jerry throwing my orange tennis ball. Chasing the squirrels and raccoons. I miss sleeping on the bed next to Jerry. I miss Cassie resting her head on my back. And kibble. A big bowl of kibble. And bacon. And cheese.

Food.

All I can think about is food.

I open my eyes. All the baby cats are snuggled into the side of the Big Cat. I can see a couple of them drinking from the faucets.

The Big Cat stares at me. Unlike all the baby cats, her eyes are gold. She stares at me for a couple of long seconds. Then she wiggles her way out from beneath the baby cats. She walks over to me and licks my head.

Stop it, Big Cat.

She licks my body.

I said, stop it!

I feel a pinch on my neck. Then I'm floating. It takes me a moment to realize the Big Cat is holding me in her mouth. She sets me down next to her belly, then nudges my head toward one of the pink faucets.

I don't want to, but I open my mouth and drink.

It's more delicious than I remember. The whole time I drink, the Big Cat licks my head.

I guess the Big Cat isn't so bad.

* * *

I've gotten bigger. And I can make noise now. It's not much. Just a little squeak really. But it's something. And we are no longer in the cardboard box.

We're in a room. I don't know what it's called. It has the same kind of floor—the kind that is nice and cool and where I used to sleep when it was too hot—as the place where Jerry takes his baths. But there is no bath.

There's a big white fence in the doorway. The fence has holes in it. They are too small for me to fit through. Trust me; I tried. But I can see through the holes. I can see a couch. I can see carpet. I can see a TV. I can see the giant she-human walking around.

She visits more often now. Sometimes she'll come into the room and sit down. She'll take turns picking us up and petting us. She is always putting us on her phone. She's no Jerry, but she seems like an okay human.

When she isn't around, mostly I've been playing.

Yeah, I know, I'm a traitor.

I'm no closer to understanding any of this dog-into-cat stuff, but I'm pretty sure it isn't any of the baby cats' faults. They just want to pounce, tumble, and wrestle. They are harmless. Well, mostly harmless. They have teeth now. These tiny little daggers (I have them too). Sometimes, the baby cats bite too hard and I have to give them a whack on the head. I learned this from Cassie. It's what she did to me when I was a baby dog and I would bite her.

These baby cats don't know anything.

That's the difference between them and me.

I'm a baby cat, but I know stuff. I know not to bite hard.

* * *

There's a sound. I look up. I feel the other two baby cats I'm curled up with look up as well.

It's the she-human. She's doing something to the big white fence in the doorway. There's a crunching sound, then the fence is moving, then it's gone.

The two other baby cats and I scramble to our feet.

I run forward to where the fence used to be, where the bath-floor turns into the carpet. The carpet is much taller than I remember carpet being. I've come to the realization I'm not living in a giant world. The giant she-human is just a she-human. Everything looks big because I'm so small.

I jump onto the carpet. It smells like I remember. I turn around and look over my shoulder. All five baby cats are on their feet, but they haven't moved. They look confused.

I let out a little squeak. My loudest yet.

Come on; it's okay.

The all-gray baby cat takes a couple of hesitant steps forward, then jumps onto the carpet. His eyes are the same color as the Big Cat's eyes now. (All of the baby cats' eyes have changed color. Some are green. Others are orange. I'm not so sure about this eyes changing colors thing.) Another quickly follows. Then another, until all five of the baby cats cross to the carpet. I wait to see if the

Big Cat will come. She raises her head for a moment, then lies back down on her side.

I turn back around and run. It's the first time I've run in, well, I'm not sure how long. I run toward the couch towering above me. I reach out my paw and scrape it against the side. Something happens. My paw sticks to the couch. (It's my little tiny nails!) I reach out another paw, a little higher, and my paw sticks. I do this again. Then again.

I can *climb*.

When I'm halfway up, I fall. I should land on my back, but somehow I flip my body over right before I hit the carpet and land on my feet.

I try to climb again. This time I make it onto the couch. Another baby cat has done the same thing. He sees me and pounces on me. We roll around on the couch.

I hear the she-human laughing and look up. She's holding her phone in her hand. Following us on the couch with it.

"You guys are so funny," she says.

Then she walks away. I see her on her hands and knees. She is following another of the baby cats with the phone.

I squirm from beneath the other baby cat and climb one of the cushions. I make it to the top and I look around. I can see the TV across from me. There are no pictures moving on it right now. Between the couch and the TV is a table. The table was the only thing Jerry wouldn't let me get on. (Couch—okay. Bed—okay. Table—*not* okay.)

I turn my head and I see it.

A window.

I know what is on the other side of the window.

Outside.

I love Outside.

I jump off the couch. I brace for impact when I hit the carpet, but it's as though I weigh nothing. Like I've floated to the ground.

I run toward the window. It's high. Higher than the couch. I won't be able to get up there. I look around for the she-human. Maybe she can lift me up.

I let out one of my squeaks.

Come here, she-human! Lift me up so I can see Outside.

She doesn't come.

There are things hanging around the side of the window. We didn't have these at Home. I don't know what these are called.

I look at the couch, then back to these *things*.

I can do it.

I climb back up the couch, then go to the far edge. Without thinking, I jump. I hold out my paws. I hit one of the things. My paws stick. I climb up the thing until I come to the windowsill. I crawl on the windowsill, which is twice as wide as I am, and press my face to the cold glass.

Outside.

I see big, tall houses that are nearly touching one another. And the street. It isn't flat. It goes down at a steep angle. There are a bunch of cars on the street. The sky is gray.

Where is all the grass? Where is the little blue pool? Where is the wild mint? Where is the sun? Where are the big pine trees?

This is not my Outside.

* * *

"Go potty," the she-human says.

She keeps putting me in this weird-shaped box filled with smelly sand and saying this.

If she wants me to go potty, then she should take me Outside. To the grass. I didn't see any grass, but surely there must be grass somewhere. Surely, every Outside has grass.

I jump out of the sand and walk toward the white fence. It's back. The she-human takes it away for a few hours a day, lets us explore the house, then she puts us back in the room. Then she puts the white fence back.

I paw at the fence.

The she-human picks me up and puts me in the sand.

"Go potty," she repeats.

I squeak.

I am not pooping in this weird sand.

But the thing is, I really have to poop. And pee. And I don't want to poop and pee on the floor anymore. It's embarrassing. The other baby-cats don't seem to care; they poop and pee whenever they want.

"Go potty," she says for the one-thousandth time.

Fine.

I go poop.

"Good job," she says, clapping her hands.

I hate being a cat.

4

"FARMERS' MARKET"

Cassie

The tadpoles are bigger. Over the course of the last month, I've watched them grow (I haven't had a whole lot else to do). Each day they are a little bigger. But each day, there are fewer of them. The ones that don't make it float to the surface. Sometimes I will give them a little tap with my paw to make sure they aren't sleeping. Sometimes they flutter, then zip around, but mostly, they just lie there. The ones that have made it this far—the Chosen ones—have tails now, zipping around the small pool like little fish.

This is my fourth year watching the tadpoles. Jerry likes to make fun of me for just staring at the water. He would say, "I bought that baby pool for you guys, not for those silly tadpoles. Don't you want to get in?"

But I don't want to go in, Jerry. I don't want to kill any of the frog babies.

Sometimes Hugo would want to get in and I would have to guard the pool. Hugo was nearly as big as the pool; he would send half the water spilling out. (Not on my watch!)

But now it's just me and Jerry. And the tadpoles.

I watch the water and count the tadpoles.

One. Two. Three. Four. Five. Six. Seven. Eight. Nine. Ten. (There are more, but this is as high as I can count.)

After another few minutes, I make my way to the fence and peek through one of the cracks between the boards. Sitting in the dirt on the other side of his yard is Storm.

I bark.

Hi, Storm.

I've known Storm since we moved here. He's a Husky. We have different walking schedules, so I've only gotten to sniff him a few times. (He has the same color eyes as Jerry!) I mostly know him through the fence. He used to come up to the fence and say hi, but he doesn't do much these days. He just lies in the dirt. And in the winter, he lies in the snow.

I bark again, but Storm doesn't flinch. I don't think he can hear anymore. (But he can still sing. I hear him singing to the moon every once in a while.)

I hear a rustling and turn around.

Jerry is standing in the doorway. He looks different. The fur on his face is gone. I can see his cheeks! And he's holding something. It takes me a moment to realize. My leash!

I bark a couple times and twirl.

Twirl, twirl, twirl.

I run to him and put my paws on his chest.

This better not be some sort of sick joke, Jerry.

"Let's go for a walk, girl," he says.

Did he just say the W-word?

Twirl, twirl, twirl.

I can't stop twirling.

Jerry clips my leash to my collar.

"Slow down!" Jerry yells.

I'm pulling him toward the gate.

Sorry, Jerry.

I sit and take a couple calming breaths. It's just a walk, Cassie. You've been on hundreds of walks.

Jerry opens the gate and I dart through.

"Cassie!"

Oh, right.

"I know you're excited, girl, but you've got to calm down."

Okay, Jerry. Only for you.

I calm down and Jerry and I start our walk. Jerry is a good walker. Sometimes when I see other dogs with their humans, the humans are always pulling them along. Not Jerry. He lets me stop and sniff things as long as I want.

I sniff a couple of flowers, then turn around and glance up at Jerry. He's wearing a head-hider, shading his blue eyes from the sun. He looks at me and his lips curve. It isn't quite a smile, but it's the closest he's come since Hugo died.

We continue down a few more streets, then I smell it. One of the most glorious smells in the world. A smell called Kettle Corn.

It's been almost a year, but I immediately know where we're going. The Farmers' Market.

Julie!

We walk another couple of blocks. I don't stop to smell anything. I just want to get to the market. To the kettle corn and Julie.

We round a corner and all the tents come into view. There are lots of humans walking around the tents and a few other dogs. One of the first tents we come to is the blueberry tent. Jerry asks for a sample. That's the thing about Jerry; he's always asking for "samples."

Jerry holds out a blueberry for me. It's huge, twice the size of the blueberries I'm used to. I take it and bite it gingerly, letting all the juices flow out and swim over my tongue. It's amazing. It's the best blueberry I've ever had.

We walk past a few more tents, then I see her.

Julie.

Julie is my favorite human. (Well, after Jerry. Jerry is *my* human. Julie is my favorite human who isn't mine. She's Alex's. I know that.)

I bark.

Julie!!!

Julie's eyes open wide when she sees me and she runs around the table filled with head-hiders. She falls to her knees and wraps her small arms around my neck and screams, "Cassie!"

Jerry

I watch as Cassie's golden/white-tipped tail helicopters and she licks Julie's face. Cassie's tail doesn't helicopter often. Only when she sees a few different people: my dad, one particular UPS delivery man, and Julie.

"Hi, Julie," I say.

Julie glances up and says, "Hi, Jerry."

Julie is ten years old. She has brown hair, big brown eyes, and adorably crooked teeth.

"Where's your dad?"

"He had to run to the car real quick. He should be back in a few minutes."

Alex, Julie's dad, is my best friend in Tahoe. It can also be said he is my *only* friend in Tahoe. We met a few months after I first moved here. He jump-started my car in the Safeway parking lot, then told me I was buying him a beer at the bar across the street.

Three beers later and we were BFFs.

Alex is a website designer, but he also owns a custom hat company, of which he sells a good many at the weekly Farmers' Market over the course of the summer.

I'm wearing one of his hats now. It's blue with the words "Tah Ho" embossed in yellow on the front. Not the cleverest of brand names but catchy enough that plenty of the tourists—primarily of the female variety, which no doubt was the driving force behind the name—will drop $25 for one of his custom "lids."

After giving Cassie a nice rub behind the ears and a kiss on the nose, Julie stands up. She's all legs. She looks like someone is pulling her apart like a piece of warm taffy.

She comes up and gives me a hug and says, "Sorry about Hugo."

The last time I saw Julie was a few days before Hugo died, when the three of us went to see the latest Pixar film. Alex split custody of Julie with his ex-girlfriend, so he has her half the week and every other Saturday.

"Thanks," I say, forcing my voice not to break.

So far, I've done a good job of keeping Hugo out of mind. But the Farmers' Market was one of his favorite places, and I can feel the soldiers of sadness getting ready to storm my brain. Thankfully, there's movement at the back of the tent—Alex dipping under the back, carrying a load of hats—and I'm able to fight back the surfacing memories.

Even after being friends with the guy for more than three years, it's impossible not to see him and smile. With his curly blond hair, giant handlebar mustache, and Buddha gut, he looks like the grown version of a rosy-cheeked cherub who has made a lifetime of poor decisions. At first glance, it's easy to write him off as a buffoon, but according to his IQ and Mensa status, he's closer to a genius.

Alex's eyes and mouth both open wide. He drops the hats, rushes around the display table, envelops me in his rotund arms, and shouts, "You finally got out of the house!" loud enough so that all the surrounding booth owners pause for a moment to glance up.

"Yeah."

He smacks the bill of my hat and says, "That's good marketing right there. A bestselling author wearing one of my lids."

I laugh.

He grabs my arm and shouts, "Hey, this is a bestselling author right here!"

I feel the blood rush to my cheeks and I stare at the ground. (Alex does this all the time. It doesn't matter where we are: the beach, the casino, the movie theater, a restaurant, the grocery store; it's relentless.) I glance up and see nobody is even looking at me.

My stomach unclenches.

"Can I take Cassie to get some kettle corn?" Julie asks.

The big kettle corn truck is at the far end of the Farmers' Market. Julie had been the one to first slip Cassie one of the sweetened pieces of popcorn a couple of years earlier and Cassie has been obsessed ever since.

"Sure."

I pass over Cassie's leash and the two disappear into the crowd.

Alex slaps me on the back and says, "So what have you been doing?"

"Sleeping mostly."

He nods.

Alex's mom died of cancer a few years before I met him. If anyone knows what it's like to lose someone you love, it's him. And if anyone knows how attached I was to my dogs, it's Alex.

"Oh, shit," he says. "You got to check out this girl behind you. She's perfect for you, man."

I turn and glance over my shoulder.

Alex and my tastes differ considerably, but for the first time, I agree with him. She's a petite brunette. She's wearing little yoga pants. And the best part: she's with her dog, a German Shepherd. She *is* perfect.

"Go talk to her, man," Alex prods.

I think about it. I think how easy it would be to go over there and say, "Hi, I'm Jerry." Then ask about her dog. But my feet are frozen. They are stuck in concrete.

I will myself to take a half-step in the girl's direction, but then I waver and turn back around.

"You're such a wuss," Alex says.

My inability to talk to women drives Alex crazy. I've attempted to be his wingman a few times at the casinos and it's never ended well. Though far from a Casanova, Alex is fearless and moreover, persistent. He will often cozy up to a girl who shows zero interest in him and wear her down over a number of hours until she finally gives up and goes home with him.

Alex would continue shaming me if not for the two young ladies approaching his booth. The girls are cute, probably sisters, either still in high school or just starting college. They are undoubtedly on a family vacation with their parents. This should deter Alex.

It doesn't.

He raises his eyebrows a few times at me, then heads back to his booth and begins hawking his wares.

I inwardly sigh.

On the attractive scale, I certainly have Alex by a point or two. Sure my hairline is running away from my forehead like a frightened gazelle, and sure, if I wear a red shirt to Target people will think I work there (I learned this the hard way), and sure, I'm somehow simultaneously both skinny and fat, but all things considered, I'm a decent-looking guy. People always comment on my eyes and how blue they are and my teeth are freakishly perfect even though I never had braces. And technically, I *am* a bestselling author. How many guys can say that?

Then there's Avery. She's one of the most beautiful girls on the planet. A ten in most men's considerations. She couldn't enter a room without all the men literally stopping for a half-second as if hit by stun guns. And I dated her. No, I was *engaged* to her.

But the thing is, *she* hit on me. She overheard me talking to my agent at the coffee shop. Chuck called to tell me a few movie studios had expressed interest in buying the movie rights to *Pluto Three*. He threw out numbers. Numbers in the high six-figures. Numbers I may have repeated within ear-shot of a stunning brunette. Avery pounced the moment I hung up. She asked if I wanted to take her out for sushi.

I suppose in the long run this was a curse. For the last three years, I've been waiting for another girl to hit on me. But that isn't how it works. Maybe in San Francisco, but not in Tahoe.

I glance back over my shoulder at the girl. She's moved over a booth, to a guy who sells honey.

I take two breaths.

Okay, Jerry, you can do this.

On three.

One.

Two.

Three.

Four.

Five.

I let out a long sigh, then walk to Alex's booth. The girls are still there. Alex glances up at me and gives me a quick shake of the head. Then he says, "Girls, this is Jerry. Jerry, this is Amanda and Hannah. They're here on vacation. And guess what, their parents got them their own room."

Cassie

The kettle corn is even better than I remember.

Julie takes a kernel out of the bag and throws it in the air. I follow it with my eyes, then snatch it out of the air in my mouth. I bite into it, hear the gratifying crunch, then swallow. The sweetness lingers on my tongue for a moment and just as it recedes, Julie throws another kernel in the air.

We play this game for a while and I catch most of them. But Julie loves it when I miss, sometimes doubling over with the giggles, so I miss a few on purpose to make her happy. I love Julie's laugh. It's maybe my favorite sound in the world. (Well, one of them. My *very* favorite is the sound that Jerry makes when he sleeps. *Urnggggggg. Urnggggggggg. Urngggggg.*)

Speaking of Jerry, I can see him standing by himself, not far from where Alex's tent is. He keeps looking at something. *Staring* at something. It's a dog. A German Shepherd. He's black and brown. And big. I think about Hugo. God, I miss him. That's why Jerry must be staring at him. He must remind Jerry of Hugo.

Poor Jerry.

"You missed another one, Cassie," Julie says.

I glance around. There are four popcorn kernels on the ground around me. This no longer matters.

I walk toward Jerry.

"Whoa, Cassie! Slow down."

Sorry, Julie.

By the time I get to Jerry, he's at Alex's tent, next to two young girls. I don't like them. They smell. Like *Her.*

Julie gives my leash to Jerry. Then she goes behind the table where Alex is. I sit down next to Jerry.

Jerry leans down and asks me, "Did you get some kettle corn?"

I bark.

Yes, I did. It was amazing.

I lick his face. He seems okay. He doesn't seem sad. He seems something else.

Before I can figure it out, the girls reach down and pet me. I want to growl at them, but I don't. I know it will make Jerry upset. So I let them pet me with their big rings on their fingers and their smelliness. I know the smell is called Perfume. Finally, after a few more pets, they start talking to Alex, putting different head-hiders on.

I turn my attention back to Jerry. I perk up my ears. I can hear a rustling. It's coming from Jerry's belly. I can hear his stomach churning. It's how he gets when he sits in front of the computer lately.

But why here? Why is the German Shepherd making Jerry's stomach rumble?

As if reading my mind, Jerry turns his head and glances at the German Shepherd. I follow his gaze. Then I realize it isn't the German Shepherd. It's the German Shepherd's human. The girl is making Jerry's stomach rumble.

I know Jerry wants a playmate. He wants another human. A female human. Especially now. Especially after what happened to Hugo.

But I'm not so sure about this. Not after what happened with Her. And I want Jerry to myself. I don't want to share him. But I know a female human playmate will make Jerry happy. And that's all I want. All I want is for Jerry to be happy.

I bark.

Go talk to her.

"What?" Jerry asks.

I bark again.

Jerry doesn't move, so I start pulling him. Pulling him toward the girl.

"Cassie!" he shouts.

The girl and the German Shepherd are a few tents away. I pull, pull, pull Jerry toward the pair.

I can hear Jerry stumbling behind me.

"Where are you going?" he keeps shouting.

Jerry

37

Cassie is dragging me through the Farmers' Market. I nearly trip over my feet trying to keep up with her. Then I see where she's headed. Toward the German Shepherd. And the girl.

How did she know?

Though I shouldn't be surprised. I learned long ago never to underestimate Cassie's intelligence. It isn't just that she's a mix of two of the smartest dog breeds (border collies are widely considered the Valedictorians of the species and golden retrievers aren't far behind, being the most common breed of service dog), it's more than that. It's a level of empathy rarely seen in humans.

I know this is because of whatever happened to Cassie at her first home. I'm pretty sure her first owner was a woman and she wasn't nice to Cassie. A year after I rescued Cassie, she got a few ticks and the vet had to shave her down in a couple of spots. In one of those spots, there was a small circular scar. I didn't think much of it until a couple of months later when an older woman smoking a cigarette bent down to pet Cassie.

Cassie's hackles raised up and she snarled at the woman. It was the first and last time I've ever seen her snarl.

Because of this, Cassie is circumspect of all females—she eventually warms up to them, but it takes a while—which is why it's even more incredible that she's dragged me through the Farmers' Market toward this particular one.

We come abreast of the girl and her dog near the honey booth. Cassie and the German Shepherd give each other a few polite sniffs and the girl turns. Up close, she is strikingly beautiful. She's holding a bottle of honey in her hand.

"Hi, honey," I say.

I see the words leave my mouth and immediately want to delete them. That's what's so great about writing. If you write something stupid, you can just highlight the words, hit a button, and voilà, it's like they never existed.

Not so much in the real world.

The girl cringes, then says, "Uh."

I feel sorry for her. Sorry she will have to endure me hitting on her.

"Because of the honey in your hand," I explain.

She glances at the honey in her hand, then back at me, then to her credit, and I suppose mine, she smiles and laughs.

The guy working the honey tent, who is approximately my age, with a heavy beard, gives me an approving nod.

I throw him a quick smile, then stick out my hand toward the girl and say, "Hi, I'm Jerry."

The Shepherd's leash is in one hand, the bottle of honey in the other and she can't shake. I should have noticed this. Most men would have noticed this. She awkwardly transfers the honey to the hand with the leash and we shake. In the awkwardness of it all, I do notice she isn't wearing a wedding ring.

"I'm Gloria," she says. She glances down where Cassie and her dog are still doing their sniffing dance and says, "She's beautiful."

"Yeah, that's Cassie," I say with fatherly pride. Then ask, "Who az dee Jarman?" I may do this in what I believe to be a German accent.

The girl pauses for a moment as if trying to decide if this is funny or offensive. Luckily, she finds it funny, laughs and says, "That's Bruce."

"Bruce?" I laugh. "That's awesome."

"Yeah, I wish I could say I came up with it. But that was his name when I rescued him."

"Same with Cassie," I say.

"She's a rescue?"

I nod.

Gloria bends down and says, "Hi, Cassie."

Cassie comes over and gives her hand a sniff, then a soft lick.

My eyebrows jump. "She likes you," I say, surprised by Cassie's obvious endorsement.

"Well, I am pretty likable."

I laugh. "Yes, you appear to be."

"So do you live around here?" she asks.

"Yeah, just a few blocks from here actually. How about you guys?"

"Not far. Over by Reagan Beach."

Reagan Beach is a dog beach a couple of miles away. I used to go there all the time with Hugo and Cassie.

I think of Hugo, remember life is short, and decide to go for it. I ask, "So, do you maybe want to grab a cup of coffee sometime?"

"Oh," she says, then adds, "No."

It takes a moment for this to register.

No.

No?

Wait, isn't she supposed to make up some excuse, say she's busy, or that she has a boyfriend, or that she's a lesbian? Isn't she supposed to water it down, to dilute it, to say, "Sorry, I'm not interested," or, "I'm sorry, but I'm gonna have to pass"? Anything but *No*.

"No?" I say, more confused by her directness than spurned by her rejection.

"Yeah, no." She smiles. "But thanks for asking."

I don't want to laugh, but I laugh. I laugh, and I say, "You're, um, *you're welcome.*"

I glance at the guy working the honey stand. He's cringing as if he's vicariously felt the trauma of what just occurred. Like I'm his character in a game of *Street Fighter* and I just had my spine removed and was set on fire.

Within a short nanosecond, my confusion gives way to visceral, palpable, universal self-consciousness.

I give a tug, probably stiffer than I would like to admit, on Cassie's leash and do an about-face. I glance across the way to where Alex and Julie are staring at me. I should go over and say goodbye, but I don't want to. Alex will make me relive it, word for word. Tit for tat.

I give a short wave goodbye, then pull Cassie through an

opening between the booths. After two blocks, I stop. Before getting *Pluto Three* published, I was rejected by hundreds of agents and publishers, so I'm not exactly sure why I feel the way I do.

I lean down on my haunches and Cassie comes and rubs her head against my chest.

I give her a rub behind the ears and say, "Well, thanks for trying."

5

"NEW HOME"

Hugo

"This one," the little girl says. She has both her hands wrapped around my belly and is holding me a few inches from her face. Her eyes are the same color as the Big Cat, a light gold, and both of her front teeth are missing. She reminds me of Julie, but not as stretched out.

A bunch of humans have come and gone over the past few days. They take turns picking us up, holding us, rubbing our bellies. Some are small, like the girl holding me now, others are bigger, others older. All have been she-humans. I wonder if he-humans, *Jerry-humans*, exist in this new world.

Two of the she-humans took baby cats yesterday. I don't know where they went. Did they go to one of the tall, skinny houses across the street? Is it weird that I miss them?

"Are you sure, Sara?" asks the she-human who came with the little girl.

"Yes," Sara says. "I'm sure. He's so cute. I like the gray stripe down his head. And his eyes, I like how they are yellow on the outside and more green on the inside."

She cradles me to her neck and squishes me with her head.

I glance over her shoulder at the Big Cat. She's standing next to the white fence. She has been standing for the last two days.

Since the first baby cat left.

* * *

I'm in a car.

I keep trying to scramble up Sara's body so I can see through the window. To see Outside. I get on her shoulder and press my face to the glass. When I did this with Jerry, he would roll the window down and I would stick my head out. I wait for the window to go down, but it doesn't.

Through the window, I see the many tall, skinny houses. And cars. So many cars. And humans, both she-humans and Jerry-humans. (They do exist!) I can see them in cars and walking on the street. Each Jerry-human I see, I think it might be Jerry, but they are gone before I can be sure.

Each time I get up on Sara's shoulder and push my face to the window, she pulls me off and sets me back in her lap.

I want to see more Outside and let out a squeak. I still can't talk, but I'm getting close. (I'm starting to figure out how these new sounds work. They are so much different than what I'm used to.)

"Did you hear that, Mom?" Sara says. "He just meowed."

So that's what that noise is called.

"I heard," Mom says. "It was so cute."

I meow again, but other than Sara laughing, it doesn't accomplish anything.

A few minutes later, the car stops.

Sara carries me toward a tall, skinny house. Like the house before, it's on a hill.

Once in the house, Sara sets me down on the ground.

"Welcome to your New Home," she says.

43

* * *

I spend most of my time at my New Home running. Running away from Sara. All she wants to do is hold me. That's the problem with being so small: if something bigger wants to hold you, it usually can.

I'm used to being the holder, not the holdee. Squirrels, birds, mice, you name it and I held it. I held it, then I killed it.

I don't think Sara wants to kill me, but sometimes she holds me so hard I think she might.

Once I scratched her and she screamed. Mom came and whacked me on the head. I don't scratch anymore. But I still squirm. And thrash. And then I get away. And then I run.

Thankfully, Sara will leave me alone when I'm eating. I get to eat a lot of kibble. But my little teeth are terrible. They make it so hard to crunch up my food, but luckily, baby cat kibble is much smaller than dog kibble.

Sara also leaves me alone when I have to go to the bathroom. I still hate peeing and pooping in the weird sand, but it isn't as bad when you're not sharing it with five other baby cats. I would still prefer to do my business outside in the grass, but as much as I scrape at the front door, it never opens.

Right now, I'm hiding under the couch. I can see Sara's eyes peeking underneath, her hair dangling over her face. "Come out of there!" she yells.

I meow.

No!

Sara reaches out her arm, but it isn't long enough. She disappears and then reappears on the other side. Her arm snakes through, but I've moved so I'm just out of reach. I've started to like this game. Mostly because it makes Sara so mad. It's fun until Mom gets involved. Mom usually brings a broom.

Sara wiggles her fingers a few inches from me, then she yells, "Cheese!"

Wait, did she say, cheese?

Does she have cheese?

I slowly crawl out from beneath the couch, poke my head out, then go sit right in front of Sara.

I meow.

I'm ready for my cheese now.

Sara picks me up, cradles me to her chest, and rubs her chin all over me.

"Ah, Cheese," she says.

This is when I realize cheese isn't a snack.

It's my name.

* * *

I'm a baby cat named Cheese.

I'm a baby cat named Cheese.

I'm a baby cat named Cheese.

* * *

I don't like Dr. V.

He has weird eyebrows. He didn't give me a treat when he first saw me. And his hands are cold. (And he said that I weigh two pounds. Two measly pounds!)

I want Dr. Josh. Dr. Josh was the best. He would always give me a treat right when he saw me. He'd yell, "Hey, Big Guy," then he'd ruffle my head and give me a treat. I liked when he called me Big Guy. Sometimes, Jerry would call me this, but it never sounded the same as when Dr. Josh did it.

But the best part about Dr. Josh was: I trusted him. I knew he wouldn't do something without telling me first. He would say, "All right, Hugo, I'm going to put this thermometer up your butt now."

Not Dr. V.

One second I'm sitting on the table. The next minute, I have a thermometer up my butt. No warning.

And that's why I scratched him.

He has a Band-Aid on his nose where I scratched him and his weird eyebrows are all squished together. He's holding a big needle in his hand. It's the biggest needle I've ever seen.

I try to jump off the table, but Sara holds me down.

"It's okay, Cheese," Sara says. "It will only hurt for a second."

I hiss.

Yes, I learned something new.

I can hiss.

I hiss some more.

Get that psycho and his needle away from me!

"Mom, come help me hold him down," Sara says.

Mom joins in, helping to pin me to this cold metal table.

This is a new low.

I feel the needle poke my butt. It hurts. It's worse than the time I got stung by a bee.

After two more shots, Dr. V finally asks me if I want a treat.

I don't.

* * *

Yellow.

That's the color of my collar.

Not red like before. Or even blue. No, it's yellow.

You know who has a yellow collar? Cassie. You know why? Because Cassie is a *girl*.

It's bad enough being a baby cat named Cheese. But a baby cat named Cheese in a yellow collar?

What did I do to deserve this?

"I got you something else," Sara says.

I recognize the white bag that she pulled the collar out of. I know it's from the Ball Shop. I know this isn't what it's called, but when Jerry would take me and Cassie there, that's what we would usually get. (At least that's what I would get. Cassie always went for the pig ears.)

Sara pulls something out of the bag and tosses it on the carpet right next to me.

I gingerly take a couple of steps forward—my butt is still sore from my showdown with Dr. V—and inspect it. It's a fake mouse. I bat at it a few times, then take a couple of steps backward and lie down.

"You don't like it?" Sara asks. "Well, then how about this?"

She pulls out a ball.

I feel my whiskers twitch.

The ball is a rainbow of colors. She tosses it on the carpet and it jingles. I bat it with my paw and it jingles some more. I don't like the sound it makes. I like things that squeak. Not jingle.

"Not that one either," Sara says, shaking her head. Her hand goes back into the bag and comes out with a package. She opens it. I take a few steps toward her. She has her back to me, but I can see her smiling. She turns around. She's holding something metal in her hand.

Red dot.

Red dot.

Weird red dot.

There is a weird red dot on the carpet.

How did it get there?

I jump on it.

I look under my paws.

It's gone.

Now it's on the wall.

Red dot on the wall.

I run over there.

I hit it with my paw, but nothing happens.

Then it's moving.

I chase this weird red dot around the room. I don't even notice that Sara is laughing so hard she's fallen over on her side. Mom is in the doorway. She's laughing too.

I don't have time to figure out what they are laughing about; the red dot is back.

I pounce on it.

I've got it this time.

I look under my paws.

It's gone.

It's back.

I charge forward, pounce on it, tumble and roll.

"I think he likes it," Mom says.

* * *

The empty cardboard box is open on the ground. It's about as tall as I am and twice as wide. It's no different than the cardboard boxes that used to magically appear on the front porch of my *old* Home. Jerry used to get these boxes all the time. He'd open them up, then leave the empty box on the ground. So there should be nothing special about this empty box.

But there is.

I want to be inside it. I *have* to be inside it.

I jump into the box, spin around a few times, then curl into a ball.

It's not very comfortable. The carpet the box is sitting on is much softer. And the cardboard is smelly.

I will myself to get up and get out of the box.

But I can't.

I never want to leave.

I'm not so sure about all this box stuff.

* * *

I've explored every inch of my New Home and it isn't so bad. There are lots of things to climb and lots of places to go under. I do this mostly when Sara and Mom are gone, which is a lot of the time.

I don't know where they go. They don't tell me.

I climb on the couch, climb up the stairs, I go pee and poop in the weird sand. I wait for Sara and Mom to come home. I think about the red dot. About where it comes from, why I can't catch it, and why it never shows up when Sara and Mom are gone.

All in all, this isn't a bad life.

A thousand dogs would kill for this life.

But it's not for me.

I climb up the curtain and look out the window.

Somewhere out there, beyond the tall, skinny houses and the hills, are Jerry and Cassie.

And I'm going to find them.

6

"PARENTS"

Jerry

I'm still on Chapter 13.

Over the past three weeks, I've rewritten it seven times. Each new version is worse than the previous iteration. I'm wondering if I should skip over it. Like that superstition about buildings and the 13th floor—that it's cursed. Some buildings don't have a 13th floor; they go directly from the 12th to the 14th. Others rename the 13th floor "12B" or "14A", or even "M" (which is the 13th letter in the alphabet). Maybe I should do the same.

I reread the two paragraphs I've written, highlight them, then hit delete. Then I delete "Chapter 13" and change it to "12B."

Worth a try.

I dance my fingers over the keyboard, waiting for inspiration to strike.

It doesn't.

"Ding-dong."

I pull the blinds apart and see my parents' white Explorer parked on the street.

"Ding-dong," my mother says a second time. This is one of my mother's many quirks: the human doorbell.

When I exit my bedroom, I see my mother standing on the other side of the screen door, her hands shielding her eyes, leaned over at the waist, peeking into the house. It's as though she's peering through a window of the Louvre and not her own home.

Behind my mother, I can see my father in the front yard. He's rolling on the lawn with Cassie, who had been taking a nap on the front steps and street watching.

"Hi, Mom," I say, striding toward the front door. I've been looking forward to (and dreading) this day. Looking forward to it because it will give me the kick in the ass I need to get out of the house and actually get some writing done. Dreading it because my parents are coming to live with me for three months.

"Hi, honey," my mother shrieks.

"You can come in," I say. "This is your house after all."

"Oh, well, I don't want to walk in on you doing anything unseemly."

My mother walked in on me doing something *unseemly* once when I was fifteen and she's been acting like I'm in the KGB ever since.

I push the screen door open. My mother pulls me into a long hug, gives me two kisses on the cheek, then pulls back. Betsy Ryman is pushing seventy, but she doesn't look a day over sixty. Her hair is fashionably dyed blonde with pink streaks. She's wearing equally pink-tinted glasses and a gray bowler hat.

"Nice hat," I say. My mother has never worn a hat a day in her life.

"I wear hats now," she says, then waving me forward adds, "Come say hi to your father."

I walk toward my father, who is on his back in the front grass, Cassie lying across his belly, her tail helicopping fast enough I fear she may become airborne.

"Hi, Dad."

He glances up and smiles. "Son!"

My dad wiggles out from under Cassie and brushes the grass off his khaki shorts. Martin Ryman is pushing seventy and looks that way. The afternoon sun reflects off his nearly bald pate (he has a bit of white fluff hanging on for dear life at the sides) which is a constant reminder of my own impending doom. Like my mother, he has glasses (though untinted) which appear to be a few millimeters thicker than his last pair. He's wearing compression socks pulled up to mid-calf and black Tevas.

My dad pulls me into a hug, then asks, "What's shakin'?"

"Not a whole lot," I say. "Just working on a new book."

"Any ladies?"

I shake my head. "Sadly, no."

"Talk to Avery lately?"

My father, like most red-blooded males, had been in love with Avery. But to his credit, Avery was especially charming the few times she met my parents.

"No, Dad. I haven't talked to the girl who dumped me three years ago *lately*."

He bobs his head from shoulder to shoulder, then says, "Well, it never hurts to give her a poke."

"A poke?"

"Yeah on Facebook. A poke."

Since my parents had both retired in the last two years, they'd gone from barely being able to send a text message to technologically savvy millennials.

Attempting to switch the subject, I ask, "You guys need help with your luggage?"

"We already brought it in," my mother says.

"I didn't see it."

She shakes her head and asks, "Do you even read my texts?"

"Sometimes," I say with a shrug.

She scoffs, then says, "We're staying at the Winston's instead. They're in Europe all summer."

The Winston's house is the one directly across the street, which on closer inspection, is where my parents' Explorer is parked.

"Oh," I say, trying to fight back a smile.

"We don't want to cramp your style," my father says. "You know, in case you do get a lady."

"Thanks, Dad."

He winks at me, then glancing down at Cassie—who after letting my mother give her a few hearty pats, laid down at my father's feet—my father says, "Speaking of ladies, when's the last time this pretty lady went for a walk?"

"It's been a few days."

My dad shakes his head shamefully, then says, "Well, why don't you go grab her leash and I'll take her for a little trot."

I go inside and grab Cassie's leash, then hand it to my father. At the sight of her leash, Cassie starts zooming around the yard.

My dad clips the leash to her and the two start down the street. Cassie doesn't give me a backward glance. Once they round the corner, my mother gingerly puts her hand on my shoulder and says, "How are you doing? You know, with Hugo being gone."

I let out a long exhale. "I'm dealing."

"It's been four months, dear. Maybe you should get a puppy."

"A puppy?" I scoff angrily, though it isn't as if I haven't considered it. Half of me wanted to get a puppy the day after Hugo died. Something to help soften the blow. But that would be cheating. Hugo deserved to be grieved. "I'm not getting a puppy."

"It was just an idea. I read on the internet that sometimes that's the best way to move on. And you have to admit, Cassie would love a new playmate."

I shake my head in silence.

My mother can see she's upset me and smiles softly, then gives me a hug. I don't want the hug, but after a long second, I fall into it.

"My heart is just so sad," I mutter, my eyes filling with tears.

She lets me cry against her, as I cried against her in nearly the exact same spot twenty-five years earlier. The only other time I have felt such sorrow.

"He was a good boy," she says. I can feel her let out a few sobs against my cheek.

Cassie, as evidenced by the past few minutes, is all about my father. It isn't that she doesn't like my mom; it's that she's weird around females altogether. But Hugo loved my mother. And my mother adored him. He was her *granddoggy*.

After a few more sobs, my mother releases me, massages her eyes behind her pink lenses, then says, "Let us get settled for a few hours and then come over for dinner."

I force a smile and nod.

Cassie

I love Martin. Partly because he spoils me. But mostly, because he made Jerry. And did I mention, he spoils me!

"Okay, last one," Martin says.

We're sitting on a bench by a big fountain. There are a bunch of people walking around and a few other dogs. I know this is the time of year when all the people come. Sometimes there will be so many people it's hard to get around them.

Martin tosses the cookie in the air and I follow it with my eyes, then I open my mouth and chomp it out of the air.

It's delicious.

Peanut Butter.

Martin wipes his hands together, shows them to me, then says, "No more, pretty lady."

Jerry calls me Girl.

The delivery man calls me Honey.

Martin calls me Pretty Lady.

"What do you want to do now?" Martin asks. "Do you want to go to the lake?"

The lake?

I haven't been to the lake since last summer.

I bark.

Yes, the lake!

Jerry

"Come on, girl," I say.

Cassie's eyes flutter open. She's been zonked out since she got back from the lake with my dad. I give her a light shake. Her golden fur is still slightly damp. "We have to go."

She raises her head for a moment, then lays her head back down.

I laugh.

I've never seen her so tired. But then again, I haven't played with her much for the past three months and she hadn't been swimming for almost a year. She's probably out of shape. Underneath these thoughts, like a nest of termites slowly eating away at my brainstem, is another reason I know she's so tired—she's ten years old. But my current psyche is too fragile to think about Cassie aging and I mentally release a bug bomb.

"Come on, Cassie. I bet my dad will feed you scraps under the table."

This gets her attention and she pushes herself up and stretches. Down-dog, up-dog, then she jumps off the couch.

(A little over a year ago, I moved from my upstairs bedroom to the guest bedroom on the first floor. Cassie was only nine at the time, but I didn't see any reason she needed to be bounding up and down the stairs several times each day.)

I watch to see if there's a hitch in her step or if her hips have that buffering lag.

They don't.

Thank God.

Before leaving, I give myself a quick once-over in the bathroom mirror. I've put on a short-sleeve collared shirt and I've styled my hair, parting the thinning strands up and to the side as is currently guy chic.

I'm not sure why I'm dressed up. Am I trying to impress my parents? Do I just want to remember how it feels to be properly attired and groomed? What am I trying to project?

I decide to switch out the collared shirt for a T-shirt and pull on a hat. Then Cassie and I cross the street and push into the Winston's house. From the outside it looks reminiscent of my parents' house, but the inside is considerably more elegant. My parents both recently retired and while they have a decent nest egg, they can't spend extravagantly for their remaining years. But the Winstons are wealthy, Mr. Winston having a few patents under his belt which made him a small fortune.

Cassie and I cross through a marble foyer onto a dark wooden floor, then into a kitchen that is Food Network worthy. My parents are both standing around the kitchen island. My father is holding a glass of white wine. My mother is sipping from a tumbler, no doubt Captain and Diet Coke. There's a plate of raw tenderloin steaks and a large bowl of salad resting on the island. A perfume of chocolate wafts from the oven and my mouth waters at the thought of my mother's world famous brownies.

My mother runs around the island and gives me a hug, kiss, kiss, as though we didn't do the same routine a few hours earlier. My father picks a carrot from the salad bowl and feeds it to Cassie. It's like watching a rerun of an old sitcom you've seen a million times.

After feeding Cassie a few more carrots, my dad opens the fridge and hands me a beer.

Several years after I moved from my hometown of Medford, Oregon to San Francisco, I went back to visit my parents for the holidays. A new micro-brewery was built in my absence and my father insisted we do a father/son beer sampling one afternoon. We sampled a dozen beers and predictably, my father wanted to rank them from best to worst (my dad always wants to rank stuff, whether it be Will Ferrell movies, to months in a year, to brands of bottled water) and after hounding a poor waitress for two pens and some paper, we did just that.

I'm not sure if it's my father's waning memory or if it's a long-running prank, but my father always brought me the beer I ranked dead last (the beer *we both* ranked dead last). An atrocity called *Backward Bill's Buttermilk Beer* which was crafted around alliteration and not digestibility.

I crack the beer open and take a small sip. It's worse than I remember. It's an abomination. It's sour dairy creamer meets Coors Light. But being the good son that I am, I give a nod and a satisfying, "Ahhhhh."

This makes my father immensely happy and I say, "Thanks, Dad."

"You bet, son. I brought seven cases."

I nearly choke on my second swig, though I can't be certain if it's because my father has brought me seven cases of this liquid nightmare or if it's simply my esophagus rebelling.

"Seven cases," I choke out. "You don't say?"

"Yep."

"Well, I hope you'll help me drink them."

He shakes his head. "I'm actually not a big fan of that one. Something about the combination of buttermilk and beer."

Yeah, because it's disgusting.

"Well, I'm gonna go throw these bad boys on the grill," he says, lifting the plate of steaks. He glances down at Cassie and says, "You want to come with me, pretty lady?" My father likes to eat little pieces of steak while they cook, and I know Cassie will also get her fair share.

The two disappear to the back deck and my mother asks, "Have you talked to your brother lately?"

My brother Mark lives in Michigan. He's eight years older than me and we have always been more acquaintances than friends. Like we've worked for the same company for thirty years but have always been in different departments.

I say, "Not in a few months." He sent me a heartfelt condolence message after Hugo died, but we hadn't talked on the phone in over six months.

"He just made partner," my mother exclaims.

"Partner? Really? That's great."

Making partner in his law firm is a big deal and I wonder why my brother hadn't at least shot me a text. But then again, maybe he worried it might feel like he was trying to rub it in my face. Here he was happily married for going on fifteen years, two great kids, nice house, and now partner in one of the Midwest's most prestigious law firms. And here I was a one-hit wonder, single, living in my parents' vacation house, and cashing royalty checks which barely covered my diet of bologna sandwiches and Chex mix.

My mom nods and says, "You know, he's really proud of you."

She must have seen me mentally tabulating my SSCI (Sibling Success Comparative Index).

I arch my eyebrows.

She says, "Every time I talk to him he's always saying how someone found out that he's related to you and they tell him how much they love your books."

On the off-chance I did talk to my brother, he usually had one of these stories, but part of me always thought they were fabricated for my benefit.

"Books or *book*?" I ask.

"Books. The second and third ones are better than you get credit for."

Tell that to *Robin_Readsalot77* who just yesterday posted a review for *Pluto Destiny*: "This book was torture. I'd rather get waterboarded for eight hours."

Anyhow, my mother is a retired English teacher and though she's completely and utterly biased, the words still feel good to hear.

"I liked them," my father shouts, who can apparently hear our conversation through the window.

My books are probably the only fiction books my father has ever read. He mostly reads biographies and WWII epics, but mostly, he surfs the net on his phone.

"Thanks, Dad," I shout.

"How's the next one coming?" my mom asks.

Part of me wants to steer her back to how Mark is proud of me, but I'm not that desperate for validation.

Or am I?

"It's coming along nicely," I lie.

"When can I read it?"

"Oh, maybe in a few months."

"Can't wait," she says.

There's a ding and my mother turns.

It's the timer on the oven.

"Brownies are done," she shouts, then gives me a few winks.

I sniff at the air. Underneath the aroma of chocolate, there's a hint of something else. Something herbal.

"Mom?" I say.

She glares at me.

"*Mommmm?*"

"What?" she says. "It's been legal for two years."

I lean my head back, smash my eyelids together a couple of times, take a long breath, then say, "What, you and Dad are like potheads now?"

"We don't smoke it. But we do like the edibles."

Two years ago, Oregon legalized recreational marijuana, and

while I knew plenty of baby-boomers were rushing to the nearest dispensary, I didn't know my parents were among them.

"When did you start?" I ask. "*How* did you start?"

"Oh, friends had us over for dinner one night and they had brownies, and after a little debate, your father and I decided to give them a whirl." She laughs. "We had so much fun!"

My mother sets the tray of brownies on a hot pad on the counter. This woman with a bowler hat, pink glasses, and pink-streaked hair, who now likes to get high, is hard to wrap my head around.

"Are you having a midlife crisis?" I ask.

"If I was having a crisis, it would be a three-quarter life crisis. But no, I'm not. Your father and I are just having fun. Living free."

"Do you listen to reggae now?"

She shrugs. "A little."

Well, there you have it. My parents have become late-stage hippies.

My mom cuts two squares of brownie and sets them on a small plate. "Do you want one?"

"Thanks, but I have enough paranoia as it is." I haven't smoked pot since New Year's Eve my senior year in college. Whatever I smoked was laced with something and I spent the better part of the night praying to God I would make it to see the new year.

My mom covers the remaining tray of brownies with foil, then shoves it into the fridge.

A moment later, from outside, my dad shouts, "Steaks are ready."

I grab the big bowl of salad, then follow my mother out to the stone patio table with a large orange umbrella in full bloom. The sky is clear and the sun is fading into the roof of the house behind us. It's the twentieth of June, the first day of summer is officially tomorrow, and the temperature hovers in the mid-seventies.

My dad plops the plate of steaks in the middle of the table.

Cassie comes over and rests her head on my lap. "Did you get some steak, girl?"

"Oh, yes, she did," my father answers for her. "Probably got herself an entire steak by the end of it."

I cut off a small piece of meat and feed it to her. She chomps it down, then I tell her to lie down. She does.

Once my father takes a seat, I ask, "So edibles, huh?"

He fights back a smile, then points his fork at my mother. "Blame her; she's the one who went to the pot shop and came back with a big ol' baggie of the stuff."

I can't help but laugh at the thought of my mother in a "pot shop."

"But it's fun," my dad says. "I can see why everybody was always smoking it when I was growing up."

"Yeah, you sure missed out," I say.

"Well, we're making up for it now," he says, then shoves a piece of steak in his mouth.

My mother clears her throat, then says, "There's actually something else we've been meaning to talk to you about." The tone she uses is flat. It's the tone you use when you tell someone you have six months to live or that you're actually adopted.

"What?" I ask, my heartbeat doubling. "Is one of you sick?"

"No, nothing like that," my mom says with a wave of her hand. "It's, well—" she pauses, then says, "You tell him, Martin."

My father chews, swallows, then says, "What your mother is trying to say is that we've decided to have an open marriage."

I cock my head to the side. "Um, pardon me?"

"An open marriage," my father repeats.

My lips purse and there's an odd high humming resonating from my throat. "An open marriage?" I sputter. "An open marriage? People in their late sixties—people who have been married for *forty years*—do not just decide to have open marriages."

My mother glances at my father. "We did."

61

"So, what, you guys are gonna like, date other people?"

"Yes, honey, that's exactly what we're going to do."

This is too much. My head is going to explode.

I grab my beer and chug nearly the entire bottle. The taste doesn't even register. I wipe my mouth on my shoulder, then shake the bottle at my mother, then my father. "This is crazy."

"It's what we both want," my father says. "Your mother and I both love one another—that's never gonna change—but we both want to see what's out there."

"What's out there? What's out there?" I'm saying this more to the darkening sky than to my parents. "What's out there is a bunch of sad, pathetic people who want what you two have found."

"I know this is a lot to take in," the woman in the bowler hat, with pink glasses, with pink streaks in her hair, who now gets stoned and wants to date other people says. "But your father is the only man I've ever had sex with and I'm the only woman your father has ever had sex with."

I put my hand up. If I hear the word sex again, I'm going to vomit.

My mother adds, "We just want to do a little exploration."

"Freshmen in college do exploration," I shout. "*NOT* women with osteoporosis and *NOT* bald men who wear compression socks."

"We've discussed this quite a bit," my father says. "And we've both decided it's what we want. And to be honest, neither of us really cares what you think."

I stand up.

"Come on, Cassie," I shout. But looking down, Cassie is gone.

I storm into the kitchen. "Cassie!"

That's when I see it.

The plate with the two brownies on it.

It's empty.

Cassie

I know I shouldn't have eaten the grassy brown squares, but I couldn't resist. They just sat there on the counter beckoning to me. And if they didn't want me to eat them, then why did they put them so close to the edge?

So I did. I ate the grassy brown squares. And they were delicious.

I can still taste them on the back of my tongue. My tongue feels heavy. But it feels smarter. But that doesn't make sense. Tongues don't have brains.

Or do they?

I stick my tongue out and glance down at it. It's pink and long. I never noticed how long it is. It's so long. What a long, smart tongue I have. I don't know how long I stare at my tongue.

A long time.

Why am I so infatuated with my tongue?

I've had the same tongue for ten years and I don't think I've ever taken the time to look at it. To really inspect it. Why now?

After another few minutes of staring at my tongue, I notice my nose. My nose was once big and black. Now it's more pink. Why is my nose changing color?

I want my black nose back.

* * *

Bird.

There's a bird in the street.

I bark.

Hey, bird.

The bird flies away.

I watch her wings (all birds are *hers* to me) flap, flap, flap, then she is gone.

How does she do that?

Fly?

I wish I had wings; I would fly everywhere.

Cassie, Queen of the Birds.

* * *

Dirt.

Where did all this dirt come from?

How did I get here?

I was watching that bird fly and now I'm digging in the dirt.

Dig.

Dig.

Dig.

* * *

I'm running.

I stop.

It's a coyote.

He pitter-patters across the street. Coyotes are always pitter-pattering.

I bark.

Hey, coyote.

He stops. He stares at me. He's skinny. Too skinny. He needs to eat. I wish I had some grassy brown squares to give him. He looks so much like a dog, but I know he isn't a dog. But he has dog in him. Or did I have coyote in me? How did that work? Were we all once coyotes?

I howl. (Or try to.)

The coyote howls.

We both have our heads back howling.

When I stop howling, the coyote is gone.

* * *

When did I lie down?
    When did I melt into the grass?
    Why is grass green?
    Frogs.
    Tadpoles.
    The Chosen Ones.
    Cookies.
    Peanut butter cookies.
    Hugo.
    Poor Hugo.
    First Home.
    Why was she so mean to me?
    Did I deserve it?
    Was I a bad dog?
    Blueberries.
    Blueberries as big as my head.
    Super blueberries.

* * *

Ten.
    Ten.
    Ten.
    I'm Ten.
    Ten.
    What is the number after ten?
    What happens when we die?
    Where do we go?
    What will happen to Jerry when I'm gone?
    Who will protect him?

* * *

Super blueberries.

Super blueberries.

Super blueberries.

Jerry

My phone rings.

I stop running and pull my phone out of my pocket. I'm guessing it's my mom calling to ask if I found Cassie yet. But it's not. It's an unlisted number. I shake my head. I don't have time for this. I have to find Cassie.

I *have* to.

I'm about to decline the call when logic strikes and I answer. "Please tell me you have my dog," I shout.

"That I do," a man replies.

Over the course of the last hour, my intestines have twisted into something resembling the knotted ball of Christmas lights Clark Griswold hands to Rusty.

"Where are you?" I ask.

"Jerry, this is Pete."

"Pete?"

"Pete, your neighbor, three houses down."

"Oh, right."

"Cassie is in my backyard."

"Thank God."

I tell him I'm a few blocks away and that I'll be there in a couple of minutes. I sprint for a block, then slow down. I haven't exercised in four months and my lungs ache.

"She's safe," I tell myself, sucking in a few breaths.

When I get to Pete's, he's standing on his front steps. He's about my age and as a paddleboard shop owner—and a once professional paddleboarder—he's lean and muscular. He's wearing a white tank top, revealing an assortment of tattoos on his biceps and forearms. I've chatted with him a dozen times in the three years I've been living in town, mostly when we were both taking out the trash. (Every time I saw him, he invited me to join him for "a paddle," and I always said, "Soon, for sure.")

I expected Cassie to be with him, for her to see me and to come bounding down the street, but she isn't. When I don't see her, my stomach immediately clenches.

What if Pete was joking? What if he didn't have her? Or what if he had, but then she ran off again?

"Where is she?" I call desperately.

"Relax," he says calmly. "She's in the backyard."

He leads me around to the fence, opens a gate, and pushes through. I hesitate for a nanosecond before following behind him. I've been in this backyard hundreds of times before. But not in over twenty-five years.

Pete walks a few steps, then points and says, "Something tripped my floodlights and I came out back and found her like this."

Cassie is sitting back on her hind legs. She's between two bushes and is staring at the fence an inch in front of her. Her entire face is covered in dirt. Her tongue hangs out the side of her mouth like a dead fish.

I don't know whether to laugh or cry.

"She ate two of my mom's pot brownies," I explain to Pete.

He lets out a light laugh and says, "Ahh." If he has questions or concerns, he keeps them to himself.

I walk gingerly to Cassie, get down on my haunches, and pet her. "Hey, girl."

She turns her head slightly. Her eyes are big and glassy. She's completely and utterly stoned.

I pick her up with a groan, cradling her under my arms.

"You want me to carry her over?" Pete asks, evidently aware of the strain Cassie's sixty pounds is causing me.

"No, I got her."

He leads me out of the backyard.

When I pass him, he asks, "Any chance you can send a few of those brownies my way?"

* * *

According to PetMD, dogs can get seriously sick from ingesting too much THC, but they have to eat much more than two brownies. More like an entire tray. As for the chocolate in the brownies, I wasn't worried. When I was living in San Francisco, Avery left out a dish of holiday Hershey Kisses. Cassie ate about twenty of them and I totally freaked out, knowing chocolate can be a death sentence for dogs. But after consulting the Chocolate Toxicity Calculator on the internet (yes, this is a thing), at sixty pounds and having consumed three ounces of chocolate, I was assured Cassie would be fine. And she was. (Well, aside from a very festive, green, red, and gold poop the next day.)

After carrying Cassie back to the house, I set her on my bed. I rubbed her head and within a couple of minutes, she was asleep and snoring. I watched Netflix for a few hours, checking on Cassie's breathing every few minutes. She woke a few hours later, still groggy, but she was able to drink some water and eat a few blueberries before zonking back out.

At this point, I popped over to the Winston's to tell my parents Cassie was okay. My mother, understandably, felt awful and was profusely apologetic. My father was asleep, but my mother insisted he felt terrible as well.

"Water under the bridge," I told her, though in the future, I expected her to be more careful with her *pot*. I also told her, "And as far as you and dad having an open marriage, if seeing other people makes you happy, then go for it."

My own words stuck with me during the walk back across the street, stuck with me as I stroked Cassie's head and ears, stuck with me as I ate two bologna sandwiches, and stuck with me as I sat down to my computer to give Chapter 12b another go.

If seeing other people makes you happy, then go for it.

Why couldn't I shake these words?

Then I had an epiphany. My parents' relationship and my relationship with writing wasn't all that different. The only thing I'd ever written were these *Pluto* books. I'd been married to these characters since I first came up with them when I was twenty-one-years-old. I've been in a committed relationship with these characters for going on fifteen years.

But I want to see other people.

I click Edit, then I click Select All.

I take a deep breath and click Delete.

It feels good.

It makes me happy.

7

"ESCAPE"

Hugo

Sara and Mom are at "swim practice." I'm not sure why you have to practice swimming. (You just paddle your legs. It's super easy!) I was a good swimmer. No, I was a *great* swimmer. Jerry used to call me "Michael Phelps," though I'm not sure what this means. But he would always be smiling when he said it, so I guess it's a good thing.

I'm hiding under the couch. I can see the bottom of the front door. I'm waiting for it to open and for Sara and Mom to walk through. That's when I'm going to go.

I wait.

I wait.

I wait.

Rattle, rattle, rattle.

Creak.

The door opens. I see two shoes and two little bare feet.

It's hard for me not to run to Sara, to lean into her little legs and purr, to let her pick me up and give me all sorts of kisses. (It took me a couple of weeks to realize it, but Sara isn't *too* bad. She smells good, she plays with me a lot, she gives great belly rubs, and she lets me sleep on a pillow right next to her head.)

I force myself to stay put.

Jerry, Cassie, Outside, the Lake.

Jerry, Cassie, Outside, the Lake.

Jerry, Cassie, Outside, the Lake.

If I stay, I will never see these things again.

There's a soft thud above me and Mom says, "Sara! Don't throw your towel on the couch."

"But I have to pee," Sara shrieks, then pitter-patters up the stairs.

"That girl," Mom says. Her shoes move around to the back of the couch.

The door is open and I can see part of a car, the top of a skinny house, and gray sky.

This is my chance.

I dart from under the couch. I run as fast as my stupid little baby cat legs will go and zip out the door.

Mom must have seen me and yells, "Cheese!"

I scamper to the sidewalk and start down the hill. When I glance back the first time, Mom is running down the hill after me. Her face is all red. When I glance back a second time, she's stopped and bent over at the waist, breathing hard.

I continue to run. There are cars lining the sidewalk all the way down the hill. And on the other side of these cars, is a long line of moving cars. I run down a hill, up a hill, then down another hill. Finally, after what seems like forever, the steep hill evens out. The street meets another street, a much wider street full of honking cars and people—lots and lots of people. On the other side of the street are buildings that shoot up high into the sky and are covered in windows. I've never seen so many buildings and people in one place.

"Hey!"

I turn my head.

It's a man. Actually, it's three men.

"Dude, it's a kitten," one of them says.

I feel my whiskers twitch.

Jerry?

No, all three men have too much hair to be Jerry. And they are all wearing these things around their necks. I've never seen Jerry wear one of these things. And none of them have blue eyes.

They aren't Jerry.

But maybe they know Jerry!

I meow.

Take me to Jerry.

"Grab him, dude," one of the non-Jerrys says.

"I got a meeting."

"Me too."

"We can't just leave a kitten out here. He's gonna get mangled by a car."

"Go for it, Rick."

The non-Jerry, *Rick*, drops a black square bag (the other two non-Jerrys have the same thing draped over their shoulders), then leans down. His hair is black, shiny, and smelly. Rick fiddles with my collar then says, "Cheese," with a light laugh.

How does he know my name?

He picks me up and carries me across the street and to a large fountain near where the tall buildings begin. He sets me down on the edge of the fountain. The water is light blue and a bunch of shiny things lay on the bottom. I remember a fountain just like it. Is this the same one? If so, then I must be close to Jerry.

But then why are these buildings so much taller than the buildings I'm used to seeing? Or do all the buildings look so big because I'm so small?

Rick takes out his phone, then he picks me up and squints at my neck. I give him a lick on the nose, well, because it's right there and I like a good nose lick.

He laughs, then does something to his phone. I know humans can talk to each other through these phones.

"Hi," Rick says. "I found your kitten."

Jerry?

Is he talking to Jerry?

"On the corner of 2nd and Mission...I work three blocks away at the *Chronicle*, can you meet me there?...Ten minutes?...Okay."

Rick puts his phone away, then picks me up.

I claw at his leg.

Was that Jerry?

Were you talking to Jerry?

Is Jerry coming to get me?

He picks me up and we walk a few more blocks. We pass lots and lots of people. Rick stops a few times to let she-humans pet me. I let them. What do I care? I'm going to see Jerry soon.

We stop in front of a large, gray building. It isn't as tall as the other buildings. There's a bench out front and Rick and I sit down. Rick plays with his phone and I sit on his lap and wait for Jerry.

A few minutes later, I see her.

Mom.

And she isn't happy.

* * *

Lockdown.

That's what Sara called it.

The weird box with the sand and my water and food bowl have been moved to Sara's bathroom and I'm not allowed out of Sara's room.

I guess I'm something called a "flight risk."

It's been a week since my first escape attempt. A week since Mom drove me back to New Home and handed me to Sara. A

73

week since Sara cried and asked, "Why did you run away, Cheese?"

Because my name isn't Cheese, I wanted to tell her.

Because I belong with Jerry and Cassie.

Because I can't be locked in a house all day.

Because I'm a dog.

I crawl up Sara's bedspread and onto her bed. There's a window next to her bed and I jump on the windowsill. I do this every day. Sit on the windowsill and watch Outside. Watch the cars go by. Watch the people walk down their steps and get their newspapers. Watch Sara and Mom come and go. Watch the squirrels run around in the tree next to the house.

Sara's window is different than the windows downstairs. There is a black thing with lots of holes behind the glass. It looks like the thing Jerry uses to catch the fish—a "net."

Usually, I can't touch the net because it's behind the glass, but today is different. Today, the glass is gone. The window is open. I can feel Outside coming through the black net. I can push against this net with my paw. It's spongy and it moves when I touch it.

That's when I realize the only thing between me and Outside is this black net. There's been a development with my nails in the last week—I can retract them into my paw—and I snap out my claws. Then I do something I've never done before (something I will later learn is called "whapping"). I whap at the net and one of my claws makes a tiny cut.

I feel my whiskers twitch.

Whap, whap, whap, whap, whap, whap, whap.

I whap until there's a small hole. I stick my paw through. I whap some more until I can wiggle my little baby cat head through the hole. I wiggle, wiggle, wiggle, and then I'm Outside!

I'm standing on something black and warm. It angles down. I walk to the edge of the black and glance down. The ground seems really far away.

How do I get down to the ground?

Jump?

Even though every time I jump off something, I land softly (I don't fully understand this quite yet), I chicken out.

It's too high.

The tree!

I pitter-patter to where the tree is. There's a branch not far from where the black stops. It isn't very thick, but I saw a squirrel out on the branch a few days earlier. If a squirrel can do it, then shouldn't I be able to? (Cats and squirrels are basically the same thing, right?)

I rock back and jump. I land on the branch softly. I scamper down the branch, then jump to a lower branch. My paws slide on a couple of leaves and I fall.

Then I'm on the ground.

And I'm fine.

I look up.

I just fell half a house and it didn't even hurt.

Are cats indestructible?

I run to the sidewalk. I think about going back down the hill, but that didn't work out very well last time and I decide to go up the hill. I run, run, run, run, then finally I get to the top of the hill. That's when I see it. It's far off in the distance, big and blue.

The Lake!

I run down the hill as fast as I can. I cross a bunch of streets. The hill evens out and I can't see the Lake anymore. It's just houses and buildings and cars. So many cars.

I cross another street and that's when I see the biggest car I've ever seen. It's right in the middle of the road. There are a bunch of humans crammed into the car, then a bunch of humans hanging off the side of it. It's coming right at me fast and I don't know which way to go.

I freeze.

I feel a rush of wind as the huge car passes.

Then I feel hands around me.

"That trolley just missed you, buddy," the she-human says, pulling me to her chest. "What are doing out here anyhow—" she fiddles with my collar, "—Cheese?"

How does she know my name?

She pulls out her phone, then talks to someone.

Five minutes later, I'm back at New Home and Mom is mad and Sara is crying.

* * *

Total Lockdown.

That's what Sara called it.

Total Lockdown is a cage.

A *cage!*

The cage is on the floor in Sara's room. My water and food bowls are in one corner, the box of weird sand in another. The cage is about the same size as the cardboard box I lived in when I was just a tiny baby cat. That seemed like plenty of space back then but I'm bigger now and I can feel the walls of the cage closing in on me.

I've never been in a cage before, but Cassie had. When she was at something called Shelter, she lived in one for many months. She said it wasn't that bad. She said it was better than living on the Street.

I disagree. It's terrible. It's the worst. I have to get out.

But how?

Even if I get out of the cage, how am I supposed to get out of Sara's room? There's still a big hole in the black "net," but the window is closed in front of it. And if I do somehow get back Outside, how do I *not* get caught by any humans and brought back to Sara and Mom?

I've given this last part a lot of thought. About how the humans somehow know my name and how they keep bringing me back to Mom and Sara. There's something on my collar.

Something the humans keep looking at after they pick me up. I'm not sure how this all works, but I know I have to get rid of my collar if I want to make it back to Jerry and Cassie.

Speaking of Cassie, I wish she were here. She's so smart. She would figure out a way. Just like she figured out how to get the carrots out of the fridge without Jerry knowing. Most dogs, like me, would eat the entire bag of carrots (or the big block of cheddar) but not Cassie. She would only eat two or three so that Jerry wouldn't notice.

What would Cassie do in this situation?

"Have they ever taken the collar off of you?" Cassie would ask.

Sara had. Once. Right before she gave me a bath.

"And why did she give you a bath?" Cassie would ask.

Because I was "gross." Because I rolled around in the weird sand after I took a poop.

I feel my whiskers twitch.

Poop.

That was the answer.

I walk to the weird sand, then think better of it. The weird sand stuck to the poop, so it didn't spread very much. I poop directly on the floor of the cage. Then I roll around in it until my entire body is covered.

I'm pretty sure I'm *gross*.

* * *

Two hours later, the door to Sara's room opens.

"Chee—Ugh—what's that smell?"

Sara leans down and looks at me.

I wag my tail.

Hi.

"Oh, my God. You're, you're...MOM!!!...Cheese is covered in poop!"

Yep.

Mom comes into the room and looks at me. She shakes her head and says, "Well, clean him off, Sara." She waves her hand in front of her nose, then goes over to the window and pushes up the glass.

I hadn't planned on this, but it works in my favor.

"I don't want to touch him," Sara says.

"He's your cat," Mom says. "This is what you signed up for."

"I signed up for a nice cat that plays with the toys I buy him, doesn't constantly run away, and DOESN'T roll around in his poop!"

"There are kitchen gloves under the sink," Mom says on her way out. I think she's smiling.

A few minutes later, Sara picks me up and carries me into the bathroom. She's wearing yellow gloves. She holds me far away from her body, her arms stretched out straight.

"Ugh...You are so gross," she says.

Mission accomplished.

She sets me in the bathtub, then starts the water.

"You even got poop on your collar," Sara says, taking off my collar and throwing it into the water in front of me.

I force my whiskers not to twitch.

I let Sara scrub me for a few minutes until I'm clean. She turns her back for a second and I make my move. I jump out of the tub —which takes me three tries because it's so slippery—then zoom past Sara and out of the bathroom.

"Cheese!" Sara screams.

I jump onto the bed, onto the windowsill, then wiggle through the hole in the black net. Once I'm Outside, I turn and look back.

Sara is standing next to her bed. Her hands are at her sides and she's staring at me. "You are the worst cat," she says.

That's because I'm a dog.

* * *

I avoid people. I avoid cars. I even try to avoid streets.

It takes me a long time, but eventually, I make it to the water. To the Lake. The sun is starting to set and I can see the water lapping at the sand and rocks. I know if I stay by the Lake long enough that Jerry and Cassie will come.

I pitter-patter down to the water and jump in.

Immediately, I know something is wrong. The water feels different. It tastes different. This is not my water. This is not my Lake.

A few minutes later, it starts to rain.

I find some rocks to hunker down in. I'm wet, I'm cold, I'm hungry, I'm thirsty, and I'm lost.

The cage doesn't seem so bad anymore.

8

"TINDER"

Cassie

I don't want to wake up Jerry. But I have to. I have to go outside. I scratch the bed softly a few times.

Jerry.

Jerry.

Jerry.

He doesn't wake up.

I know I shouldn't bark. That it's too late to be barking. But this is an emergency. I have to go outside.

I bark.

Just once.

Jerry rolls over. One of his eyes squints open. He groans, then asks, "What are you barking at?"

I trot toward the back door and give it a scratch.

I hear Jerry blow out a long breath of air, then hear his feet hit the carpet.

"What's wrong?" Jerry asks, his eyes and mouth doing their weird wake up dance. "Do you have to go pee?"

No, I don't have to pee, Jerry. I know how to schedule my pees so I don't have to go in the middle of the night.

I scratch the door a few more times.

"Are you gonna be sick?"

I can't blame Jerry for thinking this. The last time I woke Jerry up in the middle of the night to go outside, I was "sick." I think it was from the little red berries that grow on one of the trees in the yard. They give me the poops, but boy do they taste good.

No, Jerry, I'm not sick.

Jerry opens the door and I scamper onto the back porch and to the small blue pool. I can see well at night—better than Jerry, who is always squinting when it's dark outside—and I gaze into the water. I see a few of the tadpoles—some of them have tiny legs now—zipping around in the water. That's the thing about night, that's when the tadpoles come alive.

"You woke me up to come check on the tadpoles?" Jerry asks, leaning down behind me. I can hear him shaking his head.

Yes.

Yes, I did.

Ever since I ate the magic brown squares, I've been thinking a lot about the tadpoles—and Hugo. I think the two are connected, Hugo and the tadpoles. And something in the magic brownies connected them. (And I've been thinking a lot about blueberries that grow as big as my head. But I don't think these super blueberries are connected to Hugo and the tadpoles.) All I know is that after I ate those magic brown squares, I realized something: I should have protected Hugo. I should have taught him to be more careful. Taught him never to run into the street. But Hugo is gone. I can't save him now. I can't protect him.

But I can protect the tadpoles.

A frog, a Chosen one, sits on the edge of the baby pool. I lean down and give him a sniff. He jumps into the water and swims across the pool, his little legs fluttering together, then he climbs out on the edge of the pool farthest from me.

"The water in the pool is getting kind of low," Jerry says.

"Maybe we should fill it up a little bit."

I follow Jerry to the hose. He turns it on so it's just above a trickle. Then he gingerly sets the hose in the pool. The water churns slightly and I'm sure some of the tadpoles go for a little ride, but they will be fine. And they will have more room to play.

After a long minute, Jerry pulls out the hose and turns it off. "You're so silly," he tells me, then he ruffles my ears and gives me a kiss on my nose. "I'll leave the door open for you."

Then he goes inside.

I protect the tadpoles for a long time. I'm not sure exactly what I'm protecting them from, but whatever it is, it has to get past me first.

Finally, when the sky begins to lighten, my eyes grow heavy. I give the backyard one last scan, searching for tadpole predators both big and small, but see none. Then I nose the door open and climb into bed next to Jerry.

My watch is over.

Jerry

"You scrapped it? What do you mean you scrapped it?" Chuck shouts loud enough that Cassie lifts her head off my legs. After her all-night tadpole vigil, Cassie is understandably tired. I give her head a reassuring pat, turn the volume down on the phone, then say, "Exactly that. I'm not gonna write it."

Chuck sighs somewhere in Manhattan, then says, "Do I need to remind you that you signed a contract for five books? Alison was already breathing down my neck because you didn't deliver on time, now I have to tell her that you scraped the entire project."

"I don't know what to tell you, Chuck. I can't finish it. I'm done with *Pluto*."

"Is this because of Hugo? Because I can buy you some more time if you need it."

"No, this isn't about Hugo." Cassie lifts her head at the sound of Hugo's name. I scratch the fur above her nose with my free hand and she slowly sets her head back down. I take a deep breath, then say, "This is about a series that should have only been one book."

Pluto Three had initially been a standalone novel, but Chuck convinced me we needed to market the book as a series if we really wanted to cash in.

I say, "The second and third books sucked because I forced a story that wasn't there."

I wait for Chuck to tell me the second and third books did, in fact, not suck, but he's silent.

"Well," he finally says, "What do you want me to tell Alison?"

"Tell her I'm working on something new?"

"Are you?" Chuck asks, a slight perk in his voice.

"Yeah."

"Sci-fi?"

"I'm not sure yet. I'm playing with a few ideas right now. Maybe fantasy. Maybe YA."

"YA is always hot."

Young Adult is a huge market. Not only did the books sell like hotcakes, but movie studios are always looking to option the next *Hunger Games*. And they have deep pockets.

"Anything you can tell me about?" Chuck asks.

"Not yet. Soon though."

"Alright, buddy," Chuck says, his spirits apparently lifted. "Keep me posted. I'll talk to Alison and try to spin this."

"Sounds good."

We hang up.

I set the phone on the bed and lean my head back against the cushioned headboard. I'd been dreading talking to Chuck for the past week and it feels good to be done with it. But now that it is, I actually have to come up with a book idea.

I may have told Chuck that I was playing with a few different ideas, but the truth is: after a week of trying to come up with a book idea, I'd gained five pounds (I eat a lot of Kit Kats when I'm thinking), I had a dry erase board with *Mermaid Triplets with Superpowers?* written on it, and I had a pounding headache (which might be from all the Kit Kats).

I wiggle my legs and Cassie stirs. We both jump off the bed and she follows me into the kitchen. I feed her a few blueberries, then I swallow a few Advil with the aid of a half-empty club soda. The dry erase board I ordered from Amazon takes up the better part of the living room and I walk over, pick up a red marker, and draw a line through my mermaid triplet idea.

I carry the rest of the drink with me, then head into the backyard. It's the hottest day of the year so far and I slink into a chaise lounge in the shade. Cassie finds a spot near me, takes a long breath, then melts into the wooden deck.

I open the memo app on my phone and lean my head back.

Book idea.

Book idea.

Book idea.

Ugh.

I open Netflix and watch an old episode of *The Office*. I call two of my friends who I haven't talked to in months. One in over a year. Neither answers. Finally, I call my brother.

"Wow, I must really be procrastinating," I say out loud.

Mark answers on the third ring. "Little bro," he says.

"Hey, Mark."

We shoot the breeze for half an hour, mostly talking about my parents and their late-stage hippieness. We touch on him becoming partner, his wife, his kids. He tells a quick story about how one of his clients is a big fan of mine. We hang up, both promising to text more.

I snap a couple of photos of Cassie asleep, then post it to Instagram with the caption "Sleeping Beauty," which I'm sure will amuse my 906 followers.

I get a text alert, thinking it's probably Mark saying: **You said we should text more!** It's not. It's from Alex. It says: **Check out this chick.**

Attached is a screenshot of a Tinder profile. The girl is brunette. Pretty. She's wearing a red bikini and standing on a boat. At the bottom is her bio: Rebecca, 27. *Just looking for my Luke Skywalker.*

Another text from Alex: **She likes *Star Wars*, bro! This might be your only chance to ever get laid again!**

I laugh.

I check the photo a few more times. She really is cute.

"What the hell," I say.

I go to the app store and download Tinder. A half-minute later, it's installed and I'm working on my profile. I select five pictures from Facebook that make me look more in shape than I actually am and that I have a bit more hair than I actually do. One of my best pictures is with enormous Hugo on my lap and I contemplate adding it, then think better of it. But then I realize the picture makes me more happy than sad and I set it as my primary picture.

(What stage of grief does that put me at?)

Next up is my bio. I'm a writer, so this should be simple. Only, it's not. Do I want to be funny? Sincere? Laid back? Serious? Play up the *Bestselling* author thing? After ten iterations, I finally settle on:

Oregonally from Oregon (get it?) but I've been in Tahoe for the past three years. I'm a semi-famous author of a few novels. When I'm not writing, I'm playing with my dog, reading, watching Netflix, or THINKING about exercising. If you don't know what Quidditch is, then this probably isn't going to work...

Satisfied with my profile, I begin swiping.

* * *

Tinder message:

To Jess: **Hey!**

Tinder message:

To Nicole: **Hey!**

Tinder message:

To McKenzie: **Hey!**

Text message:

To Alex: **None of the girls I matched with on Tinder are messaging me back!**

Alex: **Haha. Welcome to the world of internet dating. You match with that chick I sent you? Don't tell me you're just writing "Hey!"**

To Alex: **I swiped right on that Rebecca girl. Didn't match. I might have said a few "heys!"**

Alex: **Girls hate that shit. Say something about their bio or comment on one of their pictures. And swipe RIGHT on all of them!**

Tinder message:

To Brook: **Hiya Brook. That's a pretty nice looking fish you caught. Where was that picture taken?**

Brook: **Hi Jerry! I like your dog! Caught that sucker in Tahoe :)**

Text message:

To Alex: **I got one on the line!**

Alex: **Lol. I'm sure you'll mess it up!**

Tinder message:

To Brook: **Thanks. That's Hugo. He was awesome. He actually got hit by a car a few months back and passed away**

Brook: **Oh no! I'm sorry babe! Poor puppy! :(:(:(**

To Brook: **Yeah, it was pretty brutal the first few months, but I think I'm getting better. You live in Tahoe or just visiting? What do you do for work?**

Brook: **Oh good! I live here! #tahoelife. I'm a cocktail waitress at Harrah's :) :)**

Text message:

To Alex: **She's a cocktail waitress at Harrah's!**

Alex: **Send me a screenshot NOW!**

To Alex: **[image]**

Alex: **Holy shit! Big ol fake titties!**

To Alex: **You think?**

Alex: **Yes, you idiot.**

Tinder message:

To Brook: **What are you doing tonight?**

Brook: **Work :(:(:(...But I'm free tmrw :) :) :)**

To Brook: **Awesome, we should try to get together**

Brook: **I totally forgot...my friends are playing at Live@Lakeview. We should meet up there. The first one of the summer is always a blast!!! Beer tent? 6:30?**

To Brook: **Great! I'll see you there :)**

Text message:

To Alex: **Meeting at Live@Lakeview tomorrow! You gonna be there?**

Alex: **Thatta boy! I've got to scramble a website together for a guy by tomorrow night so I probably won't make it. Julie will be there with her mom. She says to bring Cassie**

To Alex: **Will do**

To Alex: **Question: how late are tanning salons open?**

Alex: **I can't believe we're friends**

9

"LIVE@LAKEVIEW"

Jerry

Even though I live less than a mile from the lake, it's been eight months since my feet last met the sand. The last time was early November, just before the long onslaught of winter. Previous winters, I was able to take Hugo and Cassie swimming in the lake between snowmelts (the water is cold but with their heavy winter coats they didn't seem to mind) but last winter it snowed a record 700 inches in the mountains—over 150 inches at lake level—and there was three feet of snowpack around the lake until late April. By the time all the snow melted, Hugo was gone, and I couldn't stomach the thought of going to the lake with only Cassie.

Today, however, I shall make my triumphant return.

Cassie and I are halfway through the mile and a half trek to Lakeview Commons, where the Live at Lakeview concert series will take place each Thursday until the end of summer. The bike path that runs parallel with Lake Tahoe Blvd is bombarded with fellow concert-goers and Cassie and I move off the path to let a large group of twenty-something guys—I'm guessing one of the many bachelor parties that come each weekend—pass. A couple of them stop to pet Cassie and she lets them, giving an extra butt wiggle when an especially handsome one scratches her ears.

When they're gone, I laugh and say, "You're such a flirt."

We resume our walk, continuing past Heidi's Pancake House, the Bijou Shopping Center, Pyramid Peak Ski & Snowboard, Action Watersports Rentals, the Beach Retreat and Lodge at Tahoe, Beach Bear Cafe, Sierra Shores condominiums, then finally the lake comes into view.

No matter how many times you see it, no matter how many times you peer out on the expansive blue water surrounded by the still white-capped mountains, it never gets old.

It is truly *majestic.*

Nestled high in the Sierra Nevada mountains and straddling the California/Nevada border, at seventy-two miles in circumference, Lake Tahoe is the largest alpine lake in the U.S. (and the second largest alpine lake in the world). The runoff from those record snowfalls the previous winter have filled the lake to capacity and it's bursting at the seams. I've never seen the water so high.

Cassie starts down the path toward the water and I give her leash a light tug. She glares at me, then lifts her eyebrows—which are a shade darker gold than the rest of her fur—slightly.

"Sorry, girl, but we aren't going in the water," I tell her. "I have a date."

I texted Brook an hour earlier to make sure we were still on to meet at the beer tent at 6:30. Part of me wanted her to cancel, to save us both from my awkwardness. But she texted back: **Yessss! I'm already hereeeeeee :) :) :)**

Cassie glances at the lake, then back up to me.

"Okay, *maybe* on the way back."

She does a double twirl.

A half-mile later we reach Lakeview Commons. The Commons is one of the most popular beaches in South Lake. On any given day during the summer, the clean restrooms, snack bar, outdoor grills, picnic tables, beach kayak and paddleboard rental, boat launch, and large sandy beach amass a large crowd.

But on concert day, it's madness.

A stage is set up at the water's edge and a thousand people are dispersed between the beach, the auditorium-style concrete bleachers built into the sand, the large beer tent up top, and the several food trucks (including the big kettle corn truck) parked on a blocked off section of the street.

The bike path runs between the beer tent—which is less of a tent and more a fifty-yard cordoned-off area—and a grassy area dotted with skyscraping evergreens. Tethered around the trees' girthy trunks is a labyrinthine maze of different colored slack-lines. They are set at varying heights—from as low as one foot off the ground to as high as ten feet—and a faction of barefoot hipsters, tweens, and kids await their turn to traverse them.

One of these kids is Julie.

She's working her way down the length of a purple slackline two feet off the ground. She bites at her bottom lip in concentration as she takes another step, then another.

Cassie sees her and lets out a soft whine.

"She's okay," I assure her.

(The highly coordinated ten-year-old might have nothing to worry about, but the one time I attempted to traverse the two-inch wide nylon—at Julie's relentless badgering—I nearly killed myself. I attempted a line that was eight inches off the ground. I took one lurching step, wobbled for a nanosecond, then attempted to jump to the ground. Sadly, one of my feet caught the line and I flipped backward and landed on my head. In a moment of clairvoyance, Alex was recording me on his phone, a video which he then posted to YouTube, where it quickly racked up 820,000 views.)

Julie moves gracefully, one foot in front of the other, to the halfway point. The line shimmies and she nearly falls, then she regains her balance, walks steadily to the opposite tree, then jumps softly to the grass.

"Julie," I call out.

Her eyes open wide and she runs over and wraps Cassie in a hug. Cassie licks her face. Then Julie gives me a quick hug and says, "So, my dad said that you have a date."

"I do."

"Where is she?"

I cock my head at the bustling group of drinkers hidden behind a blue mesh fence and say, "Somewhere in there."

"Are you nervous?"

"A little," I confess.

"Well, just be yourself."

I let out a chuckle. "Thanks for the advice."

She shrugs me off and I pass over Cassie's leash. I tell her to leave Cassie tied up to a tree if she has to go anywhere. She takes the leash, then asks, "Can I have some money for kettle corn?"

"Where's your mom?" I scoff kiddingly.

"I don't know. Somewhere down on the beach." She holds out her hand and flashes her jumbled chompers.

I pull a five-dollar bill from my wallet and hand it to her.

"*And* a slice of pizza."

I shake my head, then add another five.

"*And* a slice of pizza for Mia."

Mia is Julie's best friend and I spot the shy Hispanic girl leaning against a nearby tree watching us. I give a light wave and she waves back.

I hold out a twenty and say, "I want change."

Julie snatches the bill from my fingers, blurts out a quick, "Thanks, Jerry," then skips toward Mia with Cassie nipping at her heels.

"I guess I'm eating tuna fish sandwiches all July," I mutter under my breath, then fall in with the bustling crowd.

I continue past the mesh fence of the beer tent and to a throng of people watching the concert from the paved concrete up top. For the first time, the riffs of rock music lift from the white noise of the crowd. Three guys and one girl fill the stage on the water, including a bass guitarist with long blonde hair clad in a leopard print Speedo.

Gutsy move.

I check the time on my phone—it's 6:22 p.m.—then glance at the entrance to the beer tent. *My next girlfriend might be in there. The next girl I have sex with might be in there. Do I even remember how to have sex?*

My chest constricts.

While I attempt to psych myself up, I glance at the thicket of people packed into the concrete stands and on the beach. A small group in front of the stage is dancing in the sand, a demographic that will increase exponentially as the sun dives closer and closer to the mountains. One of the dancers is none other than my neighbor, Paddleboarder Pete. He has his shirt off, his hat backward, and is grinding against a woman in white tights, a purple shawl, and an enormous red hat.

Pete's blistering confidence—not to mention his muscular physique—makes me suddenly aware of how I stack up in comparison. I'm headed toward DEFCON-1 insecurity when I notice a familiar bald head in the crowd.

Thankful for a reason to postpone my *first impression* a few more minutes, I pick my way down the steep steps and slide into a vacant space of concrete next to my father. He's wearing khaki shorts, a light yellow golf shirt—which has the unmistakable aura of thrift store (my dad loves a good thrift store)—prescription sunglasses, a blue fanny pack, and of course, his trusty compression socks and Tevas.

"I was wondering if you were gonna show up," the elderly Japanese tourist who ate my father says. "Are you here with Alex?"

"I actually have a date."

"A date?" he exclaims.

"Yes, Dad, a date. Don't be so shocked."

He ignores me and asks, "Where did you meet her?"

"Online."

"Tinder or Bumble?"

"*Um...*Tinder."

"Let's see."

"What do you mean?"

"Her profile. On your phone. Let's see it."

I pull my phone out and show him a picture of Brook. He gives a quick whistle and slaps me on the leg. "Hubba hubba," he says.

Hubba hubba?

"Take your sunglasses off," I tell my dad.

"Why?"

"Just do it."

He pulls off his glasses. His eyes are big and glassy.

"Are you stoned?" I ask.

"*Very.*"

I'm about to let out a long exhale of judgment, but I suck it back in. "Brownies again?" I ask.

"Nope," my dad says, unzipping his fanny pack and extracting a small bag and holding it up. "*Gummies.*"

He shakes the pack at me and asks, "Want one?"

"I'm good."

He shrugs.

"Where's Mom?" I ask.

"Dancing, I think."

I lean forward and scan the small group in front of the stage. "Where? I don't see her."

"There," he points. "With your neighbor."

"That's not—"

The shawl and hat are so big it's nearly impossible to tell, but as I watch the woman flail about—my mother dances like Elaine from *Seinfeld*: disco meets grand mal seizure—I realize this *is* my mother. Paddleboard Pete is dancing—no, Paddleboard Pete is *grinding*—against the woman who gave birth to me.

I lurch forward and dry heave.

Fighting back a second round of bile, I squeak out, "How did this happen?"

"Well, a couple of days ago, your mom saw Pete pulling up in his truck with all his paddleboards. And in all the years we've lived here, neither your mother or I have been paddle-boarding. So she asked if maybe he would take us out for a private lesson. When they started talking about payment, he said he would gladly take payment in brownies—which, by the way, he said that you told him about."

"Which, by the way, I *had* to tell him about because my dog was *catatonic* in his backyard from *my parents'* weed brownies."

He waves me off and continues, "Anyhow, he took us out yesterday, then we had him over for dinner and your mother, well, I think she fancies him."

"He's like thirty years younger than her."

"Thirty-four, actually."

I rub my temples with my fingers to keep them from going Mount St. Helens and ask, "How are you okay with this?"

He pats me on the shoulder and says, "You need to mellow out, son."

I stand and head back up the stairs toward the beer tent. After seeing your father stoned out of his mind and seeing your mother grinding her sixty-eight-year-old hips against your hunky neighbor, well, talking to a hot girl doesn't seem so scary.

Cassie

"Here, Cassie," Mia says, dangling a piece of pepperoni in front of me. Mia is Julie's best friend. Mia is Julie's *Hugo*. I lean forward and gently take the pepperoni in my teeth.

I still try to be extra gentle around Mia, even though we've been friends for a while now. She was scared of me the first time I met her and she ran away from me. Julie told me not to be upset, that it wasn't my fault and that Mia was bitten by a dog when she was younger. But I was upset. Who would bite an adorable little girl? And why am I getting blamed for this?

The next time I saw her was at Julie's *eighth* birthday party (I only know this because Julie and I are the same age) and I went and sat a few feet from where Mia was sitting and eating cake. I could hear Mia's heart beating in her chest and I thought maybe she was going to get up and run away, but she didn't. Every few minutes I would get up and go a little bit closer until I was sitting right next to her.

I looked up into her little brown face and I tried to tell her, *I will never hurt you. I will never ever hurt you.*

I could see her bottom lip quivering, so I got up and walked away. It was hard. I wanted so badly to put my head in her lap. And I wanted to lick a scratch on her knee, but I made myself get up and walk away.

The next time I saw her was here, at this same place with the music and all the people.

"Just stick your hand out," Julie said to Mia. "I promise you; she is the sweetest dog in the world. She won't bite you."

Mia reached out her hand. It was shaking. In it was a big piece of kettle corn. I slowly—the slowest I could possibly go—put my chin in her hand, then I stuck out my tongue and I licked up the kettle corn.

"That tickles," Mia laughed.

That was the day we became friends.

Speaking of kettle corn, after we finish off the pizza, Julie, Mia, and I get some kettle corn and the three of us plop down in the grass and eat the entire bag.

Jerry

The beer tent is packed to the gills with small groups conversing, people leaned over the railing and gazing at the concert below, and a long, twenty-minute line to get beer and wine.

After a few minutes of pushing through the crowd, I spot a girl up against the railing talking with two guys. She's clad in a red bikini top and white shorts and resembles the pictures I saw on Tinder.

I tap her on the shoulder and she turns.

With her dyed blonde hair and pouty lips, she looks like she belongs on a trashy reality television show. There's a large purple octopus tattoo taking up the better part of her toned midriff, the tentacles wrapping around her hips and I presume onto her buttocks.

"Brook?" I ask.

"You made it!" she shouts, pulling me in against her big—but not too big—well, maybe just *a tad* too big—breasts.

She turns to the two guys—both of whom have thick beards and are covered in tattoos—and says, "Guys, this is my friend, Jerry. We met on Tinder."

I raise my hand in a perfunctory wave.

Hey, dudes.

You guys on Tinder or what?

Brook has a beer cup in her right hand; actually, it's three beer cups stacked inside one another, and says, "Let's get you a drink."

"Okay," I say, happy not to have to make idle chitchat with the two gentlemen.

Brook grabs my hand and begins pulling me behind her. Instead of taking me to the back of the line, she pulls me up to the front and shouts, "Jake!"

A guy pouring beer from a tap—also with a beard and tattoos (I'm starting to see a pattern here)—snaps his head up and smiles.

Brook shakes her nearly empty beer cup at him and flashes

two fingers. Ten seconds later, two frothing beers are hand delivered.

No payment appears necessary.

We find an open spot on the railing and Brook says, "I'm so glad you came."

"Me too."

We cheers and she gulps down a quarter of her beer.

"So you said your friend is in the band?" I ask.

"Yeah, Tyler. He's the crazy one in the Speedo."

"That takes guts."

"Yeah, well, when you got the goods, you might as well show 'em off."

I force a laugh, then ask, "So how long have you been a cocktail waitress at Harrah's?"

"Seven years."

"You must like it?"

"Money is good, especially in the summer. You have to deal with a bunch of shitheads hitting on you and grabbing your ass, but—" she shrugs, "it is what it is."

"You ever want to do anything else?"

"Maybe a dental hygienist someday. We'll see."

I leave a few beats open for her to ask me a question. She rocks her head to the music and takes a long drink.

I take a sip of beer, then ask, "What do you do for fun?"

"Go out, have some drinks," she pauses, "I like karaoke!"

I wait a few seconds.

"What about you?" she asks.

"I'm sort of a homebody. I read a lot, watch a lot of Netflix, play with my dog."

"That's cool." She nods at my beer and says, "Finish that and I'll get us a couple more."

I take a few long chugs, dripping a bunch down my chin, then hand her what's left. She slugs my remaining beer and says, "I'll be right back."

She leaves and I check my cell phone. I have a text message from Alex telling me that Julie left with her mom and that Cassie is tied to a tree. I step up one rung on the railing and glance backward over the top of the mesh divider. I can see the top half of Cassie lying next to a tree. Mia is sitting next to her, stroking her ears.

I text Alex back that Cassie is all good. A half minute later, Brook returns.

After a few sips and a second cheers, I say, "Okay, Desert Island."

Brook slugs back two inches of beer, wipes her mouth and asks, "What's that?"

"You can bring one book, one movie, and one TV series to a desert island, what do you bring?"

She scrunches her bottom lip, which is pretty cute, then says, "Book would have to be *Style*."

"*Style*, like the magazine?"

"No, it's a book."

Oh, good.

"By Lauren Conrad," she says, "You know, from *The Hills*."

"Oh, okay." I'm vaguely familiar with the MTV reality show from a decade earlier, but I'm more familiar with Lauren Conrad because she has a series of fiction novels based loosely on her time in L.A. "She actually has a bunch of novels as well," I tell Brook.

"I heard that!" she exclaims, then continues, "Movie would have to be *Crazy, Stupid, Love*."

"I love that movie. Steve Carell is hilarious."

"Ryan Gosling is half naked in it," she scoffs. "I mean, I am *alone* on this island, right?"

I nod and smile.

"And for the TV series, it would have to be a toss-up between *The Real Housewives of Orange County* and *The Real Housewives of Atlanta*. I have to pick just one?"

I almost say, "Yep, it's a real Sophie's Choice," but considering her answers thus far, the reference would be lost on her.

"I guess if I have to pick one," she says, "I'd have to go with… Orange County."

I laugh, then say, "I would bring—"

"Let's go dance," she interrupts.

"Oh, okay."

She slugs back her beer, beckons for me to finish mine—she ends up drinking a good half of it—then grabs my hand and leads me out of the tent and down the steep steps.

As I stumble behind Brook, using my free hand to brace myself on the railing, I catch my father's eye in my peripheral. He gives me a huge grin and two *orange* thumbs-up (consequence of the big bag of Cheetos Puffs on his lap).

Brook and I snake our way to the now crowded dance section of beach in front of the stage. Thankfully, my mother and Pete are gone. (Which the more I think about, the more troubling it becomes. Wherever they are, I hope my mom still has her hat on.)

Brook kicks off her shoes, turns into me, and begins swaying her hips to the beat. She might not be well read, but damn if she can't move and the thought of where my mother and Pete are and what exactly they're doing is pushed aside by the voluptuous femme fatale. I do my best to keep up, but I'm made of cardboard and I can only fake it so well.

Brook doesn't seem to mind or is too buzzed to care. After two songs, she surprises me by leaning in and pressing her mouth to mine.

"I'm glad you came," she says, running her hands through my hair.

It's my first kiss in over a year and I expect it to burn a hole in my pants, but it doesn't.

It does nothing.

"Me too," I lie.

I fake it for another two songs, then say, "I've got to get going. I have my dog with me."

"You brought your dog?" she shrieks. "I love dogs!"

Cassie

Julie had to leave and she tied me to a tree. Mia kept me company for a little while, then she had to leave too. I don't get to see Mia very often, only a few times a year, so I gave her a bunch of extra licks when she said goodbye.

Now I'm just sitting here listening to the music (which I don't like; I much prefer music without words) and watching all the people. A bunch of people come to pet me. A few of them smell like the magic grassy brown squares. I bark at one girl, hoping she'll give me one, but all I get is a few more scratches.

(What I wouldn't give for another magic grassy brown square. There are so many doors in my head that I still need to open.)

At some point, I drift off to sleep.

"Cassie!"

I blink my eyes open.

It's Jerry.

"Hi, girl," he says, rubbing my ears. "How was your nap?

It was a great nap, Jerry.

"Oh, hey there," a girl behind Jerry says.

She takes a few steps toward me and leans down. She has big bumps on her chest. I know all girls have these bumps, but hers are much bigger than others.

I lean forward and sniff her bumps.

They smell salty.

Why do her bumps smell salty?

And why are her bumps all swishy?

I want to investigate this mystery further, but Miss Big Bumps grabs my head between both hands and says, "Who's a good doggy? Who's a good doggy?" She shakes my head when she does this.

I bark.

Kindly take your hands off my face.

"Cassie!" Jerry yells. "Be nice."

She shook my head, Jerry.

Babies, soda pop, and my head.

Things you do not shake, Jerry.

"Well, we should be going," Jerry says to Big Bumps.

Yes, Jerry.

The faster, the better.

"Oh, okay," she says. "Text me soon."

She leans forward and she presses her face to Jerry's mouth. I know this is how human's lick, but it still makes me angry.

That's my mouth!

"Bye, doggy," she shouts, then she turns and leaves.

Jerry grabs my head with both hands. (It's okay if Jerry grabs my head. If I like you, then you can grab my head.)

He says, "You don't like her?"

No, Jerry, I do not.

Her bumps are all swishy, she shook my head, then she licked your face.

"That's okay," he says. "I don't like her either."

* * *

I stop at the dirt path that leads down to the water.

Jerry stops and turns around.

"I don't feel like it, Cassie," he says. "Can we just go home?"

I want to go in the water, but if you want to go home, we can do that, Jerry. We can snuggle on the bed and watch Netflix. That's almost as good as going in the lake.

Jerry leans down and I feel him adjust my collar. Sometimes my fur bunches up and my collar gets tight.

I hear a light click.

Then Jerry stands up. He's holding my leash in his hand. He has a big grin on his face.

"Last one in the lake is a stinky, smelly, dog," Jerry yells, then he darts down the path.

I twirl, twirl, twirl, then I race after him.

10

"THE WHARF"

Hugo

The only good thing about being so small is that it's easy to hide. From my spot in the bushes, I watch the humans and cars crisscross the street. The humans are holding round colored objects above their heads, which protect them from the rain. Cars race through the street. Every once in a while, a car driving through the rising water near the curb splashes water into my hiding spot.

I'm cold and wet. What little fur I have is matted to my tiny body. I used to have so much fur. Thick black and tan fur. I could play in the snow for hours and not get cold. Jerry would always say, "How can you shed as much as you do and still have so much fur?"

That was then.

That was before I became a stupid little baby cat.

A small puddle has formed in the dirt beneath me and I lap up the water. (I drank from the lake that wasn't my Lake twice, but both times it made me sick.) The rainwater is delicious and I drink my fill.

I'm no longer thirsty, but I'm hungry. Starving. It seems like forever since my last meal of kibble, though I know it's only been two days.

My tiny stomach rumbles.

How can a stomach so small rumble so loud?

This is what Cassie must have felt like when she lived on the Street. When she said she was a "scavenger." Always hungry. Always wondering where and when her next bite of food would come.

But she survived.

Could I?

* * *

My first day on the Street didn't go so well.

After waiting at the lake that wasn't my Lake for a day and a half for Jerry to come, I finally smelled my way to a bunch of shops on the water. I know what shops are; Jerry would take Cassie and me to the shops all the time. The Bakery Shop. The Ball Shop. The Food Shop. But where there are shops, there are humans. Swarms of them. I could smell so many different types of food: fish, hamburger, cheese! But I never had a chance to find any. I was too busy running from humans.

Every time a human saw me, they would try to pick me up. I would run away from one human, only to have to run away from another. One human caught me. A Jerry-human. I hissed and I'm ashamed to admit this, I bit him.

This was the first time I ever bit a human on purpose. (I bit Jerry a few times on accident when we would play tug-o-war with my rope.) The Jerry-human yelled and dropped me to the ground, and I scampered to my hiding spot in the bushes.

I was rethinking my plan, trying to figure out how to get through all those humans and to some of that delicious food, when I saw a dog. A big brown and white dog. A boxer.

I have a bad history with boxers. The only fight I ever had with another dog was a boxer. *Gallagher.* We were wrestling at the dog park, like always, and then he went crazy and bit my shoulder. I had to go see Dr. Josh and he gave me something called "stitches." But maybe this boxer could help me. Maybe he could help me find the Lake. Or at least, some food.

The boxer was tied to a tree near one of the shops. I wiggled out of my spot in the bushes, then scampered up to him. He was brown with a white circle around one of his eyes. His face was flat and his nose upturned, the way boxers' faces are.

I lifted one of my tiny little paws and meowed.

"Hi."

His front legs stiffened. He leaned down and gave me a sniff.

"Can I ask you a quest—"

Before I could finish, he started barking and lunged at me.

"I'm not a cat!" I wanted to explain. "Well, I mean, yes, I'm a cat right *now*. But I used to be a dog."

Luckily he was tied to the tree and he couldn't get to me. I scampered away, then looked back over my shoulder at the boxer on his hind legs, straining against his leash. I ran and ran, whizzing through all the human's legs, then finally found a hiding spot under the pier.

Couldn't the boxer tell I used to be a dog? Or was all my dogness gone?

All he saw was a cat. A cat he wanted to chase, or eat, or kill. But could I blame him? That's how I saw cats when I was a dog.

What if all the cats I chased used to be dogs?

I stayed under the pier the rest of the day and night.

* * *

Thankfully, humans don't like rain and there are far fewer of them today. And although I can't smell the food as well—it's hard to smell things in the rain other than rain—I know it's there.

I wiggle out of my spot in the bushes and scamper behind a

tree, then run down the pier. Some of the shops have big over-
hangs which shields the outdoor part from the rain. I slip through
the opening in a small red metal fence to where there are a bunch
of tables and chairs. Under one of the chairs, I see them.

Two French fries.

I gobble the first one so fast I don't taste it. I try to eat the
second one slowly, like how Cassie would, knowing it might be
awhile before I get another chance to eat. But before I'm even
done *thinking* about eating it, I've already eaten it.

I continue scavenging under the tables for more food. I find a
piece of bread and a pickle. Jerry was always eating pickles when
he was working on his computer. So, of course, I love the smell of
pickles. But I hate how they taste. Still, I force myself to eat it.

"Hey! Get outta here!" someone yells.

I look up.

It's a she-human. She looks like Mom, but bigger. Like Mom,
she has a broom. She pokes the broom at me and says, "Shoo!
Shoo!"

(I don't know why she's talking about shoes. I haven't eaten
any shoes in a long time; not since I was a puppy.)

I slink back through the red bars and run down the pier. I run
past a bunch of shops, then come to a metal railing. Through the
railing I can see the lake that isn't my Lake. There are a bunch of
boats, though different than the boats on my Lake; these are
bigger and one of them blares its horn. When the horn dies, I hear
barking.

Barking coming from the water?

I follow the barking, then stop and look out through the rail-
ings. Lying in a pile, on a huge piece of floating wood, are a pack
of black dogs. (Only their legs look weird. They are flat and
pointy.)

A few of the big black dogs bark. One of the dogs pushes
another of the dogs off the floating wood and into the water. The
dog flips over in the water and dives. He's like a fish.

A black fish dog.

I get as close to the railing as I can and I shout, "Hey, do you guys know where the Lake is?"

One of them looks at me and barks.

But I don't understand him.

I must not speak fish dog.

* * *

I don't have any more luck scavenging. I'm chased by a couple more humans until finally finding my way back under the pier. Night comes and with it a chill from the rain and a light wind. The sand is cold and my body shakes. My tiny teeth chatter. I hear Cassie's voice in my head, "You have to move, Hugo. You have to find somewhere warm."

Okay, Cassie.

I will.

I slink out from under the pier. I'm still starving and I want to go look for more food at the shops, but I know finding somewhere warm is more important.

The streets are mostly empty. I scamper for a few blocks away from the lake. It's still raining and the streetlights reflect off the large puddles of water in the street. I walk between a row of buildings onto a brick walkway. I think it's called an "alley." This is where Cassie spent most of her time on the Street. Going from alley to alley.

Scavenging.

Surviving.

I continue down the alley. There's a large dumpster. Like the one on our street. A big green rectangle. I sniff at the bottom. I can smell food inside. I try to jump onto the dumpster, but it's too high and I slip down and land in a puddle. Something scurries near me. I nose around in a crack between the bricks looking for whatever it is, but it's hiding from me. I suppose no matter how small you are, there's always something smaller.

I scamper through the wet alley, then to another. And another. Looking for anywhere that could be warm. But everything is wet. Wet and cold.

Like me.

Another alley. Then I see something. Actually, I see a lot of somethings. I know from when Jerry would take Cassie and me hiking, that people live in them sometimes.

Tents.

Most of the tents are dark, but a few have light coming from inside them. I know there are humans inside the tents. I can smell them. But I don't care. I need somewhere warm.

I come to the first tent and give it a few scratches. My paws slide off the side of the slick tent, barely making a sound. I wait, scratch again. Nothing happens.

I move onto the next tent.

Scratch, scratch, scratch.

There's a weird sound and then a flap in the tent opens. A she-human sticks her head out and says, "Wha—Oh, hello."

I dart through the opening and out of the rain.

"Well, come in, why don't you?" the she-human says with a laugh.

I never thought I'd be so happy to see inside.

I shake the water off me.

"Ahh," the she-human says with a laugh. Then she picks me up. "Let me help you out, little guy."

She sits me in her lap, then pats me down with something until I am mostly dry. Then she says, "Are you hungry?"

Yes!

I'm starving.

I hear a crinkling sound and then she says, "I bet you'll like beef jerky."

I *love* beef jerky!

109

She feeds me a few strips. I gobble them down. The fry was okay, but this, this is amazing!

I paw at her face and she feeds me one more. She offers me another one after that and I want to eat it so badly, but my stupid tiny little stomach is about to burst.

"What's your name?" she asks, holding me up to her face.

Hugo.

I lick her chin.

Her face is rough. Rough like Jerry's. She has long hair like a she-human and her face looks like a she-human, but her face is rough like Jerry's.

I sniff.

And she smells like a Jerry-human.

I would give this more thought, but I'm too tired.

"Oh, sleepy kitten," she-Jerry says. "Let's make you a bed."

She wraps me in something, something that smells like her, then cradles me to her stomach.

I am warm.

11

"SUMMER OF 1991"

Cassie

I feel a thump on my head and open my eyes. Jerry's feet squirm next to my face. Jerry moves around a lot when he sleeps and sometimes he accidentally hits me in the head. (I could easily sleep somewhere else, on the carpet, on my dog bed, or near Jerry's head, but I usually fall asleep licking Jerry's feet.) Jerry's feet settle and I give them a few licks, then I hop down from the bed. I reach my front legs forward, lean my head back, and stretch.

Then I shake it out.

I pad out of the bedroom and to the big silver water bowl. I take a long drink. I hear birds chirping which means it's early. Too early for Jerry. Jerry doesn't like to get up until the birds are all chirped out.

I'm heading back to the bedroom when I stop and sniff.

Sniff, sniff, sniff.

I run to the window and look outside. Everything is wet.

It rained!

Why did it take me so long to smell the rain? I have this big nose that's supposed to detect the rain.

You let me down, nose!

I run into the bedroom and jump on Jerry.

The worms, Jerry! We have to save the worms!

Jerry

I'm under attack.

I cover my face and yell, "Cassie! Get off!"

She doesn't get off of me.

"What's going on?" I shout, thinking perhaps we're under attack by drones, or the house is on fire, or there is a raccoon in the house. Then I smell it. A powerful, unmistakable, dewy smell.

Rain.

"No, no, no, no," I say. "I'm not doing Worm Patrol right now."

At the sound of the word *Worm*, Cassie bites at my bed comforter, yanking it off of me.

I scramble for my cell phone on the night table and check the time.

6:53 a.m.

Cassie nuzzles her cold nose into my back, trying to roll me off the bed. "It's seven in the morning, Cassie. There aren't even people on the bike path right now."

Worm Patrol started last summer.

While South Lake Tahoe does get a considerable amount of precipitation, the vast majority of that comes in October through April and it comes in the form of snow. During the summer months, especially July and August, it rarely rains, which is one of the reasons Tahoe is such a popular tourist getaway.

The previous summer, after a rare rainstorm blew through, the sun came out and I took Hugo and Cassie for a walk on the bike path. On this particular day, after this particular rainstorm, the bike path was permeated with worms seeking refuge from the soaked and oxygen-deprived soil. (I Googled "Why worms come out after a rainstorm," and evidently, this is why.) Sadly, many of these worms had been flattened, cut in half, dismembered, and trounced upon by the heavy summer bike path traffic—a combination of beachgoers, runners, skateboarders, bikers, and those four-wheel monstrosity "family" bicycles.

Cassie wouldn't stop whining, then she began frantically picking up all the surviving worms in her teeth and transporting them back to the surrounding dirt. It's one of those things that makes your heart melt the first time you see it, but isn't as much fun the one-hundredth time and definitely no fun at 7:00 a.m.

"The worms will be fine for another few hours," I tell Cassie. "Please, can we go later?"

I was up until three in the morning surfing the internet, looking for inspiration for a book idea, and the thought of putting on clothes and scouring the bike path for an hour sounds as enjoyable as catching a toenail on the door jamb.

Cassie sticks her face in mine, her huge amber eyes open wide as if to say, "Don't you care about the worms?"

I let out a long sigh. "Okay, okay, I'm getting up."

* * *

Ten minutes later, we're walking down the bike path. Luckily, the path runs in front of a McDonald's and I'm able to grab a coffee and two Egg McMuffins.

While I chow down and the coffee slowly wakes me, cell by cell, Cassie moves down the bike path, scanning the bike path for *lumbricus terrestris*. Each time she comes upon an earthworm, she gently scoops the worm up between her teeth and carries it to the dirt or grass and plops him down. Then it's onto the next worm.

Two miles and seventeen worms later, the bike path ends. By this point, it's closing in on 8:00 a.m. and the first of the joggers and the beachgoers are beginning to stir. Normally, we would turn around and walk home, but this is my first time awake before noon in over four months and I don't want to waste it.

I turn to Cassie and ask, "How about a little run?"

Cassie falls into a light trot next to me and we run, walk, run, walk (Cassie is so happy to be running that she doesn't worry about the worms) down the sidewalk until the bike path resumes. We follow the bike path behind a residential area and to thick woods. Just beyond the woods, it opens up to a wide green valley.

Cassie knows where we're headed and I follow her through a trampled down section of grass. After a few minutes, we find a small patch of forest two hundred feet square that is covered in pine needles and fallen logs.

I've spent more hours in this small patch of forest than I can count. Both when I was a child and many times over the course of the past three years. But I haven't been back since Hugo died. Though this has less to do with Hugo's death and more to do with death in general.

I reach down and scoop up a handful of dirt. The soil is still soft from the rain. It will be a good day. A good day to dig a hole.

* * *

"You're late, Bear," Morgan said. She always called me Bear. First it was Jer. Then Jer Bear. Then just Bear.

"Sorry," I shouted, dropping my red BMX into the dirt. "It took seven hours to drive here this time and then my mom made me put all my clothes in the dresser before I left."

Morgan rolled her green eyes, then pushed herself up from the giant log—Lincoln Log—she was sitting on.

She was wearing her usual jean shorts and a red tank top, which was a couple of shades darker than her hair. She was an inch taller than when I last saw her over Spring break.

"Did you bring your stuff?" she asked.

I pulled my backpack off and gave it a few pats. "Yeah, right here."

Morgan smiled, revealing the small gap between her two front teeth, then rushed toward me and enveloped me in a giant hug.

I felt my cheeks redden.

Morgan was eleven, a year older than me, and she'd just finished 6th grade. We'd been inseparable since my parents first bought the house in South Lake Tahoe five years earlier.

Morgan lived three houses down from us. She was an only child and the day we first arrived—the summer after I finished kindergarten—she was drawing on the sidewalk with chalk. She asked if I wanted to draw with her. Of course I did. Especially since my brother Mark was thirteen (eight years older than me) and never wanted to hang out.

For the next five years, every day for the three months of summer, the two weeks in winter, and the week for Spring Break, I spent with Morgan. Though I had friends back home in Oregon —a few, not a lot—Morgan was my best friend.

At the beginning of the past school year, Morgan's 6th grade class made a time capsule. Everyone brought one thing to put in the capsule (preferably from the pop culture of the time) and each of them wrote a short essay about what they thought middle school would be like. Then at the end of 8th grade, they would dig up the time capsule and look at all their stuff.

But Morgan said it was too hard to pick just one thing to put in the time capsule and that three years didn't seem like a very long time.

All the stuff they put in the capsule would still be popular in three years, wouldn't it?

So during winter break earlier that year, Morgan broached the idea that we make a time capsule of our own. That way we could put in as much stuff as we wanted and we could dig it up whenever we wanted. In five years. In ten years. In *twenty* years.

After releasing me from her hug, I leaned down and picked up my backpack. I unzipped the front compartment and pulled out two sandwiches wrapped in tin foil. I handed one to Morgan and said, "My mom says hi."

Morgan took the sandwich, tore away the tinfoil, then crammed a huge bite of peanut butter and grape jelly into her mouth. We both sat on Lincoln Log and ate our sandwiches and drank our Capri Suns. When we were done with the sandwiches, Megan dipped her hand into her backpack and pulled out a foil package of her own.

I knew what was inside.

Cookies.

For the last three years, since Morgan's mother taught her how to bake, I'd been Morgan's guinea pig for her creations. Brownies, doughnuts, cakes, pies, and especially, cookies. Most of them were pretty good, but others, like her chocolate chip and Skittles cookies, were not.

Morgan unwrapped the foil and handed me a cookie. It looked just like an oatmeal raisin cookie but it was twice as fat.

"Go ahead," Morgan coaxed. "Try it."

I took a bite and it was amazing. It tasted just like a Little Debbie Oatmeal Crème Pie.

"It's amazing," I mumbled, crumbs cascading down from my mouth.

"Yay!" Morgan said, clapping her hands together a few times. "They are oatmeal raisin and *cream cheese*."

I ate a second cookie and then it was time to get to work.

* * *

"What do you think?" Morgan asked, showing me the box. Morgan had spent the last few weeks perfecting our time capsule.

It was a box that a pair of her mom's cowboy boots had come in. It was two feet square and eight inches tall. Morgan had reinforced the walls of the box with two rolls of duct tape. (Morgan was always fixing things with duct tape, a skill passed down from her father.)

"I think it will work just fine," I tell her.

She pulled a full roll of duct tape from her backpack and said, "When we finish putting all our stuff in, I'll tape it up so it's airtight. We don't want any water leaking in."

We spent the next half an hour taking things out of our backpacks one-by-one and putting them in the box. The highlights were:

Me: A stack of Garbage Pail Kids (*Barfin Barbara* on the top).

Morgan: A stuffed animal (Gizmo from Gremlins).

Me: A copy of *Where the Red Fern Grows*.

Morgan: A G.I. Joe.

Me: A crumpled $2 bill.

Morgan: A copy of *The Hobbit*.

Me: A Viewfinder with a Scooby Doo disc.

Morgan: A Gameboy cartridge, *Skate or Die* (broken).

Me: A baggy with one of my molars (that I lost the week before).

Morgan: A recipe for chocolate chip and Skittles cookies.

Once we put everything in, Morgan set about taping the box closed and I scouted the area for a good place to dig a hole. After fifteen back-breaking minutes, I found a decent spot and had a hole dug six inches deep.

Morgan looked at my meager work with a laugh and said, "Bear, you might be the slowest digger in the entire world."

We traded off digging for the next hour until we had a large hole about three feet deep.

Morgan went and retrieved the box from behind the log and dropped it next to the hole. There was so much tape on the box, I figured it would last for an eternity. Also, Morgan had made an executive decision. On top of the box, written in heavy permanent black marker on the thick rows of duct tape was: **TO BE OPENED ON 6/18/2001.**

Ten years.

* * *

Morgan and I spent the next five weeks doing what we always did: camping in her backyard, staying up late to watch *Saturday Night Live*, playing Monopoly, making S'mores, reading comic books, playing Gameboy, going to the lake, setting up a Dessert Stand so Megan could sell her cakes and cookies, and of course, riding our bikes to *our* secret spot in the woods.

The last week of July, I came down with the flu. It was terrible. I had to stay in bed for three days. Morgan came to visit me a few times, and she let me borrow her Gameboy (as long as I disinfected it once I was better).

That Sunday, I was just starting to feel better. I wanted to go to the lake with Morgan and her parents, but my mom wouldn't let me. She said I needed to rest for a few more days. I was bummed, but within the next hour, I would throw up the Cinnamon Toast Crunch I ate for breakfast.

A few hours later, there was a knock at the door, then my mother shouted, "Oh, no!"

I jumped out of bed and ran to the window. The neighbors

from across the street, the Winstons, were standing on the front porch. Mrs. Winston and my mom were holding each other and crying as Mr. Winston looked on awkwardly.

I'd never seen my mother so upset.

Where was my dad?

Something must have happened to my dad!

I ran downstairs, out the front door and screamed, "What happened? Where's Dad?"

My mom turned. She was sobbing. "It's not your father," she choked out. "It's Morgan."

"What happened to her?" I screamed. "Is she okay?"

My mom cradled my head and said, "No, honey, she's not."

She was diving for golf balls. Some of the people who owned houses on the lake would buy buckets of cheap golf balls and hit them into the lake. Every once in a while, Morgan and I would strap on our goggles and go golf ball hunting.

The lake is the second deepest lake in the United States—1,600 feet deep in some places—but in South Lake, the water is shallow going out a hundred yards. Even two hundred yards out, where the boats are tied to the white floating mooring balls, it's only eight or ten feet deep.

Not finding any golf balls in the shallows, Morgan continued out farther and farther to where the water was twelve feet deep.

That's where Morgan drowned.

I didn't eat solid food for two weeks. My mom was lucky to get me to drink a couple of Carnation shakes each day. We went back to Oregon three weeks early and I started to see a therapist.

When winter break came, I refused to go to Tahoe, so for the first time in six years, we didn't ski and we celebrated Christmas in Oregon. The following summer, I stayed with my dad in Oregon, then I stayed with my Aunt Joan when my dad would make the trip to South Lake every other weekend.

It would take me three years before I would go back in the lake.

Morgan's death destroyed her parents' marriage. They divorced a few years later. Her mother moved to Mexico and her dad drank himself to death. Their house was bought and sold a few times. Paddleboarder Pete lives there now.

Ten years later, on June 18, 2001, I'd just finished my second year of college at Oregon State and I was working a summer job washing windows.

I would not think about our time capsule once.

* * *

The area where I'm positive Morgan and I buried our time capsule is pockmarked with holes. In the three years I've been back in Tahoe, I've dug over thirty holes, but I've yet to find it.

Cassie sticks her head into various holes, sniffing and inspecting them, before choosing one to make a little deeper. Soon half her body is submerged in a hole and she's kicking up waves of dirt behind her.

I find the shovel that I've hidden in a thicket of bushes, then choose a spot and begin digging. The earth is soft from the rain and it only takes me fifteen minutes to dig down three feet.

All I find are worms.

12

"4TH OF JULY"

Jerry

Each year, over 100,000 tourists flock to the beaches of Lake Tahoe to celebrate America's independence. The most notable party is at a beach five miles into Nevada called Zephyr Cove. Hundreds of boats tie up together in the water, and the half-mile of sandy beach is overrun with thousands of revelers partaking in Spring Break-like debauchery. My first year in Tahoe, I rode my bike to Zephyr Cove to witness the madness, but by the time I arrived, the police were in the process of shutting things down. Apparently, the seventh time the ambulance is called, it's the *last* time.

The biggest party on the California side takes place at Timber Cove and currently there are people packed like sardines at the usually quiet beach tucked behind the Beach Retreat & Lodge.

A stage has been set up and a guy with a man bun pumps out music at five million decibels. Girls in matching red thongs—I recognize a few as go-go dancers from Opal Lounge in Montbleu casino—thrust, grind, and twerk under the rainbow of floodlights on stage.

Alex and I are standing in a small buffer between the outer edge of the scrum of dancing and the thicket of tents and gazebos set up in the sand. A few police officers chat in a group near the Timber Cove pier, which juts out over the rippling blue water.

The police officers keep a lazy eye on the burgeoning party, but for the most part, things are still tame. But, then again, it's only 5:00 p.m. and the world-class fireworks won't go off for another four and a half hours. That being said, if last year was any indication, there will be plenty of action for the police officers in the hours to come.

Two young women, girls really, both well-endowed, and both clad in red, white, and blue bikinis emerge from the crowd of dancers and head in our direction. When they are steps away, Alex —who is wearing short lime-green swim trunks that hug his massive thighs, the waistband nearly invisible under his protruding (and hairy) belly—tips his beer can at the girls and says, "God Bless America."

The two girls exchange a quick glance, then scurry by, disappearing into the throng of tents behind us.

"Will you stop doing that?" I protest.

"What?" Alex grins, his handlebar mustache twitching. "It's bound to work eventually."

We've been at the beach for all of twenty minutes and this is already the fifth or sixth time Alex has said this line.

I shake my head at him, knowing nothing I say will prevent him from his onslaught. My only hope is to numb my senses until his advances no longer make me cringe with discomfort.

I slug down the last of my first beer, then lean down and grab two more from our cheap styrofoam cooler. I hand one to Alex, his fourth by my count, and he takes it with a belch. "Thanks, mate."

The sky is clear and the sun pulsates overhead. According to my phone, the temperature is only eighty-four degrees, but at 6,300 feet, the sun's rays pack a wallop. It isn't uncommon to overhear a roasted tourist utter, "I was only in the sun for like twenty minutes."

I pull off my shirt and throw it to the ground. Compared to Alex, I appear malnourished, but I'm soft around the edges and my frighteningly pale love handles muffin-top above my blue swim trucks. I lather my front, my arms, my legs, then I pull off my sunglasses and massage the lotion onto my face and into the thinning hair on my forehead.

When I'm finished, I hold out the bottle to Alex and say, "Will you do my back?"

"No way," he says with a shake of his curly hair. "Ask one of them." He nods at a group of twenty-something girls huddled beneath a white tent a few yards behind us.

"Come on, man. You know I'm not gonna go ask them." I hold out the bottle. *"Please?"*

He takes the bottle with a huff, moves behind me, then proceeds to squirt half—maybe even two-thirds—of the bottle onto my back.

"You asshole," I mutter, knowing my back must look like I was just dipped in Elmer's Glue.

"Ask and you shall receive," he bellows, then instead of using his hands, he disperses the lotion using the bottom of his beer can.

Needless to say, my second beer goes down much faster than my first.

Cassie

I know Jerry is going to be gone for a while because he turns on the TV with the volume up high. On the screen, a yellow square with big eyes dances underwater. Jerry calls them "cartoons." Hugo loved them, the drawings on the screen. But not me. I prefer the real thing, like the channel with all the animals. My favorite is "Shark Week." Jerry, Hugo, and I would curl up on the couch and watch hours of these big fish swimming around in the water. I would always look for them when we went to the lake, but they must hang out in the deeper water.

Still, I curl up on the couch and watch the TV for a little while, but it's too loud. It hurts my ears. Jerry should know better.

I jump down from the couch and I go get a drink of water.

Lap, lap, lap.

The house is warm and I spread out on the floor in the kitchen, which is nice and cool.

I pant.

I'm always panting in the summer. Even when my fur falls off onto the couch and the floor and the bed, I still pant. I like summer, but I could do without all the panting.

I lie there for a while. A tiny black spider runs across the floor in front of me. I lean forward and give him a sniff. He doesn't smell like much of anything. I leave him to do his spider stuff and walk to the fridge.

I nose the refrigerator open. There's a big container of blueberries and I bite the lid open. I slurp up two of the blueberries and bite into them. They are amazing. They are the best blueberries I've ever had.

I eat two more. Then two more. Then I bite the container closed.

I pad into the bedroom.

I wonder how long Jerry has been gone.

I sniff the air.

Two hours. There is two hours less Jerry in the air.

I miss Jerry.

I find my teddy, a green alligator, near the bed and pick it up in my teeth. (My alligators—Jerry always buys me the exact same one—didn't survive very long when Hugo was around. Hugo would always tear them apart and pull all the stuffing and squeaker out.) I nose the sliding door of the closet open and sniff around Jerry's dirty clothes.

Now that's the stuff!

I fluff up his clothes for a few seconds, then lie down. Then I tuck my alligator under my chin and fall asleep.

Jerry

"Are you ready yet?" asks Alex.

"One more beer."

"You said that two beers ago."

"Come on," he pleads. "They're just waiting for us to go talk to them."

An hour earlier, three girls set up camp a few feet to our left. Real estate on the beach is scarce and the girls are only a few steps away, close enough that we can overhear them conversing. Alex said he heard one of the girls say I was cute, which is odd because the threesome isn't speaking English.

According to Alex, the girls are J-1's. (Alex hooked up with a J-1 a few years back, so he knows all the ins and outs.) J-1s are university students from overseas who are in America on work visas (the work visa is called a J-1, hence the name). In the winter months, the students are from South America—which is their summer break—and they work at the different ski resorts. In the summer, the J-1's are from Eastern Europe, Russia, Ukraine—or in the case of the girl Alex *bedded*, Romania—and they work at the many hotels, casinos, and a few other seasonal jobs.

Our best guess is that the threesome next to us are Russian, a conjecture based loosely on as Alex put it, they look "sturdy" and that they are drinking from a large bottle of vodka.

It's closing in on 8:00 p.m. and the sun is banking toward the still snowcapped mountains across the lake. I'm sufficiently buzzed, enough so that talking to a girl shouldn't be terrifying, but I can't shake the image of the last girl I hit on—the girl at the

Farmers' Market—telling me flatly, "No," she was not interested in getting coffee with me.

Also, at thirty-five, Alex and I are on the older end of the age spectrum, and sadly, we look it. Sure, there are forty-somethings, even fifty-somethings, but they are anomalies, and to be honest, when I see them dancing and frolicking about, it makes me sad. I don't want to end up as one of these pathetic old men.

But how far away am I, really? Two years? Three at most?

"I'm going," Alex spits. "Are you coming or are you going to sit on your thumb here all night?"

I pick up a beer, slug it down in its entirety, wipe my mouth and say, "Let's go."

Alex takes the three steps to where the girls are swaying to the music and says, "Howdy, ladies."

All three smile, happy to be approached by guys, even if it is by two buffoons.

Alex introduces us, then makes small talk, asking where they're from (which is Serbia) and where they're working this summer (which is Safeway).

"I thought you looked familiar," I say to the girl closest to me. She has dark hair, angular features, and is the least *sturdy* of the group. "You bagged my groceries last week."

"I bag lot of groceries," she says. Her English is heavily accented and slow. "You live here?" she asks.

"Yeah, I do. But I grew up in Oregon?"

"Oregon." She pronounces it *Orey-GAIN*. "Where is this?"

"It's right above California." I show her on an invisible map with my hands.

"Why you come here?"

"Oh. It's complicated. I was living in San Francisco and I was engaged to a girl and she broke up with me for this rich tech guy and I had to get away. My parents have a summer house here and I've been living there for the past few years. Hey, do you read much science fiction?"

She glances at one of her friends, I'm guessing looking for a lifeline (who could blame her), but before she gets any help, I ask, "So you're from Serbia?"

She turns back toward me. "Yes."

"Wow, that's so cool. I didn't know anyone really lived up there. It's so cold. Right? Super cold?"

She glares at me. "Not *that* cold."

"Really? I thought Serbia was freezing."

Her eyebrows cross and she asks, "Where you think Serbia is?"

"Above Russia. Near the Arctic Circle. Right?"

"This *Siberia!*" She turns to her two friends and shouts, "He think us from Siberia!"

I try to laugh with them, but its quickly evident that I'm being laughed at. Your average guy could probably shake this off, but I can't. I tuck tail. "I'm gonna go use the bathroom," I call to Alex as I retreat.

He gives me a half shrug, then continues to enthrall one of the *Serbians* with a story.

I weave my way through the crowd and behind the stage to the beach parking lot and the Porta-Pottys. There are easily eight people to a line behind each of the ten stalls. While I wait in line, a teenager is dragged past me by a cop. The cop gives him a light push and tells him to go home. The kid has some departing words, and I watch as the cop fights the urge to throw him in cuffs.

I glance around the line and notice it's almost entirely kids. College kids and high schoolers. All drunk or stoned. Or whatever else.

I don't belong here. I belong on my couch with Cassie watching Netflix. Or at the movies…with a *girlfriend*.

The line moves a notch closer and I pull out my cell phone. I load Tinder and start swiping. There are lots of cute girls in town because of the 4th, but I don't match with any of them.

I go to settings and look at my age bracket. I have it set to 18-

35. I once again glance around at the barrage of eighteen-year-olds. Why would I ever want to date an eighteen-year-old? Or even a twenty-one-year-old? What could we possibly have in common?

I move the bottom bracket from 18 to 27. I move the top bracket from 35 to 40, then with a light shrug, I slide it up to 45.

A forty-five-year-old? I let out a light laugh. Maybe that's exactly what I need.

I swipe for another ten minutes, then finally it's my turn in the Porta-Potty. As I'm coming out, I see Alex striding toward me.

"How'd it go with the Serbs?" I ask.

"They all have to work tomorrow at six in the morning. They're going home right after the fireworks."

"Did they ask about me?"

"They did *not* ask about you," he says flatly. He nods at the line to the bathrooms and says, "You wait in this line?"

I nod.

He scoffs. Then he walks behind the wall of stalls, where I'm guessing he takes a piss. While I wait for him to finish, or be arrested by the cop who saw him go back there—but appears not to care—I turn back to my phone.

I Google "Serbia" and discover it's in southeastern Europe, near Hungry and Romania. (So yeah, I was a little ways off.)

Then I resume my Tinder swiping.

Like.

Nope.

Like.

Nope.

Like.

Like.

Nope.

Nope.

Nope.

Nope.

Nope.

Nope.

Like.

Nope.

Nope.

Nope.

Oh, my God.

I must say these last words out loud because Alex, back from his whiz, repeats, "*Oh, my God*, what?"

I turn the phone toward Alex.

His eyebrows jump.

"Oh, my God," he says.

On the phone.

On Tinder.

It's my mother.

* * *

"Your mom is on Tinder?"

"Uhh." I can't speak.

I can feel the five beers I drank churning in my stomach.

Alex takes the phone from me and says, "Says here that *Betsy* is forty-four years old? So let's see here, if my math is correct," he begins to laugh uncontrollably, "*Betsy* had you when she was nine-years-old."

I can see his eyes begin to water and I say, "I'm glad you think this is funny."

He begins scrolling through my mother's pictures and I reach out for the phone, "Give me that." I'm going to delete my Tinder account and then throw the phone in the lake.

Alex is about to hand me the phone when he darts it into his other hand and swipes right. The green "Like" icon flashes.

"You LIKED my mother!" I scream.

I punch him in the shoulder as hard as I can.

Alex covers his mouth with his hands. At first I think it's to cover his scream from my punch, but it isn't. It's to cover his scream from what he sees on my phone.

I glance down to my phone. My picture is on one side of the screen. My mother's picture is on the other.

We *Matched.*

I matched on Tinder with my mother.

* * *

"You okay, bro?" Alex asks, still obviously delighted by my having matched with my mother on Tinder.

I shake my head.

In fact, I am *not* okay.

I toggle to my matches. There are six. I highlight my mother and am about to delete our match when a bar flashes at the top of the screen indicating I have a new Tinder message.

Please, please, please don't be what I think it is.

Holding my breath, I click on it.

Hi Honey!

My stomach wrenches and I turn the phone toward Alex and show him. He shakes his head in awe. This is even too much for him. He claps me on the shoulder and says, "I'm sorry, bro," then walks away.

I take a deep breath, then I message back my mother: **Hi Mom**

MOM: **We matched!**

ME: **I see that...I also see that you are 44-years-old**

MOM: **[Smiley face] [Smiley face]**

ME: **You do know that you don't look 44-years-old**

MOM: **I do so.**

ME: **Um...no...maybe change that to 54...or maybe your real age!?! Which if you have forgotten...is 68!!!!**

MOM: **Your father says hi.**

ME: **OMG! Is he on Tinder too?**

MOM: **Yes. He just matched with a lovely young lady.**

ME: **Young?**

MOM: **62.**

ME: **Are you guys going to pay for my therapy sessions?**

MOM: **Therapy sessions?**

ME: **Yes. Because I MATCHED on TINDER with my MOTHER!!!**

MOM: **[GIF of a crying baby]**

ME: **I gotta go. I'm gonna go drown myself in the lake.**

MOM: *OK. Have fun. [Kissy face][Kissy face]*

Cassie

Now I know why Jerry left the TV on so loud. It's *that* day. The worst day. *Bang Day.*

There's a loud bang and I snap my head to the side.

I bark three times, but my barks are no match for the bangs.

Bang, bang, bang.

I run to the closet and to my bang corner. I lie down and press my face into the carpet.

I want Jerry.

He would rub my head and tell me, "They're just fireworks, Cassie."

But who I really want is Hugo. The bangs didn't scare him. And he would lie on top of me, which made the bangs not as bad.

I close my eyes.

More bangs.

My stomach rumbles.

Sometimes the bangs give me the poops.

More bangs.

I start to cry.

It's been awhile since I cried.

Years.

Not since First Home.

But I can't stop.

I want the bangs to stop.

I want Jerry to come home.

I want Hugo back.

Bang, bang, bang, bang, bang, bang, bang, bang, bang.

Jerry

The crowd roars wildly throughout the fireworks finale, which I have to admit is beyond spectacular. Within seconds of the final glowing ember falling into the lake, a mass exodus ensues. The music dies, the stage begins to come down, people pack up their tents, blankets, and coolers, and head out. Half the party will go home, as it is a weekday and many have to work in the morning.

The other half will make their way to Stateline—the California/Nevada border a mile to the east—and to the small strip of casinos and nightclubs and party until the wee hours of the morning.

"I'm heading home," Alex states loudly, one eye half closed. He has drunk at least twelve beers, not to mention a few swigs off the Serbians' bottle of vodka. He gives me two loud claps on the back, then stumbles his way to the flood of departing beachgoers.

I'm still in a weird headspace from my interaction with the Serbs, not to mention my living nightmare Tinder chat with my mother, and I mindlessly begin tossing our pile of empty beer cans into the styrofoam cooler.

"You drink all those?"

I glance up.

It's *Brook*.

The temperature has dropped into the mid-fifties and she's wearing shorts and a hooded sweatshirt. She has American flag temporary tattoos on both cheeks. Even beneath the sweatshirt, her large breasts swell.

I smile. "My friend Alex drank most of them."

"Did he leave?"

"More like wobbled. But yeah."

She giggles.

I ask, "Who are you here with?"

"I was here with a big group. They all want to go out to the casinos, but I'm not feeling it."

"Yeah, I was thinking about that myself, but I think I'm just gonna head home."

She pokes me in the ribs with her foot. "Or we could go to Nepheles for a drink."

Nepheles is a neighborhood bar with low lights and a good wine list, and frequented more by locals than out-of-towners.

I should go home. I should make sure Cassie is okay.

"Okay," I say. "One drink."

Cassie

I hate to admit it, but I peed inside.

It just came out.

I thought the bangs were done, but then there were more, and it just happened.

I peed.

I'm so sorry, Jerry.

I'm so sorry I peed.

I'm sitting at the front door. When Jerry gets home, I will show him where I peed.

Hopefully, he will forgive me.

I sniff.

There are eight less hours of Jerry in the air.

Where is he?

I can't remember the last time Jerry left me alone for eight hours.

I hope he's okay.

What if the bangs got him?

I lift my head.

Footsteps.

I jump up and paw at the door.

I hear a jingle.

Keys.

Keys!!

More jingling, then finally, the door opens. I nose the door open and jump up on Jerry. Oh, he smells so good.

"Cassie!" he shouts. "Are you okay, girl?" he says, falling to his knees. "I was worried about you."

I lick his face.

I'm okay.

Now.

"Doggie!"

I snap my head to the side.

There's someone with Jerry.

I sniff.

Noooooooooo.

"Hi, doggie!" *Big Bumps* says, bopping my nose with her hand.

I glance up at Jerry.

She bopped me.

She...*bopped*...me.

But Jerry doesn't seem to notice or care.

Why doesn't Jerry notice or care?

"Go potty," Jerry says.

That's the thing, Jerry. I already did. In the closet. Still, I push past them and into the yard. I force a bit of pee out, then I run back inside.

Jerry and Brook are in his bedroom.

Jerry has his shirt off.

I remember this.

He used to do this with Avery.

Don't do it, Jerry.

I go and grab my teddy and I drop it at Jerry's feet. He glances down at my stuffed alligator, then me. He's all wobbly.

"Fetch?" Jerry scoffs. "Now?"

I never play fetch.

Never.

I bark.

I feel a push on my head.

Big Bumps.

She just pushed me out of the way.

First Big Bumps bopped me, Jerry.

Now she pushed me.

I want to bite her toes.

They're right there, her toenails all pink, and I want to bite them.

I don't.

Jerry and Big Bumps flop on the bed.

They're both naked.

It's been a while, but I know the smell.

I know what's about to happen.

I jump on the bed.

I nose my way between them.

"Cassie!" Jerry yells. "Knock it off."

He pushes me off the bed.

I jump back up and bark.

"Cassie!"

He jumps off the bed and he grabs me by the collar. He drags me toward the door, then he opens it.

"Outside," he says.

Then he pushes me outside and closes the door.

13

"AFTERMATH"

Jerry

Ebola.

That's what I keep thinking about.

This is what people with Ebola must feel like.

Except instead of a microscopic virus, mine is caused by copious amounts of wine. Three bottles if my memory serves me, which at this point in time, it may not.

I push myself up in bed, the resulting nausea commensurate with twenty minutes on the Teacups. I run to the bathroom just in time to fall to the floor and vomit, half in the toilet, half on the base. I groan, push myself up, splash some water on my face, then glance over my shoulder at the bed and the bare back and the snaking tentacles of a purple octopus.

The previous night comes rushing back.

The beach party. The Serbians. Tinder. My mother. Brook. Nepheles. The wine. Getting home. Cassie.

Where is Cassie?

I run from the bedroom. My heart thrums against my ribcage.

"Cassie?" I shout.

She doesn't come running.

I grit my teeth against the rising bile in my throat and concentrate. I remember getting home and Cassie, well, she was here. I remember that. Then the bedroom. Yes, she wouldn't stop barking. Me...oh, no...me dragging her outside by her collar.

I sprint to the back door and rip it open.

"Cass—"

I see her, lying on the back porch, near the baby pool.

"Oh, thank God."

I amble toward her, my eyes beginning to water.

"Hi, girl," I say softly.

She glances up, her amber eyes huge.

"I'm so sorry—" I creak, my voice breaking.

The video of dragging her from the bedroom by her collar replays over and over.

I gently rub her head and her neck. "I hope I didn't hurt you, sweetie."

I'm openly crying now and Cassie pushes up from her spot on the porch and nestles her head into my neck.

She gives my face a long lick.

I don't deserve her kindness.

Cassie

I'm mad at Jerry.

He left me alone on Bang Day (for *eight* hours).

Then he brought *her* home.

Then he dragged me to the door by my collar.

Then he left me outside all night. I even got thirsty at one point and had to drink out of the baby pool. (What if I drank up a frog baby, Jerry? What then?)

I'm going to ignore him.

For three days.

Justice served.

But then he came outside, and he said sorry, and he stroked my head like he does. Then he started crying.

I can't stand to see Jerry sad.

So I lift the ban and I lick his tears and I kiss him and love him. I can't help it.

I love him *so* much.

He is my everything.

Jerry

"Hey," I say, giving Brook's shoulder a soft nudge.

She rolls over onto her back—her enormous synthetic breasts defying gravity—and smiles, "What time is it?"

I'm not sure, but I know it's time for her to go.

Cassie may have forgiven me for being such a jerk, but she wouldn't come inside. I had to bring her food and water bowl out onto the back deck. And I know it's because of Brook.

I find her bra and panties and toss them onto the bed.

She pushes them aside, then crawls onto her knees. "Come here," she says.

A primitive urge thrums through my body.

I fight it down.

"Um, I have to get to work," I lie.

"Awww," she says, playing up pouty lips.

I find her shorts and sweatshirt and add them to the pile. She gives a soft nod, accepting defeat, then begins pulling on her clothes.

Her eyes are clear and she doesn't appear to be suffering any lasting effects from last night's binge.

"Are you, like, not hungover?" I ask.

"What? From three bottles of wine?" She scoffs as if this preposterous. "Why? Are you?"

Well my heart rate is around 170, I have tunnel vision, my head feels like it's a test site for the Manhattan Project, and I've been holding in a second round of puke for the last three minutes.

"No, I feel great," I say. Then I add, "Do you need a ride?"

"No, I'll just call Jake."

"Jake?"

"Oh, did I not mention Jake?"

"Not that I recall."

"Oh, he's my, not exactly boyfriend, but you know, we *look out for each other.*"

I have absolutely no idea what this means. Is that what we were doing last night, *Looking out for each other?*

She picks up her phone and asks, "What's your address?"

I tell her.

She sends a quick text, finishes pulling on her clothes, then ambles forward. She notices my bookcase and hunches down. "Is this one of your books?" she asks, pulling a book out, then reading the title, *"The Catcher in the Rye."*

"No," I say, literally biting my lip. "That's a pretty famous book written by J.D. Salinger."

"Right," she shrugs. "I thought maybe you went by J.D. or something."

I wait for her to ask which of the books are mine, but she tosses the book atop the bookcase, then walks past me and out of the bedroom.

I slip one of the most famous books of all time back into the bookcase, then follow Brook to the kitchen, where she's standing in front of the open fridge, slugging orange juice out of the container.

I slept with this monster?

Thankfully, there's a chirp and Brook checks her phone. "My ride's here," she says, setting the orange juice on the counter and kicking the refrigerator closed with her foot.

She walks past me, gives me a big pulpy kiss on the mouth, and says, "Don't be a stranger." Then she exits the front door.

I make my way to the window and watch as she gets into the passenger side of a low slung sedan. I recognize the guy driving. *Jake.* He was the guy who filled up our beers in the beer tent.

He leans over and gives her a kiss. Then he notices me staring out the window and gives me a fraternal head nod, one I read as, "Hope you had fun, bro."

Then they speed away.

When they are out of sight, I go throw up.

* * *

I toss the pine cone twenty feet over my head, deeper into the lake, and Cassie swims for it. I dive under the water and try to beat her there. I pop up right next to the pine cone and grab it right as Cassie clamps her jaw around it. We wrestle for it for a few seconds, then I toss it back into the turquoise shallows and we continue our game.

After spending ten minutes puking up my guts and my self-worth, I forced myself to eat some breakfast and swallow four Advil. I wanted to crawl into bed and watch Netflix all day, but I was compelled to make things right with Cassie.

So I sucked it up, grabbed Cassie's leash, and we made our way to the beach. When we first arrived, I felt like the walking dead, but after a dive into the icy water, I felt at least human.

Cassie and I play in the water for another ten minutes, then I go lie in the sun, while Cassie chases a few little kids around— including one tiny guy in a water diaper who she lets pull on her tail and yank on her ears.

When we leave the beach, I'm rejuvenated in body, if not entirely in spirit.

Next stop on the Redemption Tour is Cold Stone Creamery. It's located across from the Heavenly Ski Resort gondola in Heavenly Village, which, outside of the casinos, is the hub of the summer madness. The line is out the door and it takes Cassie and me thirty minutes until we are inside the shop.

Cassie rears up and puts her paws on the glass shield and I ask, "What flavor do you want?" but of course I already know.

Strawberry.

With Sprinkles.

We sit by the fountain and I spoon feed Cassie ice cream. She clomps down on the spoon, then smacks her lips together, then she rests her head on my knee when she's ready for another scoop.

Our final stop is the pet store next to the Raley's across the street.

We plod inside and I tell Cassie she can pick out two things.

Cassie

What a day.

First the beach and then Strawberry Ice Cream with Sprinkles! I usually only get this on my birthday!

And then to top it off, the Toy Shop.

And I can get two things.

Two.

But there's so much to choose from. Usually, I go right for the pig ears. I love a good pig ear. But I also could use a new teddy. My alligator is missing the squeaker from when Hugo played with it. But they don't have my alligator here. (I know my alligator gets delivered by the nice UPS man.) Still, I head for the stuffed animals and give them a few sniffs. There's a yellow lamb that intrigues me, but the more I think about it, the less I want a new teddy. I like my old one. I can still smell Hugo on it.

I'm sniffing a few other toys, waiting for one of them to call out to me, when I feel a presence standing over me.

I snap my head up.

"Oh, hi there," *she* says.

She reaches the back of her hand out and I give it a light sniff. It smells good. It smells like cookies.

She leans down and says, "Hi, I'm Megan."

Megan has a huge smile. It's like Jerry's eyes if they were teeth. She rubs my head a couple of times. I let her. Only because she smells like cookies.

"What's your name?" she asks, fiddling with my collar. "Cassie?"

Yeah.

I'm Cassie.

"You are so beautiful, Cassie," she says. "Did you know that?"

My coat *is* pretty shiny.

I lick her face.

I mean, when someone tells you that you're beautiful, it's only polite to give them a lick on the face.

I like her smile. And her eyes; they are light brown. They remind me of Hugo's.

You are beautiful too, I want to tell her.

"Do you want a treat?" Megan asks.

Well, if you're giving out free treats, then, of course, I want one, Megan.

She reaches into her pocket and gives me a little treat.

Dried chicken.

Yum.

* * *

My dad called the moment we walked into the pet store, asking if I wanted to meet them out for dinner (which I decline as the second coming of my hangover is gathering steam), then we chat about nothing in particular for a few minutes.

Once we hang up, I track Cassie down at the back of the store.

A young woman in a red apron is squatted next to Cassie and is rubbing Cassie's chest.

Cassie wiggles her butt and clowns it up for her.

"Hey," I say, interrupting the girls' party.

The woman turns and glances up. She has straight blonde hair held back in a ponytail and light brown eyes. Her face is roundish and a big dimple craters in her right cheek. She stares at me for a long moment, her face in a daze. After a long moment, she shakes her head and says, "Oh, hi."

I realize Cassie must know the girl from coming here with my father and I say, "I see you two know each other."

"No, we just met." She gives Cassie a tickle in the armpit and says, "She's such a little lover."

I cut my eyes at Cassie.

Who are you and what did you do with my dog?

The woman stands and brushes her hands on her apron. "I'm Megan," she says.

"Jerry," I say, giving her hand a light shake.

"Have we met before?"

She's more girl-next-door than runway model, but she's attractive enough to be memorable. "I don't think so."

She cocks her head to the side. "You sure we didn't go to school together when we were kids?"

"Not unless you went to school in a small town in Oregon."

"I did not," she says, her gaze soft, her brain seemingly somewhere else. After a short pause, she asks, "So are you guys in town for the 4th?"

"No, we live here." I add, "So maybe that's why I look familiar."

She shakes her head as if to say, *Naw, that's not it.*

I ask, "Have you lived in Tahoe all your life?"

"I left for college, but I've been back for a little over a year now."

"Where did you go?"

"The Art Institute in Sacramento?"

"You're an artist?"

"A *culinary* artist."

"What are you doing working here?"

"I only work here a couple of days a week. I'm the pastry chef at Jimmy's." Jimmy's Restaurant is inside a boutique hotel on the lakefront. It's one of the most upscale restaurants in South Lake. "I want to open up my own dog bakery at some point," she continues, "so I picked up this job to learn the ropes."

I nod toward the glass-encased bakery near the register. "You make any of that stuff?"

"All of it," she says, flashing a radiant smile.

She takes a few steps toward the bakery window and I follow.

"What's your specialty?" I ask.

"Hmmm," she says, holding her chin in her hand for a brief moment. "I'd have to say it's a toss-up between the Pawcake and Woof Creme Pie."

"Well, in that case, why don't you give me one of each."

She walks around to the back and pulls out a little cupcake with coconut sprinkles, then a layered cake with white in the center and a chocolate frosting.

"Is that chocolate?" I ask.

"No, it's carob. It tastes similar to chocolate but is safe for dogs."

"And what's that in the middle?"

"Honey yogurt."

"Tasty."

"You want to give one a try?"

"I'll pass."

"Your loss," she says with a snicker, then wraps both treats in wax paper and puts them in a box. As she's doing this, Cassie walks over and drops a pig ear at my feet.

"You can get one more thing," I tell her.

Cassie smiles and pants.

"Are you sure?"

She sits down.

"Okay, but don't say I didn't offer."

I pick up the pig ear and put it on the counter.

Megan rings me up and I pay.

"It was nice to meet you," I say.

"You too," she calls, then makes her way around the counter and squats next to Cassie. "And it was nice meeting you, sweetie." She plants a big kiss on Cassie's nose.

Cassie's tail helicopters.

My headache is starting to return with force and I say, "Okay, Cassie, let's go."

I give her leash a light tug and we start toward the door. When I have eclipsed the opening of the propped open door, I feel a sharp resistance and glance back over my shoulder. Cassie is lying on the floor just inside the shop.

"*Cassie,*" I call, giving a light tug. "Come on, time to go."

She doesn't budge.

"Seriously, Cassie, we need to go." The Advil have officially run their course and my temples are beginning to pulsate. I shake the box of treats at her and say, "When we get home, I'll give you a Woofcake."

"Woof *Creme Pie,*" I hear Megan mutter from somewhere within.

"Right. When we get home, I'll give you a Woof Creme Pie."

Cassie shakes her butt and barks.

She's in protest mode.

"What?" I ask, shaking my head. "I don't know what you want."

Two more barks, which land like explosions on my eardrums.

I lean down. "Please," I beg.

She pushes herself up and I let out a satisfying breath. Then I feel her pull—pulling me back into the store.

"No!"

She barks four times.

I've only heard Cassie bark four times in a row a handful of times and each time she was trying to protect something Hugo was trying to hunt.

Finally, I lean down and pick her up and carry her to the car.

* * *

An hour later, I'm lying in bed watching Netflix in my pajamas. Cassie has her head on my chest. Her eyes flit open and closed as she fights off sleep. I move the half-eaten pig ear from beneath her snout and toss it lightly to the carpeted floor. I softly rub the white fur above her nose, until her eyes close for good.

It took me a long time to realize what Cassie was trying to tell me at the pet store.

She did want a second thing.

She wanted *Megan*.

14

"CHINATOWN"

Hugo

Some people call her Chris.

But most people call her Rayna.

She's great.

She feeds me three or four times a day (these little tins of food that taste really good) and she gives amazing rubs. We spend a lot of time in her tent. Snuggling. Wrestling. Eating beef jerky.

Each night she leaves for a few hours. She puts on these tall shoes and smelly spray and she goes. She keeps the tent open a few inches in case I want to leave.

Each time she goes, she says, "Okay, little man (she calls me *little man*), I'll be seeing ya. If you're here when I get back, I'll have some jerky for you."

Well, of course, I'm not going to leave if you're going to have jerky for me.

But it's more than the jerky. I like Rayna. And I don't think she really wants me to leave. When she gets home each night, I can smell it. Sadness. (Some smells are light. Some smells are heavy.

Sadness is one of the heaviness smells.) But after some wrestling and a few well-placed face licks, this goes away.

But I can't stay here forever. I know that. And I think Rayna knows that. That's why she leaves the tent open.

On the fifth night, Rayna leans down and picks me up. She gives me a little kiss on the nose and says, "Okay, little man, I gotta go to work."

I give her a lick on her chin. (It's rough. Rougher than the day before, but I don't let this stop me.) I give her a bunch of licks.

Maybe she can store them up for later.

* * *

I go through a bunch of alleys. It's been a few days since it last rained and the alleys are dry. I can smell food in every direction, but I'm not hungry. Rayna left out a tin of food and I ate it right before I wiggled my way out of the tent and into the darkness.

I pitter-patter down the dark alleys and down a few sidewalks. It's noisy. There are humans walking and a bunch of cars, but I'm able to stay in the shadows and no one sees me. I dart down another alley. Then another. When I poke my head out of this last alley, I gaze upward. All the buildings have green metal roofs that slant downward at a steep angle. There are a bunch of rounded red lights hanging everywhere. But the craziest things are the smells. They are sharp and twisty.

What is this world?

I'm about to investigate further when I hear, "Pssst."

I whip my head around.

Standing on top of a green dumpster a few feet behind me is a cat. He's white with black markings on his face.

"Don't go out there," the cat says, hopping silently to the alley floor. "It's not safe."

I take a couple of small steps back into the shadows.

The big white cat slinks toward me and leans down. Half of one of his ears is missing. "What's your name, kid?"

"Hugo," I meow.

"You lost, *Hugo*?"

I've never been lost before, but Cassie used to talk about *lost* dogs. She said most of the dogs at the Shelter were lost. She called them "*Strays*."

"I think so," I tell the stray.

"Well, the last place you want to be lost is out there, kid. It isn't safe."

"Why?"

The big cat lifts his head and sniffs. "You smell that?"

I sniff. I smell a lot of *cooking*.

"You know what that smell is called?"

I shake my head.

"That smell is called Lost Cat."

* * *

"Where are we going, Gus?"

"You'll see," he says without turning his head.

I scamper behind him, my little legs needing three strides for each one of Gus's. We run through two alleys, then down some steps, through a door, and into a musty basement. Light from the street shines through two broken windows. Nestled against the wall are a bunch of boxes and lying on the boxes are three cats. All three jump down as Gus and I approach.

One of the cats is orange with white stripes and a pink nose. Another has long gray hair and bright blue eyes. The third is tan and black with a flat face and big bulgy eyes.

"Found this little guy about to walk onto Sizzle Street," Gus says.

The orange cat slinks around me and gives my butt a long sniff. The cat with the long gray hair does the same. (Finally, something I understand.) The orange cat is Ringo. The blue-eyed cat is Harriet. The flat-faced cat, though we never meet *officially*, is Eddie.

"Chinatown is no place for a kitten," Harriet says, giving me a push with her gigantic paw. "What are you doing here?"

I'm about to push her back, but then I realize the big cat will clobber me.

"I think I'm lost," I say.

"Little lost kitten," Harriet says, about to give me another push. Luckily, Gus hisses at her and she backs away.

"Where are you trying to go?" Ringo asks.

"Back to the Lake and the Mountains."

Harriet falls over laughing. "The *mountains?*"

I don't like Harriet.

"You're a long way from home," Ringo says, his whiskers twitching. "A long way from home."

"How far?"

"Don't know," Ringo says. "I've never seen them. But I've heard stories."

"How do you know about the mountains?" Gus asks.

"I lived there for a long time."

"You lived there for a *long time?*" Harriet snorts. "You're barely off the teat."

I don't know what a teat is, but this makes all the cats laugh.

"I lived there when I was a dog," I shout. The words come out before I have time to think how crazy they must sound.

Gus scrunches his nose and leans his head forward. "Did you just say that you lived there when you were a *dog?*"

"Oh, uh, yeah," I mumble. "I used to be a dog."

Harriet bounds up the boxes, then down, then back up. She can't control herself. "A dog?" she shrieks, giving Eddie a shove. "He thinks he used to be a dog."

"Take it easy on him, Harriet," Gus says. Then turning to me, he asks, "What makes you think you used to be a dog?"

"Because I was. I was a big dog too. I lived in a house with Jerry and my best friend, Cassie. We lived in the Mountains next to a big Lake. Each year it would snow. Big white clouds of snow. And Jerry would feed me bacon and cheese. And I would sleep in bed next to him. And Cassie would sleep with her head on my belly. And I would chase squirrels and birds. And I would chase cats. Yeah, cats! And then I chased a rabbit into the street. And then something happened. And now *I'm* a cat."

I stop.

All four cats are staring at me, even Eddie, who was busy licking his paw. After a long few seconds, Harriet lets out a loud wail, "He thinks he was a dog!"

Ringo and even Gus join in the laughter.

I begin to slink back toward the stairs.

"Hey."

I turn.

It's the flat-faced cat.

Eddie.

"Follow me," he says. "I think I know someone who can help you."

* * *

"She won't see you for free," Eddie says, swiveling his head back and forth, scanning the alley. "You have to bring her an offering."

"An offering?" I ask, trying to keep up.

"Yes, a *gift*."

"And what happens when I give her this gift?"

"Calandia will answer all your questions."

Calandia?

"Oh, okay. So what can we bring her?"

Eddie stops and turns. "Mice, Hugo. We bring her mice."

* * *

I don't have any luck catching any mice, but Eddie catches three.

"Wow," I say. "You make it look easy."

"It is," Eddie says, batting at one of the mice with his paw. "Just wait until you get a little older."

Eddie carries two of the mice in his mouth and I carry one. We sneak down a few alleys, but we have to cross two streets. We scamper under the big red hanging lights and then we squirm into a black opening in the street that I know is called a "sewer."

It's only a four-foot drop and Eddie slinks through and jumps. I follow. The mouse falls out of my mouth when I land and I pick it back up. The sewer is dry and smells like Cassie's farts after she ate Jerry's scrambled eggs that one time.

Eddie and I scamper down the dark tunnel, then come to a metal grate. Eddie lets the two mice fall from his mouth, then lightly scratches his claws against the metal. The sound echoes through the tunnel.

A few moments later, there's a rustling and glowing orange eyes appear in the darkness. Eddie pushes his two mice through the small openings in the grate, then I do the same. The three mice disappear and the grate swings open.

"Good luck, Hugo," Eddie says, then turns and disappears back the way we came.

* * *

The orange eyes belong to the biggest cat I've seen. He is twice the size of Harriet and twice as poofy.

"I'm Rajah," he says. "Calandia has accepted your offering."

I follow behind him, my little heart thudding against my ribs.

Is this huge cat leading me to my death? Is this all a big joke? Did I think Eddie was helping me, but actually he's the worst of them all?

"Right through there," Rajah says, stopping at an opening to another tunnel. I wait for him to leave, but he sits next to the opening. He reminds me of Cassie standing guard over the tadpoles.

I remind myself that everything I'm doing is to get back to her. And to Jerry.

Be brave.

"Go ahead," Rajah prods. "She's waiting."

I peek my head into the opening and slowly take a few steps. Sitting on a ledge, surrounded by three mice, is the strangest looking cat I've ever seen. It has no fur. Its skin is pink and wrinkled. Its ears are large, raised, and pointed. And one of its eyes is green, the other blue.

"Hello, Hugo," it says.

* * *

"Are you Calandia?" I meow.

"I am," she says, blinking her eyes twice slowly.

"They said you could help me."

"I will try."

I sit back on my butt, then say, "I'm lost."

"We are all lost." She pauses. "Do you want to be found?"

I remember back to Sara holding me in her arms and screaming, "I'm so glad we *found* you."

"No," I say. "I want to go Home."

"And where is home?"

"The Lake in the Mountains."

"Oh, yes."

"Have you heard of it?"

"I have."

"Do you know how to get there?"

"I do not know how to get to the lake, but I know how to find the mountains."

If I can make it to the Mountains, I know I can find the Lake. "Please, tell me."

"I must warn you; it will be a dangerous journey."

"I can make it," I assure her.

"I fear that you won't."

"I can make it."

I have to.

"Very well."

Calandia leans down, picks up one of the mice by the tail and slowly sucks it into her mouth. The mouse slides down her throat in a lump, then vanishes.

She licks her lips, then says, "Follow the morning sun. Then walk above water. Follow the brightest star for two nights. Then follow the morning sun once more."

* * *

Calandia makes me repeat this back to her until I have it memorized. It would have taken Cassie only a few minutes, but it takes me a long time. When I finally have it down, Calandia says, "Is there anything else you want to ask me?"

It's as if she already knows.

"I used to be a dog," I tell her.

She nods lightly.

I ask, "How can I be a dog one moment and a cat the next?"

She blinks her eyes. "Hugo, do you know what a soul is?"

"A soul?" I say, shaking my head. "I don't think so."

"There's a part of you that never dies. A part of you that lives on forever. This is called your soul."

"Okay."

"When you died, your soul stayed here."

"I died?"

"Yes, Hugo. You died."

I've seen plenty of dead things. Dead frogs. Dead bugs. Dead squirrels. Dead birds. I even saw a dead bear once. I know what dead is. And I know what dead smells like. But I never thought that *I* died.

I ask, "So how did my soul end up in a baby cat?"

"If we are good and we die, our souls become stars, living forever in the sky. But sometimes a soul stays here on Earth. It is very, *very* rare. You see, the exact moment your soul was heading up to become a star, a baby cat was in need of a soul. And since yours was the closest, your soul went into that baby cat."

"So I became a cat instead of a star?"

"Yes."

"Why?"

"There are many reasons. I cannot say why your soul stayed here. You will have to ask the Maker."

"The Maker?"

"Yes, Hugo. The *Maker* of the souls."

* * *

Calandia spends a few minutes trying to explain this Maker to me, but it's all very confusing. Not only did this Maker make all the souls, but the Maker made everything: all the humans, all the animals, the Lake, the Mountains, the sun and the moon. I don't know if my brain is big enough to understand all this Maker stuff.

* * *

I point to the lone mouse next to Calandia and ask, "Aren't you worried those mice could have once been dogs or cats?"

She picks the mouse up in her paw and sucks it into her mouth, then chokes it down with a loud gulp. She says, "You remember how I said the good souls become stars?"

"Yes."

"Well, the bad souls," her whiskers twitch, "they become mice."

15

"BEACH DATE"

Jerry

"They seem to be getting along," Megan says, nodding at Cassie and Wally chasing each other at the edge of the lake.

Wally is a one-year-old Shih Tzu-terrier mix. He has a teddy bear face and shaggy white, black, and tan fur. He's very Ewok-y. He went wild the second he laid eyes on Cassie, dragging Megan forward like the pair was in the Iditarod.

At first Cassie was a bit wary of the overly excitable fifteen-pound dog, but she warmed up to him quickly.

"Yeah, they do," I say.

The day after meeting Megan at the pet store, with my wits about me once again, I tracked her down on the internet. Jimmy's Restaurant at The Landing had a Megan Klipp listed as the pastry chef and I found her on Facebook easily enough.

After learning she was only twenty-five years old, I nearly aborted the mission, but then again, in the short three minutes I interacted with her, she appeared markedly more mature than Brook, who was in her thirties. So I wrote her a message, asked if maybe she and her dog—who was prominent in most of her pictures—wanted to meet for a playdate sometime.

"How about Saturday?" she wrote back a few hours later.

And so here we are.

The beach is crowded to the point of absurdity, but there is a football field length of narrow beach—between the public beach and Hotel Row—that is only sparsely occupied. The temperature is in the low nineties, which is as hot as it ever gets in Tahoe. Megan and I are sitting in beach chairs, shaded by a beach umbrella in the sand. I picked up some sandwiches from a local deli and they are packed in a cooler with a few bags of chips and some sodas.

"Oh, a wedding," Megan says, nodding toward Hotel Row, where a bunch of chairs are being set up in neat rows and facing a white arch.

Megan is wearing tan shorts, a yellow bikini top, and a green ball cap. Her hair is braided and falls onto one of her freckled shoulders.

"Did you know there are over five thousand weddings in Tahoe each summer?" I ask.

It isn't uncommon to see three or four wedding ceremonies taking place on the beach on a Saturday afternoon. Tahoe is an ideal and easy destination wedding for the seven million people who live in the Bay area (San Francisco, Oakland, and San Jose) just three and a half hours southwest. One day, after seeing six different weddings, I Googled the statistic.

"That actually doesn't surprise me," Megan says. "Sometimes there are three or four ceremonies a day at the beach in front of Jimmy's. Jones-Rogers at noon. Smith-Johnson at two. White-Palmer at four. It's like a wedding factory."

"Does your restaurant do any of the receptions?"

"Yeah, there are two ballrooms at The Landing, so we pretty much have two wedding parties every Friday and Saturday night for the entire summer and most of the fall."

"Are you responsible for the desserts?"

"Sometimes."

"Do you ever make any of the cakes?"

"I have."

"Really?"

She pulls her cell phone from her knit beach bag, scrolls for a moment then passes me her phone. On screen is an intricate three-tiered wedding cake.

"You made that?"

"I did."

"That's incredible."

"I'm very talented," she says with a laugh.

I hand back her phone, then ask, "Did you always want to be a chef?"

"Well, initially, I wanted to be a princess, but it turns out that is a difficult field to break into."

I smile.

"But I always loved to bake." She pats a soft little curve of belly and adds, "And eat."

I laugh and say, "Speaking of which."

I pull out two turkey sandwiches and hand her one. Then I pass over a bag of chips and a lime club soda.

After a bite of sandwich, she asks, "Did you always want to be a writer?"

"Not really. I mean, I always loved reading, but I never thought of myself as a good writer. But then my junior year of college, I came up with this idea for a story."

"*Pluto Three?*"

I cut my eyes at her. "Are you stalking me?"

"Hey, you're the one who tracked me down on Facebook," she pauses, "*stalker.*"

I feel my cheeks redden and she says, "I'm just kidding. Getting your message was a nice surprise." She throws a potato chip at me, then says, "So, you come up with this idea—"

159

"Right, I came up with this idea for a story, but other than a rough outline, I never did anything with it. After graduating, I started writing an hour here and an hour there and after four long years, I had this finished book. It took me another year to find an agent, then another year for my agent to sell it. Then the book came out and it was this surprise hit. I ended up winning the award for best sci-fi book of the year and I got a book deal and a big advance."

"Then what?"

"Then I moved to San Francisco."

"And how did you end up in Tahoe?"

"I grew up coming here each summer when I was a kid. My parents bought a second home in Tahoe in the mid-eighties and since my mom was a teacher and had the summers off, we would stay here the entire time."

"That sounds amazing."

"It was." At least until I was ten.

"What about your dad?"

"He would drive down each weekend and stay with us."

"From Oregon? Isn't that a long drive?"

"Medford is twenty miles from the California border. It's only a six-hour drive." I take a bite of my sandwich, then continue, "Anyhow, it turns out that San Francisco is ridiculously expensive and after my second book flopped—not to mention a movie deal for my first book falling through—I had to move. And since I'd blown through most of my advance, I moved into my parents' house here." I decide to leave out the part about my getting my heart ripped out of my chest by Avery.

"What about you?" I ask.

"I grew up here in South Lake, then moved to Sacramento for culinary school. After graduating, I worked at a restaurant in Sac for a couple of years, worked my way up to head pastry chef, then I got tired of the city—and the heat. A hundred and ten degrees in the summer? *Ugh.* I wanted to be back in the mountains and landed a job at Jimmy's."

"Parents? Siblings?"

"Parents split when I was little. Dad moved to Reno, where he still lives. After I graduated from high school, my mom moved to Tennessee of all places. I see my dad maybe once every couple months and I spent last Christmas with my mom. No siblings. What about you?"

"One brother, eight years older. Lives in Michigan. We aren't very close."

"And your parents? Are they still in Oregon?"

I laugh.

"What?"

"They still live in the same house I grew up in, but at the moment, they're here in Tahoe, living in the house across the street from me."

I spend the next ten minutes explaining my parents' and my unorthodox living situation. Then I proceed to disclose my parents' late-stage hippieness and how they dropped the open marriage bomb on me at dinner. When I confide how I matched on Tinder with my mother, Megan falls out of her chair laughing.

Cassie

Wally looks like a dog and he smells like a dog, but I'm not so sure. I think he's at least partly hummingbird. Which would explain all the zipping around he does.

Some small dogs are mean. The meanest dog I ever met was half the size of Wally. It was when we lived in the City. She lived a couple of houses away from us. A tiny little white dog named Rainbow. (Which is odd because rainbows are a lot of different colors and white isn't one of them.) Every time Jerry and I walked by Rainbow's house, she would push her head through the metal fence, show her little teeth, snarl, then yap, yap, yap.

But Wally is nothing like Rainbow. Wally is just energetic. He's maybe the most energetic little dog I've ever seen.

I bite at Wally's back leg and he goes tumbling into the sand. For a moment, I think maybe I hurt him, but he pops up, shakes the sand from his fur, then runs toward me. I roll onto my back and Wally nips at my face and ears.

I realize how much I miss this.

How much I miss *playing*.

Jerry

"I saw another dog in your Facebook pictures," Megan says, following my gaze to where Cassie and Wally wrestle in the sand. "A Bernese Mountain Dog."

"His name was Hugo," I say with a crampy grin. "He was such a stud." A montage of Hugo swimming in the water and rolling around with Cassie plays over my eyes.

I point to Cassie, fight back a sniffle, and say, "Wally is the first dog I've seen Cassie play with since Hugo died."

Whenever my dad took Cassie to the beach, I would ask him if Cassie played with any of the other dogs, but he always said she never seemed interested.

"When did you lose him?" Megan asks. She's scooted her chair a couple of inches closer to me.

"Back in February. His collar broke and he ran into the road after a rabbit." I glance at her and say, "I'm trying to get over it, but it's been hard."

Megan goes silent for a long moment, then says, "You won't get over it, so don't even try. You will grieve *forever*. You just have to learn to live with it." She grabs my hand and gives it a light squeeze. "You will be whole again, but you will never be the same."

I don't know if these words are her own or if she stole them from a greeting card, but they burrow through my flesh and into the marrow of my bones.

A tear runs down my cheek.

"So what made him such a stud?" she asks, giving my shoulder a light shove.

I wipe the tear from my cheek and I tell her about Hugo. I tell her how big, goofy, and lumbering he was. How much he loved Cassie. How when I said the word "cheese" he would get so excited that sometimes he would pee a little. How he would roll over on his back and whine until I kissed his belly. How he would sleep with his head on the pillow like a human. How uncoordinated he was as a puppy. How he would slobber in his sleep. How he would sort of gallop when he ran. How in the winter he would nose his way under the comforter. How when he was thirsty he would plop down next to the water bowl and basically put his entire head in the bowl. How wherever Cassie went pee, he would have to go over and pee on her pee. How he would tap my leg, just every so softly, over and over again until I played with him. How he had no boundaries; how he wasn't satisfied just sitting on my lap; how he wanted to breathe the same air as me.

I tell her about how Cassie and I picked him out at a farm in Sacramento. About how he and I have the same birthday and how last year I got him fifty of his orange tennis balls and by midnight he'd already destroyed more than half of them. I tell her about the first time he got in the lake and how I've never seen anyone or anything so happy.

I haven't spoken to anyone about Hugo since he died and celebrating his life is therapeutic. The well of sadness I thought may never go dry feels less full.

Megan holds my hand the entire time I talk.

* * *

"Desert Island," I say a few minutes later.

Megan's dimple flashes and she asks, "Are we talking food here because I'm bringing a hot tub-sized *tub* of peanut butter."

"I was thinking more book, movie, and TV show, but I fully endorse your peanut butter decision." I pause. "Wait, are we talking chunky or creamy?"

"Uh, creamy."

"I don't think this is going to work out," I say, shaking my head.

"You're a chunky?"

"*Extra* chunky."

We both laugh, then she tilts her head back and says, "Okay, give me a minute to think here."

"Do you always lean your head back when you're deep in thought?"

"Only when making life or death decisions." Thirty seconds later, she snaps her head down and says, "Okay, I got it."

I rub my hands together and say, "Let's hear it."

"What should I start with?"

"Book."

She lets out a long breath and says, "Don't judge me."

"I make no such promises."

She grins, then says, "Okay, the book is *Harry Potter and the Chamber of Secrets.*"

I cringe.

"What? Don't tell me you don't like *Harry Potter*. Because I will go grab my dog and leave right now!"

I hold up my hands to calm her, then say, "When the last *Harry Potter* book came out, I was twenty-six years old and I waited in line at midnight at a Barnes and Noble with all the little kids dressed like wizards."

"Really?" Megan snickers. "Then why did you cringe?"

"Because everyone knows *The Chamber of Secrets* is the worst of the seven books."

"How dare you!"

"Come on, *Goblet of Fire, Prisoner of Azkaban, Half-Blood,* or even the first one. But *Chamber?*" I shake my head in disapproval.

We both laugh, then she says, "So you standing in line with a bunch of kid wizards is *sort of* embarrassing, but I have you beat big time."

She lifts her hips and unbuttons her shorts. Underneath is a matching yellow bikini bottom. She folds down the yellow fabric on her hip, revealing a small tattoo of a wand and the word, "Expelliarmus!"

"Holy smokes!" I roar.

"Yeah, not my best decision."

We both give a good laugh, then she asks, "How about you, what book are you taking to this island?"

"*To Kill a Mockingbird.*"

"Really? You're going to spend your eternity with Scout and Atticus. I would have thought you would have picked some science fiction book."

"There are a few science fiction books that are in my top five. I mean, *Jurassic Park* is one of my all-time favorites. But if you go back and read *Jurassic Park,* you're gonna react to it the same way you reacted to it when you read it the first time. Every time I've read *To Kill a Mockingbird*—probably five times—it's always moved me, changed me, in a different way than before."

Now, Megan cringes.

"What?"

"Nothing, it just makes me think about how sitting on that island rereading *Chamber of Secrets* over and over again is going to get old really fast." She puffs out her cheek and says, "Can I change my answer?"

"Nope, it's Quidditch and Dementors for you until that rescue boat shows up."

"But I have a TV series and a movie right?"

"Yes."

"Okay, so TV series is hard, can I take two?"

I shake my head. "Rules are rules."

"Okay, well, it's between *Friends* and *Cupcake Wars*, but if I have to choose—"

"Wait, did you say *Cupcake Wars*? This is a show?"

"The *best* show."

"What do they do?"

"Um, they bake cupcakes."

She spends the next couple minutes explaining the premise, which is exactly what it sounds like, a cupcake bake-off. In the end, she picks *Friends* because "looking at all those cupcakes is just going to make me hungry."

I tell her my TV series is *The Office*, which she's seen but isn't crazy about. Then we move to movies. She makes me go first.

"*Shawshank Redemption*," I tell her.

"Oh, good one!" she says, clapping her hands.

We talk about how great the story is and how amazing his escape is. Then I ask, "Did you know that the movie is based on a short story by Stephen King?"

"*Rita Hayworth and the Shawshank Redemption.*"

"Wow, look at you go."

She smiles and says, "Okay, so my movie is *The Princess Bride*."

"That's *inconceivable*," I shout, and we both laugh.

* * *

It takes me a few minutes, but finally, I coax Megan into joining me in the lake. She slips off her shorts, then slowly tip-toes the twenty feet to the water.

Even in the shade, it's blisteringly hot and I needed to cool off. I'm lying on my chest in the shallows, splashing and wrestling with Cassie and Wally.

"It's not cold," I call out to Megan.

The middle of the lake is freezing, probably no warmer than

sixty degrees, but the sun heats the shallows near shore and it's well into the seventies.

Megan shakes her head. "It's not the cold I'm afraid of."

"What then? The sharks? This is a lake, not the ocean."

She rolls her eyes, then dips her toes in the edge of the water. "I just don't like the water."

"Oh, okay."

I don't press further.

To her credit, she sits down at the edge of the beach until her feet are entirely submerged. Wally runs and sits in her lap, gives her a lick on the chin, then runs into the water and swims out ten feet to where Cassie is swimming in lazy circles.

Megan throws a pinecone to Cassie for a few minutes, then she glances up and says, "The wedding is starting!"

I glance down the beach and see that all the seats are filled and a man in black robes is standing beneath the arch.

"Let's go watch," Megan says, clapping her hands together, then pushing herself up.

I give my head one last dip in the water, then jog up the beach to join her. Wally and Cassie follow in behind us. When we're thirty yards away, Megan plops down in the sand. I follow suit. Cassie and Wally, who have been playing nearly nonstop for the past hour, flop down in the sand at our feet.

The bridal party is grouped at the top of the beach. Seconds later, the first bridesmaid and groomsman lock arms and begin their procession between the rows of chairs, then split and take their respective places near the officiant and the arch. The remaining bridal party makes their way down the aisle, followed by the ring bearer, then the flower girls.

"Oh, look at them," Megan gushes. "They're so cute."

The groom finally makes his way to the arch. He's smallish, with glasses and a goatee.

The music begins to play and everyone stands. Even Cassie and Wally perk their heads up.

The bride is wearing a strapless low cut wedding dress and a long veil. The bride and a man on her opposite side—it's hard to see, but I presume it's her father—disappear behind the wall of people, then reappear at the arch. The father lifts the bride's veil and gives her a light kiss.

"Holy shit," I mutter.

The bride.

It's Avery.

* * *

"Wait," Megan smirks. "You know her?"

"I was actually engaged to her at one point."

Megan covers her mouth with her hand. "Did you know she was getting married?"

"No."

"What's her name?"

"Avery."

At the sound of Avery's name, Cassie snaps her head up.

"Settle down," I say, pushing her back down.

She wiggles out from under my hands. She turns toward the large group of people, then she leans forward.

I watch as Cassie's eyes lock onto Avery and the fur above her shoulders—her hackles—lifts two inches.

And then I hear her growl.

Cassie

"Cassie!" she yelled in her high nasal screech. "Get over here."

I was lying next to the front door, waiting for Jerry to get home. I had to pee. Avery should have taken me out to pee hours ago. But I was used to it. Used to holding it when Jerry was gone.

"Cassie!" she yells again.

I know it's better to go to her. If I ignore her, she'll only get more upset.

I push myself up and plod to the kitchen.

Avery is holding a broom. On the ground is a dustpan. It's full of golden and white fur. My fur.

"You see this!" Avery shouts, pointing at the dustpan. "You see all this stupid hair!"

She walks toward me and slinks her tiny bony hand under my collar. She yanks me—she might be small, but she is freakishly strong—toward the dustpan. She pushes my nose into the hair and says, "Stop shedding. *Stop…shedding.*"

Okay, Avery, I'll stop shedding just as soon as you stop breathing.

She picks up a handful of hair and she pushes it toward my mouth.

"Here," she says. "Eat it."

I lock my jaw.

She drops the broom and tries to pry my jaw open with her hand. She might be strong, but she isn't getting my mouth open.

Keys jingle in the front door and Avery scoffs and whacks me on the head. Then she picks up the dustpan and tosses the hair in the trash.

Jerry comes in and Avery runs around the corner and throws her arms around him. "Hi, honey."

Then she grabs my leash off the hook on the wall and says, "I was about to take Cassie for *another* walk. You want to come with us?"

That was the last time I saw *Her.*

"Cassie!" Jerry yells, trying to hold onto my butt. "Don't do it!"

I wiggle out of his grip, then I run.

Jerry

"Cassie!" I scream, chasing after her.

She tears through the sand like a greyhound at the track. I've never seen her move so fast.

She slips under the ribbon cordoning off the wedding.

I arrive five seconds later to a fracas of screaming and people leaping from their seats. Cassie has her teeth sunk deep into Avery's flowing wedding dress and is whipping her head from side to side.

Avery is screaming.

Two bridesmaids smack at Cassie with bouquets of flowers, but they might as well be fruit flies. Cassie gives a hard tug on the bottom of the dress and Avery trips and crashes to the sand.

I push my way through the mayhem and yell, "Cassie! Stop! *CASSIE!*"

"Where did that dog come from?" someone screams.

"Whose dog is that?" shouts another.

"Do you think it has rabies?" cries a third.

When I reach the arch, the groom is hiding behind the priest, who is hiding behind a bridesmaid. Two groomsmen have fled toward the beach. One groomsman is holding Avery's arms and trying to pull her away from Cassie.

An old woman is slumped over in the front seat, who I recognize as Avery's grandmother. She may or may not have fainted.

I pull at Cassie's back legs, which in theory is supposed to make a dog release their jaw, but Cassie's grip remains firm. Her body squirms back and forth in my arms, her growl only getting louder.

"Let her go, Cassie!" I scream.

Avery lifts her head and glances down. "Jerry?" she shrieks, her eyebrows knitted together.

Hi.

How ya been?

Congratulations!

"Uh."

A half second later, there's a loud tear and Cassie and I fall backward. When I glance up, Cassie is running toward the lake with Avery's entire wedding dress in tow.

I turn and look at Avery.

She's lying in the sand. There's a red garter around her right leg and flesh pasties over her breasts, but nothing else. Bad day not to wear panties.

Avery covers her crotch with both hands and lets out a long wail.

I sense movement behind me and turn.

It's Avery's grandmother stirring.

She blinks her eyes a few times, then sees me and opens them wide.

"Hi, Nana," I say.

16

"THE FARM"

Hugo

I slide out from beneath the newspaper where I'm hiding. The sky is still mostly dark, but there's a bit of pink growing behind a few of the buildings.

I've been repeating Calandia's words over and over in my head since I left her. I know the words as well as I know "Tillamook Medium Cheddar."

Follow the morning sun.

I keep to the alleys, zig-zagging my way through the buildings and closer and closer to the growing ring of pink in the sky. It doesn't take me long to make it beyond all the buildings and back to the lake that isn't my Lake. The sun is just above the water and the sky has turned from pink to orange.

I walk down the rocky bank and to the edge of the water. The only way I can get any closer to the sun is if I go swimming.

Walk above water.

But I'm not supposed to swim. I'm supposed to *walk*.

But how?

I scamper back up the rocks and scan the water. There are a

few boats on the lake, but not as many as where I first was with all
the shops and the black fish dogs. To the far right, there's a bunch
of fog and disappearing into the fog is something long and red.
The long red thing appears to be floating above the water. I can
see things moving on it.

Cars.

It's a street *above* water.

If cars can drive above water, then I can walk above water.
Right?

It takes me a while to find the entrance to this street above
water. The sun is fully awake and the sky is blue. All the cars are
awake too. I've never seen so many cars in my life. They are all
lined up to go on this street.

How am I supposed to walk on this street with all these cars?

But then I notice the cars are barely moving at all.

"Hey, kitty," I hear.

I glance up.

It's a she-human. She's gotten out of her car and is walking
toward me. I run forward and hide under the car in front of her.
I've grown some in the last few weeks, but there's more room
under the car than there was under the couch at New Home.

"Come out of there," the she-human shouts. She's on her hands
and knees and is reaching her arm under the car.

"Hey, get away from my car," someone yells.

"Chill out. There's a little kitten under your car."

"Big whoop," a Jerry-human says. "I got places to go."

"Traffic on the bridge isn't even moving, you moron."

A car door opens and I see another face. Then another. They
are all reaching for me.

I dash forward under another car. That's when I realize: I can
walk under the cars for the entire street!

And that's what I do.

* * *

It takes a long time.

Hours, I think.

At one point, the cars start to move faster and I squirm my way through some bars onto a sidewalk. I see down—way, way, down—to the water below. (I'm definitely above the water. Way above!)

There are a few people on bicycles. I scare a few of them and a few of them get off their bikes and try to catch me, but I'm too quick and they give up.

Finally, the street above the water ends.

Follow the brightest star for two days.

Nothing to do until nightfall.

I nestle into some bushes and scratch out a place in the dirt. I haven't slept since my last night with Rayna and I'm tired. I close my eyes and sleep.

* * *

When I wake up, it's dark. I wiggle out from the bushes and glance up at the stars. There aren't as many cars on the street as during the day, but there are still plenty and their lights make it hard to see the stars. I wait for an opening on the street, then I dart across the road. I hear a loud honk and a screech, but somehow I cross the street without getting hit.

Whew.

I run down a side street that doesn't have many cars, then I look back up at the stars. There are so many.

Are all these stars dogs' souls?

I scan every part of the sky, then find one star brighter than the rest. For the rest of the night, I walk toward this *soul*. Luckily, one of the big streets is pointed right at it and I walk in the dirt on the side of the road.

I walk and I walk and I walk.

When the stars go away, I find a place to hide. The sun rises and hours later, it begins to rain. I drink my fill, then I climb a tree and find a crook between two branches. My stomach rumbles for food, but I force myself to think of Jerry and Cassie. And all the bacon I'll get to eat when I get Home.

* * *

I walk all night again. I rest when the stars disappear, then wait for the sun.

Follow the morning sun once more.

I'm starving.

All I can think about is food.

Part of me wishes I was back in the tent with Rayna. (Beef jerky!) But when the sun begins to rise, all my thoughts of Rayna, the tent, and jerky go away. Behind the cloud of pink is the faint outline of jagged peaks.

The Mountains.

* * *

The sun is directly overhead and I can feel it cooking my tiny body.

It's so hot. And I'm thirsty. And hungry. And the Mountains aren't any closer.

I've been walking all day.

The street started to point away from the Mountains, so I started walking through the grass. Sometimes the grass was so high I wouldn't be able to see the Mountains for a long time. Then I would find a rock or a tree to climb and make sure I was going in the right direction.

Now I'm on a street, but it's dirt. The dirt street goes on forever, pointing at the Mountains, but they are so far away. I'll never make it there if I just walk.

So I start running.

I run and I run and I run.

And then I trip.

And I roll and I roll and I roll.

I push myself up and try to walk, but I can't put one of my front paws down.

I sprained my ankle.

I did this once before when I was a dog. I was chasing Cassie on the beach and my foot went into a hole in the sand. Jerry had to carry me to the car (which wasn't easy from the way he was grunting) and I had to go see Dr. Josh. (*"Hey, Big Guy. What happened?"*) He wrapped my ankle in this weird red stuff and he said I couldn't play for two weeks. (Two whole weeks! It was terrible!)

Now I did it again.

I guess cats *aren't* indestructible.

I try to take another step, but the pain is too bad. I roll back onto my butt. I can't walk, I'm thirsty, I'm hungry, I'm hot, and I'm in the middle of nowhere.

Calandia was right.

I'll never make it.

* * *

"Well, hey there, lil' feller."

I blink my eyes open.

A Jerry-human is leaned over me. He has on a big hat and he has a bunch of white hair around his mouth.

"What are ya doin' way out here?"

Going Home, I want to tell him, but I can't speak. My mouth is too dry.

I feel a hand scoop me up. "Whaddaya say we get you out of this hot sun?"

He carries me into his car. It's nice and cool. I know this is called "air conditioning."

"Here you go, lil' feller," he says, setting me in his lap, then cupping his hand and filling it with water from a bottle. "Bet yer mighty thirsty."

I lick greedily from his hand. It's the most delicious water I've ever tasted.

"A lil' longer out in that sun and you would've been a goner."

He fills his hand a second time and I drink until my stomach feels like it will burst. When I'm finished, he sets me on the seat next to him. I try to put my front paw down and wince.

"You got a bum leg there?" He pinches my ankle and I whine. "I'm sorry. Didn't mean to hurt ya." He sets me back in his lap. "We'll get you fixed up, lil' feller. We'll get you fixed up real good."

* * *

"How old do you think he is, Hank?" asks the she-human. Like *Hank*, she's wearing a big hat. Her hair is also white; it's just not on her face.

"From the looks of 'em, I'd say 'round three months. He still has his baby teeth."

"How'd he get way out here?"

"Maybe from a litter at one of the neighboring farms. Heard the Witlits were 'specting a litter."

"Of puppies. Not kittens."

"You're right. It was pups."

Hank and she-Hank have been fussing over me for a while now. They gave me a big bowl of milk and some turkey—she-Hank said, "You're just skin and bones there, aren't ya?"—then they set me on a big bed.

"You think it's broken?" Hanks asks. "His lil' leg there?"

"I don't think so. Probably just a sprain. He'll be right as rain in a couple of weeks."

She-Hank has wrapped my leg in something white. (She said, "I'll make him a little boot.") It still hurts, but not as bad as before.

"He can barely keep his eyes open," she says. I feel a few good rubs behind my ears. "Go to sleep, little angel. Go to sleep."

* * *

I feel wetness.

On my face.

I open my eyes and I see a big tongue. It slobbers its way down my ear and across my eye.

"Stop licking me," I meow.

"Oh, sorry," the dog curled around me says.

He's brown and black with a white stripe down his nose. He has large droopy eyes and the longest ears I've ever seen. He has big folds in his fur like he's wearing the fur of a dog twice his size.

"Who are you?" I ask.

"I'm Leroy," he says, scratching one of his big floppy ears.

"I'm Hugo," I tell him. I want to sniff his butt, but my leg hurts too bad to move. I settle for giving his wiener—that's what Jerry calls it—a few sniffs.

"What happened to you?" Leroy asks.

"I hurt my ankle."

He gives my ankle a few licks. It's what Cassie would have done. I like Leroy.

"What is this place?" I ask.

"A farm."

"What's a farm?"

"It's where they grow food."

"What kind of food?"

"Lots of kinds."

I sense movement and a cat springs onto the bed. He's big and fat. He's gray with white feet. His back is arched and all the hair sticks up on his neck. He hisses at me and Leroy, then jumps off the bed.

"Who is that?" I ask.

"That's Socks."

"He doesn't seem very nice."

"He's not."

"Do you like cats?"

"Nice cats, like Charlotte."

"Who's Charlotte?"

"She's an outside cat. You'll meet her later."

"An Outside cat?"

"Yeah, she stays outside mostly. Does whatever she wants. Comes in to eat every so often."

"What about Socks?"

"He's an indoor cat."

"So he never leaves?"

"No. He just sits around all day doing nothing. But that makes him happy."

"I'd rather be an Outside cat."

"Okay," Leroy says.

"I used to be a dog," I tell him. "But I wasn't an Outside dog. I could go Outside, but not whenever I wanted. Only when Jerry said it was okay."

I wait for him to ask about me being a dog, but he doesn't seem to care.

"Who's Jerry?" he asks.

"My human. He's the best."

I tell him all about how great Jerry is. Then I tell him about Cassie. And how amazing she is. "You remind me of her," I tell him.

This makes him happy and he gives me a few more slobbery licks.

"I want to meet Charlotte," I say.

"You will," Leroy says. "And the *others*."

* * *

I don't get to meet the *others* for three days. Hank and *Bess* (she-Hank) move me to a little room with a tiny bed on the floor and a litter box. I can barely walk and I stay in bed all day. I get to eat a bunch of food. (Bess keeps trying to "Fattin' me up.")

Leroy comes by a few times a day to keep me company. Socks struts by every once in a while and hisses. I don't think he likes that I'm using his litter box. Finally, on the fourth day, I can put my paw down and it doesn't scream.

"I'm ready to go Outside," I tell Leroy on one of his visits.

"Let's go," he says.

I hobble behind Leroy through the house. (His long ears nearly touch the ground when he walks!) At one point, we pass Bess and she says, "Look who's walking." She picks me up and gives me a kiss on the nose, then inspects my leg with a few light pinches —"that boot seems to be working pretty good"—then sets me back down.

I follow Leroy through a rubber door that flaps and into the hot sun. The first thing that hits me is the smells. Big, round, powerful, amazing smells. There's a lot of dirt, then tall green grass in every direction. Beyond the grass, I can see the jagged peaks of the far-off Mountains.

So far away.

An animal the size of a medium dog comes hopping toward us and Leroy says, "That's George." George is white and has two horns growing out of his head.

"He's a goat," Leroy explains.

"Hi, George," I say to the bouncy animal.

"Hiiiiiiiiiiiiiiiiiii!" he says, jumping up and down. He comes very close to jumping on me.

"Be careful, George," Leroy says. "He's just a little kitten."

"Careful, careful, careful," George repeats, then gives Leroy a little headbutt, then bounces away.

I'm not so sure about George.

Off in the far grass, there's a big white animal with black spots.

"Who is that?" I ask.

"That's Winnie."

"Is she a goat too?"

"No," Leroy says. "She's a cow."

"Oh."

I follow Leroy around the farm and he points things out: *That's where they keep the chickens. Those are the pigs. That's my doghouse. That's where they grow all the food. That's Hank way out there on that big yellow thing.*

My ankle is starting to hurt from all the walking and I ask, "Where is Charlotte?"

"She usually hangs out in the barn when it's this hot out," Leroy says, nodding toward another house. The house is oddly shaped. I've never seen a house quite like it. He plods toward the *barn*, his big ears flapping as he rumbles forward.

I hobble behind him.

There's a large door open a few feet and I follow Leroy inside. It's much cooler out of the sun. There's dry, yellow grass all over the ground that crunches under Leroy's feet. (I don't think I'm heavy enough to crunch anything.)

The first thing I notice is a tall, brown animal. (It's even bigger than Moses, the huge Great Dane I used to play with.) It has black hair on its neck and a thick black tail that swishes back and forth.

"Hey, Dale," Leroy says.

"Who's this?" the giant asks.

"I'm Hugo," I tell him.

His lips fold back, showing huge teeth, and he says, "Just what this place needs," he says. "Another cat."

"Don't mind him," a voice says from high above. "He's just a cranky old horse."

I look up.

Lying on one of the wood beams that crisscross ten feet above is a cat. She slinks down the wood, jumps onto Dale's back, then hops silently to the hay-covered floor.

"You must be Hugo," she says. She is entirely black with yellow eyes.

Charlotte.

* * *

"So you're an *Outdoor* cat?" I ask Charlotte.

Leroy is snuggled up in the hay taking a nap and Dale is in the back of the barn ignoring us.

"Sure am," Charlotte replies, giving one of her paws a lick.

"What do you do all day?"

"Whatever I want."

"I want to be an Outdoor cat," I tell her. "I don't want to be like Socks and lie around all day."

"Well, then you came to the right place."

I think about it.

Was this the right place?

Hank and Bess seem pretty okay as far as humans go. I would always have food. And Leroy is great. And Charlotte seems great too. I'm not so sure about George and Dale (and Winnie), but they didn't seem all bad.

Could I stay here?

But what about Jerry and Cassie?

I miss them so much. But could I really make it back to them? I walked for hours and hours and the Mountains didn't get any closer. And if Hank hadn't found me, I probably would have died. Why would next time be any different?

Charlotte slinks over to Leroy and curls up into his side. "So what do you think?" she asks. "Are you going to stay?"

I hobble over and climb onto Leroy's back. I find a comfortable place between his big folds and lay down my head.

Yeah.

I am.

17

"THE DINNER"

Jerry

I've been dreading this day for more than five months.

The big 3-6.

As I tread dangerously close to middle age, I could dwell on the fact I'm living in my parents' house, or that after brainstorming book ideas for going on six weeks, I don't have squat, or that my hair is thinning to the point of tumbleweed status, or that my last royalty check couldn't cover a tank of gas. But I don't. I'm actually—dare I say the word—*happy.*

Megan and I have been seeing each other for close to a month. After the debacle at the beach with Avery's wedding, part of me thought Megan would never want to see me again. Thankfully, she was a good sport and she gave me another chance the following week. She even admitted it was kind of funny. We went for Mexican, drank a few margaritas, and that same chemistry we found on the beach (before Cassie went Code Red Berserko) was undeniable.

Over the past weeks, we've been on several dates, but there were yet to be any sleepovers. I have high hopes for tonight, seeing as: A) It's my birthday. B) Wally is currently at my house having a playdate with Cassie. And C) Megan was yet to give me a present.

Knock on wood.

"Are you ready for this?" I ask Megan as we pull up to the valet at Riva Grill.

Riva Grill is a restaurant in the Ski Run Marina. The marina is full of boats and WaveRunners that, hours earlier, were zooming around the lake. The two-story restaurant faces the water, where the last vestige of dusk disappears behind the far mountains.

Megan is dressed in blue jeans, a cream colored blouse, and her blonde hair cascades onto her shoulders. She gives my hand a squeeze, then says, "Don't worry. Parents love me."

The last girl I introduced my parents to was Avery. That was more than five years earlier. So when my parents set up a birthday dinner for me and I told them I wanted to bring Megan, they couldn't have been happier. My father's words, *verbatim*, were, "I was starting to worry, son." (About my sexuality or that I'd simply given up, he didn't specify.)

I was a tad nervous when I broached the idea to Megan—I mean, we *had* only been dating for twenty-nine days—but while watching the opening previews for *Wonder Woman*, I leaned over and asked if she wanted to come to my birthday dinner and meet my folks. Megan's mouth opened wide and she slapped my leg. "I get to meet the Rymans!" she shouted loud enough that a few people hushed us.

I hand the keys to the valet and Megan and I make our way toward the restaurant entrance. Once inside, the young female hostess asks if we have a reservation.

"Ryman, party of four," I tell her.

She glances at the computer screen, wrinkles her forehead, then says, "I have a Ryman party of *six*."

Before I can answer, before I can tell her it must be a typo, she says, "Actually, the rest of your party is already here."

"Six?" Megan whispers as we fall in behind the hostess.

I've just begun to brainstorm who the other two people could be—the Winstons back from Europe? My brother and his wife in town from Michigan?—when I see our table.

Sitting next to my mother is a man in a gray linen suit with a slicked-back mane of white hair. Next to my father is a woman with a large purple ribbon in her hair and a chunky gold necklace.

That's when it hits me.

My parents had both brought *dates*.

* * *

"You must be Megan!" my mom shouts, jumping up from her seat. She's wearing a gray bowler hat, which stops just above the pink lenses of her glasses, a tan jacket, and red leather pants. She hugs Megan tight, pushes her away to give her a deep appraisal, then hugs her again. "Oh, it's so marvelous to meet you."

My father, unlike my mother, is dressed casually in a black T-shirt, khaki shorts, and yes, compression socks and Tevas (I'm starting to think he might sleep in them). He gives Megan a less invasive hug, then beckons me toward a woman who I can only describe as *full* hippie.

My father adjusts his glasses on his nose—a nervous tic of his —and says, "Son, this is Sequoia."

"Like the tree," she says.

"Oh, so not like the full-size SUV," I reply harsher than I intend.

I'm not sure if Sequoia or my father react to the barb as I'm spun around by my shoulder. "Honey, honey," my mom sputters. "This is Teddy."

"Heyya, Teddy," I say, giving his hand a real good shake. "Glad you could come to *my* birthday dinner."

"Glad for the invite," he says. If he can feel my angst, he doesn't show it.

As Megan and I take our seats, I notice Megan biting her lip to keep from smiling. I'm not sure if this is a Freudian Nightmare, a Greek Tragedy, or a Shakespearian Comedy, but whatever it is, Megan is enjoying it immensely.

"Shall we order some wine?" Teddy offers.

My mother puts her hand over Teddy's and says, "Teddy has an incredible palate. What was that delightful bottle you had us drink the other night?"

I lock eyes with Megan. She gives my thigh a light squeeze under the table, one I decode as, *Come on, you can survive this, Champ.*

I give her a light head shake in reply: *I'm not so sure.*

"I think it was a Zin," my dad says.

"Right you are, Martin," Teddy (my mother's *date*) says to Martin (my mother's *husband*).

This is when I realize with absolute certainty that I'm in the midst of a traumatic event. That this next two hours will forever be referred to as "The Dinner."

I want to inquire when the three of them shared this bottle of wine and if Sequoia "like the tree" was there, or if anyone was going to bring up the gigantic elephant in the room, but I simply say, "Go ahead, Theodore. Order us some wine."

I will not survive this sober.

Cassie

Wally's little butt is high in the air. He wiggles it, his tail whipping back and forth. His front paws are stretched out and he makes this rumbling little bark.

I know you want to play, Wally.

We've been playing since Megan dropped him off an hour ago. We played Chase. We played Tumble. We played Tug. We played Hide. But now it's time to play Nap.

Wally's rumbling bark gets louder and his furry head darts from side to side.

There used to be a time when I could play nonstop like Wally. Hugo and I used to play all day and all night. We'd play until Jerry would beg us to stop. But not anymore.

The day after I first met Wally on the beach—the day after I saw Avery and went what Jerry calls "Code Red Berserko" (I plead insanity, by the way)—I could barely walk. My hips throbbed. Every step sent a sharp pain down my leg. I tried to act normal when I was around Jerry, but I couldn't fake it anymore.

A few days later, Jerry took me to see Dr. Josh. Now, I *love* Dr. Josh, but he pushed and pulled on parts of my body I didn't even know existed. "I know it hurts, sweetie, I know," he would say after each push and pull.

If you know, then stop doing it!

Then he called me something he'd never called me before: a *senior* dog.

How dare you, Dr. Josh! (Storm is a senior dog. Not me. I'm pre-senior. Maybe even *pre*-pre-senior.)

After my exam, Dr. Josh said a bunch of strange words I've never heard before, words Jerry has been repeating a lot lately: *Rimadyl, Glucosamine, Omega-three.*

One of these words is a pill. Jerry tries to hide it in a little treat, but I know it's in there. (Come on, Jerry, give me some credit.) The other words come in bottles and Jerry adds them to my kibble each morning. One of them tastes funny. The other one tastes like fish. I eat them to make Jerry happy. But a few weeks later, I actually feel better. (My hips don't creak when I walk and I'm not as sore.)

I roll over on my side. Wally gives one more throaty bark, then gives up in defeat. He rushes forward and puts his front paws on my belly, then gives the side of my face a few licks with his little pink tongue. Then he zooms down the hall and disappears.

I watch Wally zoom back and forth, back and forth, back and

forth, then stop, pant for a quick second, then zoom some more. (I remember when Hugo used to do this. Jerry called them "Zoomies.")

Finally, after five minutes of zooming, Wally collapses to the carpet, panting heavily. I snuggle up around him and a few minutes later, he's snoring.

I soon join him.

Jerry

"I already saw it," I say, passing the phone back to my mother. "You texted it to me three times."

It's a video of a black bear that climbed over the Winston's fence and was sniffing around my mother's compost pile.

Bears are a part of life in Tahoe. At least once a week, you'll see one rifling through someone's trash or walking down the street. The first few times you see one is exciting, but by the twentieth bear, it's lost its thrill.

"Well, you never texted me back," my mother snaps. "No thumbs up. No happy face. Not a *single* emoji. Nothing." She glances at Teddy and he shakes his head in obvious disapproval.

Appetizers and salads have come and gone. Teddy—who I learned was a pilot for Delta for thirty years before retiring to the small town of Minden, Nevada—has ordered a third bottle of wine ("a real gem of a pinot"), which is open and breathing.

I toss back the last half inch of wine in my glass and feel it slink into my belly and crawl into my legs. "It's just that you send *a lot* of videos, Mom," I say with the same practiced smile I've pinned to my face for the last half hour. What I don't say is, *"What I didn't get is the text informing me that you're bringing the ghost of Howard Hughes to my birthday dinner."*

An awkward few seconds pass, then my father says, "So, Jerry, why don't you tell everyone about Cassie and the dress?"

I'm buzzed enough that I'm considering dropping a grenade on this celebration, something along the lines of, "So when exactly does Maury Povich come out?" but somehow, I restrain myself and begin to chronicle how Cassie destroyed my ex-fiancé's wedding.

I recount how Cassie ripped the dress off Avery, then dragged it fifty yards out into the lake. How Avery was completely naked other than some small pasties on her boobs and a red lace garter on her thigh. How after locking eyes with Avery's Nana, I pushed myself up, only to have Avery's father rush me and tackle me to the ground. How I wiggled out of his grip, then ran down the beach with Cassie, Megan, and Wally, and how we didn't stop until we reached the CVS four blocks away. How luckily, I had a twenty-dollar bill secreted away in the swim pocket of my swimsuit and I bought a Hawaiian shirt and a big hat and snuck back to the beach and got all our stuff.

"Did they go through with the wedding?" Sequoia asks. So far, she'd been quiet and reserved. Contemplative even. Which isn't surprising as she is a self-proclaimed, "Healer...well, and an accountant."

"Her Instagram is public and she had a bunch of wedding photos on there," I say. "The dress looked pretty much the same. Knowing Avery, she probably had a back-up."

Teddy asks, "Did you hear from her afterward?"

"Not her directly. But I did get an email from her father saying I owed him two thousand dollars for the dress, plus another thousand for the two extra hours they had to rent the beach." I pause, then add, "And he said if I didn't pay him he was going to call animal control and have Cassie put down."

Sequoia inhales sharply, as if the thought of this is so appalling she might die. I hate her a little less because of this.

"What did you say?" Teddy asks.

"I told him the engagement ring I gave to Avery cost seven thousand dollars and since she never returned it, by my calculations, *they* owed me four thousand dollars. And I said that if I even got a whiff of animal control, I would email the IRS about his offshore accounts in Panama his daughter was always bragging about."

"And?"

"*And* I got a check in the mail a week later for four thousand dollars."

Teddy slams his hand down on the table and grins wildly. His teeth are stained pink from the wine.

Three servers appear and drop off our entrees. Teddy gives the go-ahead for the waiter to pour the wine and he fills our glasses. After everyone takes a few bites of their dishes, my father turns his attention to Megan. I'd only told my parents the bare bones about her: that she was born here, then went to culinary school in Sacramento, and that she was now the pastry chef at Jimmy's Restaurant. But my father wants to hear it all from her lips. He prods her about her upbringing, her parents, her parents' jobs, her schooling, her work history, the genealogy of her last name, stopping just short of asking what day her menstrual cycle normally begins.

"Didn't know you were coming to a congressional oversight hearing, did you?" I mutter between questions.

My dad smirks, but this doesn't slow him down. After several more questions, he asks, "So, how do you like working at Jimmy's? Betsy and I love that place."

"Who?" Megan asks.

"Betsy?" my dad says, nodding at my mother. "My wife."

"Oh, right," Megan says with a dramatic nod. "Your *wife*."

I choke on a bite of pork, cough, then finally flush it down with a swig of water. The elephant is out. And I wasn't even the one to pull the trigger.

I give Megan's leg a light pinch under the table.

Thank you.

An awkward few seconds follows, but before the elephant

can take a big fat dump on the table, Megan says, "I do love working at Jimmy's. They give me total freedom to play with the dessert menu. I can rotate my favorites, run a special for a night, or run five specials for a night. Plus, we have a wedding party each weekend and I've been making a lot of the wedding cakes lately."

"Is that what you want to do full-time? Make wedding cakes?"

"I do love making wedding cakes, but what I really want to do is open a dog bakery."

"A dog bakery?" Teddy scoffs. "Is there any money in that?"

"You'd be surprised," Megan says. "People spend astronomical amounts of money on their pets." She smiles, then adds, "And why shouldn't they? Our pets are the only thing that will ever love us more than we love ourselves. And we only get them for these brief periods. We *should* spoil them. They spoil us with their love every day."

I'm not sure if it's the wine or Megan's milk chocolate eyes as she says these words, but my heart begins to tingle. I grab for Megan's hand under the table.

After a few beats, my mother asks, "So, Megan, have you read any of Jerry's books?"

If genealogy, college resume, job status, and life ambition are of consequence to my father, that my significant other has read my books is of *great* consequence to my mother.

(When my mother learned that after having dated Avery for over a year, she still hadn't cracked open one of my books, my mother took me aside and said, "I don't know about this girl, Jerry. I just *don't* know.")

I put my hand up and say, "Give her a break, Mom. We've only been dating for a month."

Megan and I had discussed books on several of our dates, but I made a point never to mention *my* books. In a few more months, if I hadn't scared her away, I would consider giving one of my books to her. Which is why I'm as surprised as anyone when

Megan says, "I've read the first two and I'm halfway through the third."

I turn toward her, all thirty-two of my teeth on display. "Really?"

"Of course. I downloaded the first book on my Kindle the day you messaged me on Facebook."

"So what do you think?" my mom says, stealing my thought bubble.

"Well—" she grimaces.

My stomach churns.

"—I think they're amazing."

"Oh, come on," I say, grinning wildly. "*Amazing?*"

"The first one, yeah, *amazing*. Probably one of my favorite sci-fi books ever. The second and third are still good, way better than the reviewers make out." She turns to me and confesses, "I may have tracked down *Robin_Readsalot77* on Instagram and told her to eat shit."

Everyone at the table erupts in laughter, then my mom says, "She's a keeper!"

* * *

In hindsight, I should have noticed when our waiter never dropped off dessert menus. Or at the very least, I should have known something was amiss when Megan disappeared to the bathroom for much longer than normal.

Ninety seconds after Megan returns, and fifteen seconds after Teddy bellows, "Who do you have to know to get some Tiramisu around here?" our waiter appears holding a flaming birthday cake.

"What did you do?" I ask Megan, who is fidgeting in her seat and trying extremely hard not to smile.

"Nothing," she says innocently. Then adds, "Well, maybe I'm friends with one of the chefs here and maybe I made a birthday cake for you and maybe they've been keeping it in their walk-in."

The waiter leans over the table and sets the cake in front of me. It's rectangular with intricate blue frosting. On one side of the cake are flaming "3" and "6" candles and on the other side is simply a "3". It looks as though I'm turning 336, but it makes sense once you read what's written in blue icing: "Happy Birthday Jerry & Hugo." Or once you see the face of a Bernese Mountain Dog skillfully drawn in black, brown, and white icing.

I'm subjected to an unnecessarily loud singing of "Happy Birthday," and by the time it's finished, I can't fight back the tears.

"He must really hate birthdays," I hear Teddy murmur as I pick my napkin from my lap and bury my face in it.

All I hear is muttering in the background, no doubt my mother explaining how I share my birthday with my dog, who tragically died at the end of February, and who would've been three years old today.

This is my third time crying in the last twelve hours and this bout has an edge to it. I'm sad, but I'm also angry.

How could Megan do this? Doesn't she know Hugo will never celebrate another birthday? He can't. He's dead. Plus, she never even met him. *What gives her the right?*

Megan pulls the napkin away from my face. I don't want to look at her. I want to teleport home and curl up with Cassie. But then she lifts my chin slightly and stares at me. She waits patiently until I lift my gaze to hers. Then she says calmly, "Just because he's dead, doesn't mean he doesn't go on living." Then she gives my heart a light pat.

All my anger falls away. Pushed out by this overpowering feeling of love. Love for Hugo. And love for this woman next to me who risked upsetting me at my birthday dinner—in front of my parents, who she is meeting for the first time—to help me celebrate my precious dog's life.

This would be a turning point in my grief. A moment of clarity. Hugo might not be turning three on this earth, but he was turning three in my heart. And he would always be there.

"Come on, son," my father beckons, "blow out those candles."

So I blow out my candles and I blow out Hugo's candle.

And I make a wish.

* * *

The cake, chocolate mousse, is so delicious that after his first bite, my father says, "Holy shit!" Which is the first time I've heard him curse since he stubbed his toe ten years earlier.

Once we've each polished off a piece of cake—though not the section with Hugo's face on it, I want to save that—Sequoia beckons to Megan and says, "Give me your hand."

Megan cuts her eyes at me in what I can only describe as amused bewilderment, then offers her hand to the purple-shawled healer/accountant.

"Twenty-five years old, you said?" Sequoia mumbles as she takes Megan's hand in hers and begins inspecting Megan's palm.

I don't remember Megan saying her age, but Megan nods and says, "Yes, I'm twenty-five."

"You show a great deal of wisdom for such a young woman," Sequoia says squinting, her face an inch from Megan's open hand.

Megan shrugs.

"But not such a shock now that I see your lifelines." Sequoia takes a long, measured breath, then her mouth softens into an almost-smile. "You have an old soul, my dear. An *old* soul."

Cassie

The sound of keys rattling in the door startles me awake. Wally darts around the couch and to the front door and begins barking wildly.

I love Wally, but he sure is barky.

The door opens and Jerry and Megan step inside. Wally runs

into the bedroom and comes out with my green alligator in his mouth and shows it to Megan.

Look at my new toy, he tells her.

I'm too excited to see Jerry to care (too much) and he leans down and lets me lick his face and neck. His face is salty and I know he's been crying.

Why were you crying, Jerry?

But he doesn't seem sad, so maybe they were happy tears. I know this happens to humans sometimes.

Megan leans down and lets me kiss her and Jerry gives Wally some good scratches, then he says, "Cassie let you play with her teddy? Wow, I'm impressed." He turns to me and nods lightly.

I didn't *let* him do anything, Jerry.

Jerry opens the freezer and puts the white bag he's holding inside. Then he opens the fridge and pulls out the blueberries. He feeds Wally and me a bunch of blueberries—they are the most delicious blueberries I've ever tasted—then he puts them away.

This is when Megan attacks him and starts licking Jerry's face.

And then Jerry and Megan go into the bedroom.

Wally follows them into the bedroom and barks. He wants to play. I walk up behind him and bite him gently on the tail, then I give him a light pull.

Let's let *them* play together for a while.

It takes me a few tries, but I finally get Wally to snuggle up with me on the couch. We fall asleep to the sounds of Jerry and Megan playing.

18

"THE MOUNTAINS"

Hugo

"Come on, slowpoke," I say, turning and glancing at Charlotte twenty feet behind me.

We're running through the fields between the spongy green rows of something called alfalfa. With four graceful strides, Charlotte catches up to me, then zooms ahead.

I race to keep up.

Over the past month, my ankle has completely healed. (Cats might not be indestructible, but they sure do have magical healing powers.) And I've grown a bit. I'm still a baby cat, just a bigger baby cat. And best of all, most of my little dagger teeth have fallen out and bigger teeth grew in. (They still aren't great—nothing like my big dog teeth—but they are much better than before.)

I chase Charlotte through the fields. The dirt points at the Mountains, but I'm more concerned with catching the wily cat in front of me than the long-off peaks.

I speed up and leap onto Charlotte's back. The two of us go rolling in the dirt, then end up tangled in a row of greens. We wrestle for a few minutes, then take off back toward the farm.

This has become a routine of ours: running free through the fields. Every once in a while, Leroy will come with us (I love watching his giant ears flap when he runs), but mostly it's just me and Charlotte. Sometimes we'll go to one of the neighboring farms and chase their chickens, or we'll walk along the small fence that surrounds Winnie, or if it's too hot out, we'll climb up in the rafters of the barn and knock dirt onto Dale's back. (He doesn't like this very much.)

When we return to the farm, Charlotte heads toward the barn. I head toward the main house, push through the flap in the door and into the kitchen.

"Bootsie!" shouts Bess, reaching down and scooping me up. "My baby boy, Bootsie!" This is my name. Well, this is Hank and Bess's name for me anyway.

(Better than *Cheese*, I guess.)

"You ready for some din-din?"

Yes, please.

Bess opens a can and dumps it into a small bowl. The smell hits my nostrils and I feel my tail begin to wag. This is my new favorite smell.

It's called Tuna.

I devour the tuna, take a long drink, then I find Bess in a rocking chair in the living room. Socks is lying on the windowsill. He gives me a lazy glance, but nothing more. (Since I no longer use his litter box, Socks has pretty much left me alone.) Bess has two sticks and a bunch of rope in her lap and she's making something. (I hope it isn't another little hat for me!)

I jump on her lap and she sets the sticks down. Then she scratches my head and ears. She is an amazing scratcher.

Hank comes home a little later and he picks me out of Bess's lap. He puts me on the table and he scratches my back while he reads the newspaper.

This is our thing.

When Hank goes to bed (Hank goes to bed really early, but he also gets up really early), I go back outside.

I make my way to Leroy's doghouse and look inside. Some nights he sleeps in the barn with Charlotte. But not tonight. I snuggle up into his side.

He licks my head until I fall asleep.

Farm life is pretty good.

* * *

I'm chasing Charlotte again. In the dirt. But the dirt is lighter in color. It's not dirt. It's *sand*. I'm chasing Charlotte through the sand. I can see her up ahead. Or at least, her shadow. She's so far away. I run toward her. There's something blue to my right. Water. Not just water. The Lake. I must be at the beach.

Why am I chasing Charlotte through the sand on the beach?

I run, kicking up sand behind me. Charlotte's shadow grows bigger and bigger.

And then.

It's not Charlotte.

It's Cassie.

Her tail is helicoptering back and forth.

She barks at me.

Bark, bark, bark.

Come home, Hugo.

Come home.

My eyes open.

"Are you okay?" Leroy asks.

It takes me a long moment to realize it was all a dream.

"I'm okay," I tell him.

But I'm not.

For the past month, I've tried not to think about Cassie or Jerry. I've tried to enjoy this new life. But as much as I love Leroy and Charlotte and Hank and Bess, I don't belong here.

I wiggle my way out of the doghouse and I gaze at the Mountains under the full moon.

I'm coming home, Cassie.

Or I'm going to die trying.

* * *

"Good luck, Hugo," Leroy says. His droopy eyes are even droopier than usual.

"You're going to make it," Charlotte says. "I just know it."

"I don't know," Dale says. "It's pretty far. Seems to me that you're probably going to die."

"Don't listen to him, Hugo," Charlotte says. "He's just a dumb old horse."

I give Leroy one last lick on his long ear and he lets out a loud whine. Then Charlotte and I exit the barn and go into the moonlight.

As we run into the fields toward the Mountains, Leroy's rumbling cries echo behind us.

* * *

"Okay, Hugo," Charlotte says. "I've got to head back."

Charlotte has run with me all night. Through many farms, through roads, around houses. For miles and miles. But now the sun is beginning to rise.

"Thank you for teaching me," I say to Charlotte.

"Teaching you what?"

"That life as a cat isn't so bad."

She rubs against me and nestles her head into my neck. She whispers, "You are a cat. But you have the heart of a dog." Then she races away.

* * *

For three nights, I run.

Slowly, the Mountains begin to grow.

On the fourth day, I reach the hills that lead to the Mountains. I know the Mountains are close and that the big pine trees will start popping up any second, but I may never see them.

I'm so weak.

My legs feel like they are stuck in mud. I found a small stream early yesterday, but I haven't had anything to drink since. I ate a couple of peaches and some almonds at a farm, but that was on the second day.

After each step, I wonder if it will be my last.

* * *

"Another step," Cassie barks. "Take another step."

Okay, Cassie.

I will.

For you.

I force myself to keep going. I can barely keep my eyes open, stumbling ahead blindly. And then I trip.

I open my eyes and look at what I stumbled over.

A pinecone.

I glance up and see a giant pine tree.

I made it.

* * *

I pick my way through the tall evergreens, through the thick brush, up and over the fallen logs, through the bramble. The air is nice and cool. It takes me half the day, but I make it up and over an entire mountain.

And then I hear it.

At first it's a low rumble. But as I get closer, it grows into a mighty roar.

A river.

I race to the edge of the river and watch as the water rushes over rocks in a wave of white. I scamper upstream to where the water is less excitable. There is no river bank, just rocks. I crawl to the edge of a rock and I dip my head toward the water. I reach out my tongue, but the water is out of reach. (My awesome dog tongue could have reached it, but my cat tongue isn't very long.) I scamper farther upstream and find a tree that has fallen into the water. The log is wider than I am and I jump onto it, then lean down. I lap at the cold river water, quenching my thirst.

I'm heading back for a second drink when one of my back paws slips off the log. I scramble to hold on with my front paws, but it's too late, and I fall into the water.

I've been in rivers before, so I don't panic. I paddle against the current. But my tiny paws don't work well as paddles and the river sweeps me away from the log.

Now I panic.

I turn around in the water. I can see the bubbling white water ahead. I paddle as hard as I can toward the rocks, but the mighty river doesn't care.

The white water comes fast. I slide over rocks and then I'm underwater. I get my head back above water and cough in a breath, but then there's more white water and I'm back under. I try to get my head back out, but I can't. I'm flipping and spinning. I don't know which way is up. My chest begins to burn. I need to breathe. I need air.

I'm going to die.

I feel a sharp pinch behind my neck and then I'm free of the water. I suck in air and cough, cough, cough.

What happened?

How did I get out of the water?

I'm dizzy from all the spinning, but I can feel myself floating in the air. And I still feel a pinch on my neck. I think back to when I was a baby cat. The Big Cat, holding me in her teeth.

This is the same.

Something has me in its teeth!

I whip my body from side to side and fall to the ground. I flip over and look upward.

There's a giant cat gazing down at me. It's gray and tan with black spots, light green eyes, a short tail, and is three times the size of any cat I've ever seen.

And then I remember. I remember Cassie telling me about these giant cats that live in the Mountains. She'd seen one before. When she was hiking with Jerry. Before I came along.

Not a cat.

A *bobcat*.

* * *

I'm about to thank the bobcat for pulling me out of the river when he puts one of his giant paws on my chest. He leans down, until his green eyes are nearly touching me, and says, "You're in my territory, kid."

Territory?

"What's, uh, a territory?" I mumble.

"My *area*," he snorts.

He slowly takes his paw off my chest and I scramble to my feet.

"Get moving," he says.

"Wait, what's your name?"

The bobcat opens his mouth wide, revealing two large fangs, and then he growls, "Scat!"

I turn and run.

After a few minutes, I stop and sit down on a rock.

Why was that bobcat so mean? All I wanted to do was thank him for pulling me out of the river. I didn't know I was in his area —sorry, *territory*. I didn't even know animals have territories. And if he was so mad that I was in his territory, then why did he save my life?

Mean old bobcat.

There's a shallow pool of water near where I've stopped and I go and take a long drink. With my thirst quenched, I realize how hungry I am. It's been nearly three days since I've eaten anything.

I resume my journey, looking for anything that might be edible. I find a few green berries on the ground and I eat a couple. They are tart and they make my eyes water as I swallow them. Still, they quiet my rumbling stomach and I eat a few more.

Energized from the berries, I climb farther up the mountain. It's getting late in the day and the sun is starting to dim behind me. And another thing: my belly is starting to hurt. Maybe eating those berries wasn't such a good idea.

I'm only able to walk for another few minutes before I have to stop.

I'm sick.

I was sick a few times when I was a dog. Most of the time it was because I ate one of my tennis balls. But I usually felt better right after I barfed it up. I would try to wait until I was outside, but sometimes those things can't wait. Jerry would look at my big pile of orange barf and say, "I was wondering where all those balls went." Then he would clean it up and wipe off my chin with a paper towel.

I can tell this is different. This is like the time when I couldn't stop barfing and I couldn't stop pooping. Jerry said that I must "have gotten into something," though I'm not sure what this meant. I slept in the bathroom that night because the floor was nice and cool and Jerry grabbed a couple of pillows off his bed and he slept right next to me.

That's how I feel now.

Only worse.

All I want is for Jerry to rub my belly and tell me I'm going to feel better soon.

I barf and poop until the stars come out. Then I curl up in a ball and moan. At some point, the moaning gives way to sleep.

* * *

My belly still hurts when I wake up in the morning. I force myself to take a drink from the river, but it makes my stomach hurt even worse. I get sick a few more times and then I start to feel better. By the afternoon, I'm able to drink from the river and I'm ready to continue my journey home.

I continue through the trees, picking my way up, over, and through the thick brush. I have no idea how far away the Lake is from where I am, but I'm guessing it's a long way. And walking in the Mountains is so much slower than walking next to the road or in the grass. It could take me weeks to make it back to the Lake at this rate.

I try to pick up the pace, but my body is still weak from being sick and I slow back down. That's when I smell a familiar smell. A smell I know from when I was a dog.

Bear.

I turn around and see him, a large black bear. He's fifty yards behind me, crashing through the brush. I think about racing toward him and barking my head off, but that won't work. I'm not a dog anymore. And this bear doesn't look like he wants to eat our trash. He wants to eat *me*.

There's a tree nearby and I dart toward it. I jump and try to dig my claws into the bark, but my claws aren't sharp enough and I slide down the trunk and roll to the dirt.

I turn and glance up. The bear is rumbling toward me on all fours, his head swaying back and forth. He's going to wrap his enormous mouth around me in a few seconds.

I close my eyes. I'm going to die. I'm going to become a star (hopefully).

I feel jaws sink into my flesh and then I'm yanked upwards. I wait for darkness, long darkness, like what happened after I died the first time, but it doesn't come.

Instead, I hear snarling and a loud tearing. But it's not me

204

that's being torn into, it's the tree. Below me, the bear is attempting to climb the tree, his large claws biting into the thick trunk, then climbing a few feet, then falling back down.

I'm lying on a thick branch fifteen feet above him.

I turn.

Next to me on the branch is the mean old bobcat.

"Xanthus," he says. "My name is Xanthus."

* * *

"Thank you for saving me," I say, then add, "Twice."

Xanthus shakes his head but says nothing.

After a few minutes, the bear gave up and Xanthus and I made our way down from the tree. Then he told me to follow him.

"You aren't from the mountains, are you, Hugo?" Xanthus asks, his butt rocking as he takes long strides through the bramble.

"No," I tell him. "I used to live near the Mountains, but not in the Mountains."

"I thought perhaps you were kidding at first about not knowing what a territory was. But you are unlike any cat I have seen before. And then I saw you eat those green berries and I knew you must really know nothing."

"You watched me eat those berries? Why didn't you say something?"

"Sometimes nature is the best teacher."

Xanthus leaves me to think about this for the duration of our walk.

A bit later, we reach a large tree with a hole near the bottom. "We're here," he says.

I sniff at the musty hole and say, "You live here?"

"Sometimes," he says. "I have many dens scattered throughout my territory, but this is my main den."

"Do you live all alone?"

"Yes."

I want to ask him where all his friends live, but I already know, he has no friends.

I ask, "Were you following me the whole time?"

"No, but your scent was easy to pick up."

I'm set to ask about the bear, when Xanthus asks, "How did you come to be in these mountains, Hugo?"

I consider telling him my entire saga, but something tells me that he won't understand. He may never have seen a human before in his life. So I tell him, "I'm trying to get home."

"Is this where you used to live near the mountains, but not *in* the mountains?"

"Yes, it's next to a large Lake."

"I have heard of this territory."

"You have?"

"Yes, though I've never been there. It's many, many days' travels." He doesn't say it, but I can tell by the way he's looking at me —it was the same way Calandia looked at me—he thinks I will never make it. That I will never survive.

And maybe he's right.

If it wasn't for him, I wouldn't be alive now. I would have drowned in the river, or I would have been mauled by that bear.

"Are you hungry?" Xanthus asks.

I nod. I've never been so hungry in my life.

Xanthus motions for me to follow him. We walk a short ways from the tree, then he begins digging in the dirt. He digs for a few moments then uncovers a small carcass. He picks up the carcass and drops it at my feet. It's half eaten, but I know the smell.

Squirrel.

When I was a dog, I killed a few squirrels, but I never ate one. In fact, I've never eaten anything I killed.

"Go ahead," Xanthus says. "Eat."

I bend my head down and open my mouth. Part of me doesn't want to eat this animal. This squirrel could have been a cat or even a dog. But then again, Calandia said my case was rare, that it almost never happened. Still, this squirrel had to have a soul at some point.

Right?

But its soul is gone. Gone to wherever squirrels' souls go.

I decide that while I will never kill a squirrel, it would be foolish not to eat this one. So I do. I rip away a small piece of the squirrel's flesh and I swallow. It's no bacon, but it's pretty good.

After I eat my fill, I glance up at Xanthus and ask, "Do you think I can make it? Do you think I can make it to the Lake?"

"There are many dangers in these mountains. Many things that would like to make a meal of you, just as you made a meal of this squirrel. You have many things you must learn in order to survive."

He gives me a light cuff on the head with his paw and then says, "And I shall teach them all to you."

19

"CAMPING"

Jerry

"This looks like a good spot," I say, pulling my car into a flat section of dirt among the tall pines. There's a wooden picnic table and a circular pile of rocks surrounding a mound of black ash.

For the past hour, we've been driving on one of the many dirt roads that wind through the forty-mile-wide stretch of mountains west of Tahoe. It's the last weekend of August, but camping season is still in full bloom and all the campgrounds I called were reserved (some we would learn, you had to reserve a *year* in advance). Even most of the campsites off the beaten path, tucked back deep in the Eldorado National Forest—where we've been searching for the past hour—are filled.

"Perfect," Megan says, her dimples flashing, relieved to have finally found a vacant spot.

A moment later, we're parked and Cassie and Wally are off inspecting every inch of the campsite. I watch as Cassie trots to the picnic table, sniffs one of the legs, then pees on it. A moment later, Wally walks over, sniffs, then lifts his leg and does the same.

I pop the hatch on my compact SUV and slide out the blue

husk of a tent. I carry it thirty feet to what I deem an appropriate location to set it up and toss it to the ground. A puff of dust, half from the ground and half from the thick layer covering the tent bag, wafts in the light breeze.

When Megan first broached the idea of going camping, I was tempted to rush to the nearest sporting goods store to drop a few hundred dollars on a new tent, some sleeping bags, and an assortment of other camping goodies, but I lacked the funds.

After careful consideration, I used the money Avery's father sent me to repay my parents for the eight months they'd been letting me live in their house rent-free. (They only charged me $500 in rent, a fraction of what they could be renting the place out to an actual tenant.) Then after a few unexpected expenses—a new car battery, a trip to see Dr. Josh for Cassie's semi-annual ear infection, a pair of running shoes, and the biggie, a new laptop (my old one basically self-destructed)—plus a couple expensive dinners out with Megan, and my savings was running on fumes.

So I rummaged around my parents' house for the old tent that Morgan and I would set up in her backyard. I finally found it crammed in the attic near two sleeping bags that I'm guessing also hadn't been used in over twenty-five years. (I'd never once heard of my parents going camping and my brother Mark was far from the camping type.)

"This is going to be so much fun," Megan says, tossing the two sleeping bags next to the tent. She's wearing khaki shorts, a light green T-shirt, sneakers, and a red "Tah ho" hat. As for me, I'm clad in *full* lumberjack: jeans, flannel rolled up at the sleeves, and hiking boots. I would be baking at the lake, but tucked back twenty miles into the forest and at an elevation of around 7,500 feet (1,200 higher than lake level), the temperature is in the high sixties.

Megan lunges toward me and pulls me into a long kiss, then breaking away, she says, "Camping!" She claps her hands a few times. "We're camping!"

"Well technically, right now, we're just standing in the dirt, but—"

She gives me a soft slap on the shoulder, then we spend the next few minutes pulling all our camping gear—firewood, lantern, cooler, backpacks, dog paraphernalia—out of the car.

Megan sets the cooler near the picnic table and pulls out two beers. She hands me one of the cold cans and we cheers. I take a long swig then locate Cassie and Wally. Cassie is busy digging a hole at the edge of the tall pines and Wally is barking at a large pinecone.

"So what do we do first?" Megan asks. "Fire? Tent? *S'mores?*"

We spent far longer than we anticipated on the road and it's closing in on six o'clock. The sun won't set for another hour and a half, but it's already darting behind the mountain behind us.

"Let's get the tent up while we still have the sun," I say.

It takes us twenty minutes to get the blue, four-person tent up and tethered. The tent is in better shape than I suspected, save for two tears in the nylon. One tear is only two inches, but another is eight inches long.

"A couple tears," I say. "But it will work." Then I add, "Unless it rains."

On this note, I couldn't find the rain tarp for the tent. But thankfully, the forecast didn't call for any rain, though there are a few clouds making their way in from the west that could be threatening.

Megan grins, then opens up her backpack and extracts two large rolls of duct tape. One yellow. One green.

"What color do you prefer?" the Queen of Duct Tape asks.

"What? No blue?"

She smiles. "My blue roll is holding up the bumper of my car."

"Oh, right. How could I forget?"

We decide on yellow and after a couple minutes and much more duct tape than is necessary, Megan has covered both tears in a large yellow asterisk.

"Good as new," she proclaims.

* * *

"I'm getting hungry," Megan says.

There's a hiking trail leading away from our campsite and we've spent the last hour exploring the area.

We encountered several other campsites, many of which had dogs, and Cassie and Wally were eager to say hello. All the dogs were friendly except for a little Chihuahua who nipped at Wally when he went in for a sniff.

After maybe a mile, the trailhead came to a small stream. Both Cassie and Wally splashed around, while Megan and I snuggled up on a warm rock. We let the dogs tire themselves out, then we headed back.

"I'm hungry too," I say as we round the final bend and our tent comes into view. We'd picked up sandwiches before heading into the mountains, but that was four hours earlier.

"You build a fire and I'll get the food prepped," Megan says, then gives my butt a light slap.

"Yes ma'am."

I stack several pieces of firewood on top of the ash and crumple up a handful of pages from the *San Francisco Chronicle* I'd purchased. Out of the corner of my eye, I watch Megan pull a tupperware container of homemade potato salad from the cooler, a pack of hotdog buns, a giant package of jumbo hotdogs, then an assortment of condiments. (Megan was *insistent* we eat hotdogs on our camping trip.)

I light a match and ignite a corner of newspaper. It doesn't take long until the fire is blazing.

Megan nestles up beside me and says, "I can't find the hotdog skewers. Are you sure you packed them?"

The hotdog skewers are actually telescoping pitchforks that you can use to roast hotdogs and more importantly, marshmallows. My mother bought the skewers for Morgan and me three decades earlier.

I suck air between my teeth and say, "Bad news...I think I left them in the dishwasher."

"That's okay," she says, shrugging. "I think it will be even better using a good stick." She claps twice. "So rustic!"

She tousles my hair and says, "Operation: Hotdog Stick!" Then she scampers into the trees.

Cassie

Two chipmunks chase each other around the tree, skittering their way up the trunk and disappearing into the thick green pine needles. (Chipmunks look a lot like squirrels, only they are smaller and they don't have the big bushy tail.) I think they're playing, but I can't be sure. They might be fighting over a nut.

One of the chipmunks races down the trunk of the tree and jumps to the forest floor. He has a big nut in his mouth. (I'm not sure why, but squirrels are all *hers* and chipmunks are all *hims*.) I watch as he runs a few more feet, then stops to nibble on his prize. His little whiskers twitch back and forth.

I bark at him.

Hey, chipmunk! Enjoy your dinner!

My bark startles him and he dashes deeper into the forest.

I'm about to bark for him to come back, that I just want to watch him eat his nut and watch his cute little whiskers twitch some more, when I hear a sound behind me.

It's Wally.

He's waddling toward me, struggling to hold something large and rectangular in his mouth. He plods the last couple yards, then drops his find at my feet. His little tail whips back and forth.

Wally's teeth have cut a small hole in the package and the smell wafts upward. It's an amazing smell. A smell even better than Kettle Corn.

It's called Hotdog.

Wally has stolen a big pack of fat, plump hotdogs.

I shake my head at Wally.

We can't eat these!

These are for Jerry and Megan!

Wally ignores me, ripping into the package, then slinking one of the giant hotdogs out. He wraps his little paws around it, then begins tearing little chunks away and gobbling them down.

I look around, searching for Megan and Jerry—knowing they're going to be upset when they find out that Wally stole their hotdogs—but I don't see them anywhere.

I decide what I'll do. I'll guard the hotdogs so Wally can't eat any more. I lean down and pick up the pack in my teeth. I can't help but notice that there are a lot of hotdogs in the pack.

I count them.

Nine.

There are nine hotdogs.

Some of the juice from the hotdogs drips into my mouth and I feel my eyes nearly roll back in my head. I've never tasted anything so amazing in my life.

Maybe if I just have one?

Megan and Jerry won't miss one measly hotdog!

I set the package down and I gingerly pull one hotdog out. It's much fatter than the hotdogs I've seen before. I glance up at Wally. He's still working on his hotdog, his little butt wiggling as he chokes down little pieces.

I take a little nibble of my hotdog and swallow.

Wow!

How is it possible that something this delicious even exists?

I take another nibble, but it isn't a nibble. It's a gobble. (I eat the entire hotdog!)

I'm just like Hugo! I've become Hugo.

But there's nothing I can do now.

I ate the hotdog.

It's gone.

I close my eyes and take a deep breath.

When you open your eyes you will be the Guardian of the Hotdogs!

I open my eyes.

But I'm too late.

Wally is slinking out his second hotdog.

He drags it a few feet away, then starts digging into it.

Well, if Wally is having another one, I suppose I could have another one. I mean, how many hotdogs do Jerry and Megan need?

They won't miss one more.

I slowly pull a second hotdog from the pack.

Savor it, Cassie.

But I don't. I eat the second hotdog faster than the first.

Dang it, Cassie!

I watch Wally talking small little bites and swallowing them down. He's so happy.

I glance back to the pack of hotdogs.

There are still six left.

Maybe if I have just one more.

Jerry

It takes Megan and me ten minutes to complete Operation: Hotdog stick. As we venture back out from the trees, I feel a sting on the back of my leg.

"Ouch!" I say, whipping my head around. "Did you just whip me with your hotdog stick?"

Megan giggles and says, "Maybe."

I chase her through the trees until I'm able to give her butt a

THE SPEED OF SOULS

nice swat. She grabs her butt in her hands and wheezes, "Okay, okay, we're even."

We call a truce, but when I go in for a handshake, she whips me on my thigh. I whip her back and she lets out a loud yelp. Then when she sees that my hotdog stick is broken, she gives me two hard lashes on my shoulder.

"Not fair," I howl.

We call a second truce, which we sign with a kiss, then Megan helps me locate another stick. She finds one within a short fifteen seconds, then we march from the trees and to the picnic table.

"Did you do something with the hotdogs?" Megan asks, her forehead wrinkling.

I survey the table. The potato salad, buns, and condiments are all there, but the big package of Ballpark Jumbo Franks is missing.

Megan shakes her head lightly from side to side and says, "Do you think a bear or a—" Her eyes open wide. "Wally!" Megan whips her head around and begins searching for the fifteen-pound Ewok.

"Wally?" I ask. "Really?"

"Oh, yeah. That little stinker is always running off with my food. I went to the bathroom once and came back and he'd dragged half a pizza under my bed and was eating it."

We find Wally on the opposite side of the camp, lying on his side, panting. I make a quick scan for Cassie, but I presume she's off exploring somewhere.

Megan squats next to Wally and rubs his bulging little belly. "This is a total hotdog belly!" she shouts.

Wally wiggles his tail.

"Don't you wiggle your tail at me, buddy. Now, where are the rest of the hotdogs? I know you can't fit ten jumbo franks in that little belly."

That's when I see the corner of plastic sticking out from beneath a small pile of fresh dirt. I walk over and pull the plastic out. It's an empty pack of hotdogs. All that remains is a small pool of pink liquid near the bottom.

I pick it up and show it to Megan. "They're all gone," I say.

Cassie

I can hear Megan and Jerry calling my name outside. I want to run to Jerry, but I can't. I can't bear to see him. Not after what I did.

A few minutes later, there's a rustle at the front of the tent. I hunker down behind the rolled up sleeping bag, making myself as small as possible.

"Cass—" Jerry says. "There you are!"

"She's hiding in the back of the tent!" he yells to Megan.

I feel the sleeping bag pushed out from in front of me. "Look at me, Cassie," Jerry says.

I don't.

I *can't*.

"Cassie...Cassie...*Cassie*."

I move my head up a few inches.

Jerry is squatted next to me. He's shaking his head from side to side. He waves the hotdog package at me and says, "Did you do this?" He waits a second, then he grabs my snout (not hard) and tilts my head up. "*Did...you...do...this?*"

I break.

I can't hold it in.

I can't live with the guilt.

I let out a loud whine.

Yes, Jerry.

I did it.

I have no self-control and I ate all the big, fat, plump, juicy hotdogs.

I couldn't stop.

They just kept begging me to eat them.

Eat me, Cassie! Eat me!

They were so delicious, Jerry.

I've never tasted anything more delicious in my life.

I couldn't stop.

Oh, and it gets worse, Jerry.

It gets so much worse.

After I ate all the hotdogs I went and did something just awful.

Just horrible.

Wally still had half a hotdog left and I'm not proud of this, Jerry. I stole Wally's hotdog.

Who steals a hotdog from a cute little adorable dog?

I'll tell you who.

Me, Jerry...Me!

I'm a hotdog monster, Jerry.

A hotdog monster!

I understand if you don't want me to be your dog anymore.

I'll just go live in the forest. I'll just go live with the chipmunks, Jerry.

If that's what you want, that's what I'll do.

"So you did do this?" Jerry says. He's biting his bottom lip and his face is turning red.

Yes.

I'm guilty.

Eight counts of hotdog homicide.

"And then you dug a hole and tried to hide the evidence, didn't you?"

I had to, Jerry.

I had to hide the evidence.

I couldn't stand to look at that empty package.

I had to bury it.

I had to bury my shame.

Jerry's face turns even brighter red and then his face explodes.

He's laughing.

Why is he laughing?

The tent rustles a second time and Megan crawls in. "Oh, my God," Megan says. "She was hiding back here?"

Jerry is lying on his back, holding his stomach. "Yeah, behind the sleeping bag," he says between fits.

"Look at her poor ears," Megan says. "Oh, she feels so bad." She reaches out and pets my head, "It's okay, sweetie. It's okay."

Really?

You mean, I don't have to go live with the chipmunks?

Jerry pushes himself up from the tent floor, then crawls to me. He gives my nose a big kiss and then says, "My precious little Hotdog Bandit."

Jerry

Dinner is potato salad, S'mores, and beer.

It's dropped twenty degrees since the sun went down. Megan and I have both pulled on thick hooded sweatshirts, but it's still chilly and we huddle next to the fire.

Wally is snuggled up in Megan's lap and Cassie is in the dirt next to me. I reach down and rub the top of her head. It's been two hours since I found her huddled in the back of the tent. After assuring the Hotdog Bandit that Megan and I weren't mad, that she was just being a dog, and that I still loved her to the moon and back, her spirits rose. That being said, she was still skulking around with droopy ears and sad eyes.

"I think I'm going to have one more," Megan says, reaching for the bag of marshmallows and pushing two of them onto her stick.

"A fourth S'more?"

"Hey, don't be counting my S'mores," she says with a laugh.

When the marshmallow is just beginning to sizzle, the first raindrops begin to fall.

"Ahhh," Megan screams. "My marshmallow!"

It's a race against the clock to get her S'more made before the light drizzle turns into a torrential downpour.

Cassie, Wally, and I seek shelter in the tent and Megan joins us a minute later, her hair dripping wet and wearing a pouty frown.

"My S'more died," she says.

"Oh, I'm sorry. Should we take a moment of silence?"

"I think that would only be appropriate."

So we have a moment of silence for her lost S'more.

*　*　*

"Let's see," Megan says, adding up her total. "Triple letter score on the K...that's fifteen...sixteen, seventeen, eighteen, nineteen, twenty...then a double word score...forty points."

She adds her score to the memo app on her phone, then says, "I'm up by fifty-four."

She looks down at Cassie, who is lying right next to her and says, "Did you hear that Cassie? I'm beating your dad by fifty-four points."

I shake my head lightly at her.

Megan had been challenging me to a game of Scrabble for the past week and she bought a Travel Scrabble board for the trip.

I warned her that I was pretty good—I mean, I am a professional writer—but so far, she's creaming me.

I look down at my letters. After several minutes of grunting, some humming, and clicking my tongue against the roof of my mouth, Megan says, "Will you please go before I strangle you?"

"Fine."

I grab three of my shitty one point tiles and using the P from Megan's "K-A-P-U-T", I spell out "P-U-L-T."

I start counting, "Two, three, four, five...Triple Word Score...fifteen points."

Megan cranes her neck under the light from the lantern and says, "Pult?"

"Yeah, *pult*, like, I *pult* it from the ground."

"Um, no."

"Yes. I pult a muscle in my leg."

"No, you pulled a muscle in your leg."

"No, pult."

"Challenge."

"Oh, come on. It's a word."

"We shall let the Scrabble Official Dictionary decide that." She pulls up the app on her phone and puts in my word. "Sorry, Charlie," she says, turning her phone toward me. "Not a word."

I sigh.

"How are you so bad at this?" she asks.

"I don't know."

I pull back the L tile, leaving me with "P-U-T" which no longer reaches the Quadruple Word Score, totaling me a whopping four points.

"Four points," I say.

"This is crushing you, isn't it?"

"Definitely a blow to the ego."

"Well, if it's any consolation, you look really cute when you're losing."

I laugh. "Oh, thanks."

"My pleasu—" Megan stops mid-word. Her nose wrinkles and her face appears to have a small seizure.

I'm confused for half a second until the most unimaginable rank smell invades my nostrils. I feel my face mirror Megan's.

"Cassie!" I scream.

Cassie

I'm sorry, Jerry.

I've got the toots.

I think it's from the hotdogs.

The eight and a half hotdogs.

My stomach is all flippy and floppy.

And I can't stop farting.

Maybe it's karma.

Divine justice.

Punishment for being the "Hotdog Bandit."

I know you said that you forgive me but it's going to be awhile until I can forgive myself.

Eight days.

One day for each hotdog.

One day for each delicious, fat, plump, juicy hotdog.

"Unzip the flap!" Megan yells.

"It's gonna let the rain in," Jerry says. His eyes are all squished together and he has his face tucked into his sweatshirt.

"I don't care!" Megan yells. "I can't breathe."

I'm so sorry, Megan.

I'm so sorry that my stinky toots are making it so you can't breathe.

I'm so sorry you're poking your head outside into the rain because it smells like "the inside of a dead walrus."

Jerry, I'm so sorry that my toots are making "your eyes burn."

"Okay, okay, I think it's gone," Megan says, crawling back toward me. "Wow, Cassie, that was um, *impressive.*" She gives my butt a few soft pats.

A few seconds later, everything is back to normal. Jerry and Megan are back playing their game and Wally is sitting in Jerry's lap.

That's when I see Wally's little tail flutter. Then his whiskers twitch.

Then Jerry screams, "Wally!"

He must have the toots too!

Jerry

For the next thirty minutes, Cassie and Wally continue to turn the small tent into a stinky dirigible. (Thankfully we weren't playing

Scrabble by candlelight or it could have ended like the Hindenburg.)

Finally, Cassie and Wally's savage farts subside and Megan and I can resume playing Scrabble. We finish up our first game, which she wins by one hundred and seventeen points, then I beg her for a rematch, hoping to at least be competitive in the second game.

But halfway through the second game, I'm already behind by seventy points.

"How are you so good at this?" I ask.

"Well, aside from being really, really, *really* smart, I've been playing Words With Friends religiously for the past ten years."

"Ah, well that makes me feel a little better."

"It shouldn't."

"No?"

"No. You are terrible."

I laugh, then say, "Well, let's see what you think of me now."

I pull all seven of my tiles and with the help of an X on the board, I spell out "M-A-X-I-M-I-Z-E."

"Wow!" Megan exclaims. "Look at Ryman go!"

With the fifty-point bonus for using all my letters and a double letter score on the second M, I net seventy-eight points.

"He's in the lead," Megan says, adding my score to her phone.

I moment later, Megan plays, "I-L-U-V-U."

"Iluvu?" I ask, super competitive now that I have a chance of winning.

Megan raises her eyebrows and nods.

"Challenge."

She smiles and hands me her phone.

I put the word in, then turn the phone to her and say, "Sorry, not a word."

Her dimple is flashing in her cheek, deeper than I've ever seen it. It's a crater. She nods at her word on the board and says, "Jerry."

"What? It's not a word."

"*Jerry*," she says, dragging my name out.

I look down at the word.

Iluvu.

And then it hits.

It's like getting hit with a balloon filled with warm honey.

I look up, take a deep breath, and say, "I love you too."

* * *

After exchanging our first "I love yous", the Scrabble board was pushed (more like thrown) to the side of the tent and Megan and I made love.

The tent was damp from the rain and it was still a tad combustible, but somehow it was perfect.

Afterward, Megan and I cuddled up in the sleeping bag. I was still awake, running through a montage of Megan's and my two-month journey. From meeting her in the pet store, to our first date, to our second, third, fifth date, my birthday dinner.

I thought that I'd been in love with Avery, and maybe to some level I was, but this love, this shared lightning bolt I had with Megan wasn't just in a different world. It was in a different realm.

One I didn't even know existed.

I watch Megan's chest rise and fall. I comb a few stray blonde hairs back behind her ear.

As I'm watching her, I see her eyes twitch beneath her eyelids. Her breaths quicken. Her hands flex.

I rub her head and say, "It's okay, it's okay."

Cassie lifts her head next to me, glancing up to see if everything is okay. Cassie was no stranger to nightmares.

Megan's breath continues to quicken, until she is sucking in breaths spasmodically.

I give her arm a gently nudge.

Her eyes open, then blink a few times.

"You're okay," I tell her. "You were having a nightmare."

She takes a couple long deep inhales. I can still see the terror in her face. Her eyes are rimmed in it.

"What were you dreaming about?" I ask.

"It's the same nightmare I always have," she says. "I'm in the lake. And I'm drowning."

20

"SEPTEMBER"

Jerry

"You got something for me?" Chuck asks.

"I do," I tell him.

"Really?"

"Don't sound so shocked."

"It's just that the last time you texted me you had something, it was that YA mermaid thing."

"Yeah," I laugh. "Thanks for not shooting that down too hard." I think Chuck's exact words were, "Eh, so what else do you got?"

But now, I really do have something.

"So what is it?" Chuck shouts impatiently. "Young Adult?"

"No."

"Sci-fi?"

"Nope." I pause. "Literary Fiction."

"Oh." I can hear his disappointment.

As far as fiction goes, mysteries, sci-fi, and YA are where the big money is, but a good literary fiction novel can still be a cash cow.

"Alright, let's hear it," he says.

"9/11."

"9/11?"

"Yep."

"Okay, I'm intrigued." He waits for me to continue.

"So, you know how they rerun all the 9/11 stuff on 9/11?"

"I do. I love that stuff."

"Yeah, well, it's been a few years since I watched any of it, but when they were playing it yesterday, I stumbled on it. When they started talking about all the first responders who ran into the buildings, I started thinking about if I'd been one of those first responders."

"You?" Chuck says with a laugh.

"Well, not me, but somebody like me."

"So a wimp?"

"Exactly."

"I like where this is headed."

"Yeah, so this guy, maybe he's a paramedic, or maybe he's a cop or even a firefighter; when his entire squad is running into the building, he chickens out."

"And then when the buildings fall," Chucks says, "and all those people die—"

"—everyone assumes this guy died too."

"*And?*"

"And he's so ashamed and he feels so guilty, he flees the country. Goes into hiding. Goes down to Mexico or whatever. His family, his friends, everyone thinks he's dead. And then fifteen years pass and he's forced to come home."

"Why does he have to come home?"

"I haven't gotten that far yet. But for whatever reason, maybe he gets arrested in whatever country he's in and is sent back to the U.S., or he just figures it's time. But for whatever reason, he comes back and his whole story comes out. And he has to deal with the fallout from the press, his family, his friends, maybe an ex-girlfriend." I stop. This is as far as I've gotten in the outline.

"Well," Chuck says, "I definitely think there's something there."

"Yeah?"

"Absolutely!"

"That's a relief to hear."

I knew the idea had merit, but I never got that magical feeling I had when I first came up with *Pluto Three*. But I'm coming to find out that magical feeling is rare—*super rare*, in fact. More often than not, it's a seed of an idea that is flushed out over time.

"You have a working title yet?" Chuck asks.

"Not yet." Some authors are adamant about having a title for their work. A title that might change multiple times over the duration of the project. I'm the opposite in this regard. It's one of the few things I'm patient about. The title will surface at some point—I didn't have a title for *Pluto Three* until the fifth draft—you just have to wait.

"Well, I'm excited, buddy. Sounds like you've got a winner here. Keep me updated."

"Will do."

We hang up.

I lean forward and glance through the window. Cassie is lying on the porch next to the baby pool. She's staring intently at the water. I glance at her for a long few seconds. Finally, she turns and looks at me. I stick my tongue out to the side and cross my eyes.

Her tail helicopters.

Then I walk to the refrigerator and grab a jar of pickles out of the fridge. Then I sit down at the computer.

I have work to do.

Cassie

I love Jerry's silly face. He's been doing it a lot lately. And I know this has a lot to do with Megan.

Megan stays over at our house two or three times a week. That means plenty of rubs for me. And lots of "samples" from her cooking. (Megan is an amazing cook!) And the best part: lots of Wally! (Talk about silly, Wally is such a silly little dog.)

I'm about to go inside and give Jerry some licks when I hear the top of the pickle jar open. I haven't heard the pickle jar open in a long time. I know not to disturb Jerry when it's pickle time.

I turn back to the water. Back to the frog babies. Except, they aren't frog babies anymore. In fact, they are Almost Frogs. They are almost the Chosen Ones.

They look like frogs, but they still have tails. If they make it to Frogdom, their tails will disappear. There are only seven. Of all those hundreds of little tadpoles, only seven of them have made it this far.

One of the Almost Frogs jumps off the side of the baby pool and swims across the water. His grassy green body flutters through the water, then he climbs out onto the pool edge closest to me. He's no bigger than a piece of my kibble. He has tiny little black eyes rimmed in orange.

I lean forward and give him a sniff.

Hi, Almost Frog.

He jumps off the edge of the pool and onto the porch.

Hop, hop, hop.

I follow him.

He hops off the porch and into the grass. I keep watch on him. He would be a tasty snack for one of the birds flying around. I keep guard until he finally makes his way back to the pool.

I don't want to name him yet—because he still might not make it to Frogdom—but I can't help it. I keep watch the rest of the day.

I keep watch over Hugo.

Hugo

The mouse pokes his head out of the small hole in the dirt. His little nose twitches in the moonlight. The mice in the forest are a bit different than the mice in the city and at the farm. They are the same size, but they have slightly bigger eyes and they are darker in color, which makes them harder to see at night. (I wonder how the Maker decides what kind of mouse you become. Is mountain mouse worse punishment than city mouse?)

I hunker in the long grass. My back legs flex. Xanthus' words echo in my head, "*Stealth and patience, Hugo. Stealth and patience.*"

I don't want to make the same mistake I made yesterday. If I pounce too early, the mouse will simply dart back in his hole. I need to wait for him to scurry into the bushes in search of *his* dinner (an insect or some berries).

But the mouse isn't my only worry. This is my first night alone. My first night without Xanthus by my side. Tonight for the first time, I'm not just the hunter. I'm also the *hunted*.

I'm at least a couple miles from the shelter den where Xanthus and I stayed last night (and many, many miles from Xanthus' main den). Once the stars came out, I set out. I headed downwind, then I splashed through a small stream, hoping to mask my scent.

I climbed a few small trees, jumping to the connecting branches. The entire time, I stayed on high alert.

"*You can hear much farther than you can see,*" Xanthus always said. So I listened to every rustle, every hoot, and every pitter-patter.

It took me a few hours to find the small hole where the mouse lived. I could smell him. He shouldn't poop so close to his hole.

Now, the mouse twitches his whiskers once more, then he scurries from the hole.

I leap from my spot in the grass, take two long strides, and then I pounce. I can't jump as far as Xanthus (he can jump ten feet, at least), but I can still jump pretty far, and I sink my teeth into the mouse's backside. I shake him a few times, then drop him to the ground. He's still alive and I pin him down with my paw.

There's a soft rustle, but by the time I snap my head up, I'm on my side and Xanthus has his teeth wrapped around my neck.

"You're dead," he says.

Over the course of the next few hours, I die three more times.

Jerry

"What is that?" I ask, peering over Megan's shoulder at the sizzling pan on the stove.

"Gnocchi, with a sage butter sauce."

"Gnocchi? What is that again?"

"Potato dumplings."

"Right. Well, it smells amazing." Megan has been cooking dinner at my place a few times a week and she continues to astound me with her cooking skills.

I give her a kiss on the neck, then grab a fork out of the nearby drawer and stab one of the small, buttery, gnocchi. Megan tries to slap my hand away, but I'm too quick and I pop the dumpling in my mouth.

"Get out of my kitchen!" Megan shouts, trying to fight back a smile.

I'm tempted to tell her that it's actually my kitchen, but I like her choice of pronoun.

I retire to the couch with Cassie and Wally and we watch the first quarter of the Sunday Night Football game. I'm not a huge sports fan, but I do like to watch the NFL, and with Wally in my lap and Cassie curled up next to me, the three of us watch the Atlanta Falcons drive down the field and score a touchdown. After a commercial break and a kickoff, Megan yells, "Dinner's ready."

The four of us head out to the back porch. Megan has filled both of Cassie's and Wally's bowls with kibble and a few pieces of gnocchi and sets them under the table.

The four of us eat as a family.

After we eat, Megan and I play a few hands of gin-rummy, then we grab the dogs' leashes and take them for a walk. I grab for Megan's hand and we walk the half-mile to the beach. The sun is in the process of setting, the sky a soft pink and quickly dissolving into a light gray. The lake is as still as I've ever seen it, not carrying a single ripple.

We unleash Cassie and Wally and let them romp around as we walk. Megan and I make small talk, mostly about a few movies that are due to come out soon, then she switches topics.

"Who was your first love?" she asks.

Megan and I had talked about our past relationships a few times, but this question had never been broached by either of us.

"Hmmm," I say.

"Was it Avery?"

"No," I scoff. "In fact, I'm not sure I was really in love with her. I think, maybe I was in love with the idea of her, but not her really."

Megan nods, then asks, "Who then?"

"Actually, my first love was this little girl I met here in Tahoe when we used to visit." I feel a grin crawl onto my lips as I continue, "I was five years old and she was six. We were basically inseparable for the next five years any time I came here. It was different, I mean, we were just little kids, but when I got a little older, eight or nine, there's no doubt that I was in love with her."

I consider telling Megan that she died. That she drowned in the very lake we're standing next to at this very moment. But I don't. Megan is *already* afraid of the water. Megan *already* has nightmares about drowning in the lake. And moreover, it was just eerie: Morgan drowning in the lake and Megan having nightmares about that very thing.

Even though things with Megan and I are going amazingly, part of me keeps waiting for the other shoe to drop. That it's too good to be true. I can't control these thoughts; there's a well-trodden neuron path in my brain wired for insecurity. I'm still nervous about doing or saying something that might send her running for the hills. And though irrational, I fear Morgan's drowning could be one of those things.

I will tell her about Morgan's death someday.

Just not today.

I wait for Megan to ask what happened to her, to ask why we were only friends for five years, to ask if she moved away, but she doesn't. Megan is silent. Almost in a trance.

"What about you?" I say, giving her arm a light shake. "Who was your first love?"

She gazes out on the water, then blinks twice, snapping from whatever reverie she's in. Then she turns to me and says, "You are, Jerry. You're my first love."

* * *

Indefinitely.

That's the word my parents used when I asked how long they would be staying in Tahoe.

Indefinitely.

The last time I saw them was two weeks earlier, over Labor Day weekend. Labor Day is usually the signal for the end of summer and I eagerly anticipated my parents heading back to Oregon. But no such luck. Evidently, they were having too much fun here. Having too much fun with Teddy and Sequoia, who, not to my surprise, were in attendance at my parents' Labor Day barbecue.

Megan and I made a compulsory pop-in, but when the Fearsome Foursome (that's what they called themselves) broke out the weed Rice Krispy Treats, it was our cue to leave. I can only handle so many "golden age of flying" stories and so many claims about the healing power of crystals.

Currently, Cassie is lying on the couch on her back. Her paws are in the air and the white of her belly fur statics upward. I give her belly a scratch and ask, "Are you ready for this? They're pretty weird." The most disconcerting thing about this last part is that I'm not sure if I'm talking about my parents or Teddy and Sequoia.

Cassie wiggles her entire body on the cushion and barks.

"Okay, but I warned you."

I've been dreading having dinner with my parents all day. Mostly because without Megan there—she has to work—I won't have anyone to help soothe my discomfort. But it's more than that. Over the past couple months, Megan has become my best friend. (Sorry, Alex.) She's funny, she's kind, she's insightful, she'd even helped me work through a few problems in the outline of my new book. And most importantly, she likes almost all the same shows as I do on Netflix, which I think is the single most important test of compatibility.

I lean down and blow a raspberry on Cassie's belly, then say, "Okay, let's go."

* * *

"Where are they?" I ask.

"Who?" my mother says, taking a sip of white wine. We're centered around the kitchen island.

Who? *Who* do you think?

I almost say, "The ghost of Howard Hughes and Full-size SUV," but I don't. "Um, Teddy and Sequoia."

"Oh," my mother says. Her eyes cut toward my father, who is feeding Cassie carrots and asking her to do tricks. I have a quick flash of déjà vu from the first dinner with my parents nearly three months earlier.

My father glances up and says, "So, about that." He tosses one last carrot and Cassie snatches it out of the air, then he wipes his hands on his khaki shorts. "Your mom and I have decided—"

233

He pauses.

"What?" Please say the words. Please. *Please*. There's still hope my parents haven't done irreparable damage to my psyche. There's still hope I won't have to spend thousands of dollars talking to a therapist about "The Dinner."

"Well," my father continues, "we've decided that an open marriage isn't right for us."

I throw up my hands in celebration. "Are you serious?"

My mother walks around the kitchen island and puts her hand on my father's back. "Turns out that your father's wrinkly old balls are the only ones that I want."

This should disgust me, but it doesn't. "Thank God," I say.

My dad laughs. "Yeah and there's more. We're headed back to Oregon tomorrow."

"Cheers to that," I say, even though I don't have anything in my hand.

On this note, my father goes to the fridge and pulls out a frosty bottle of my arch nemesis and hands it to me. I crack open the beer and the three of us cheers.

Backward Bill's Buttermilk Beer never tasted so good.

"Wow, the tourists have really cleared out," Megan says a week later.

We're in the same spot we came to on our first date. The beach was overrun with tourists then, but today there are only a handful of people. Tahoe will be slow for the next two months, at least until mid-November when the ski resorts open and the winter tourist season kicks off.

Megan and I are sitting in the sand. It's warm out, but the burn of summer is gone. I glance up the beach where Cassie and Wally are splashing at the edge of the water and say, "And good riddance."

Megan smiles, but it seems forced. She has a tell: her dimple doesn't surface.

"What's going on?" I ask.

Megan was supposed to stay over the last two nights but canceled both times. Now she's acting strange. Dour, even.

I feel my stomach gurgle. I've been broken up with before. I know the signs.

"Are we okay?" I ask before she has a chance to answer.

Megan is sitting Indian style and her head hangs. She cuts her eyes at me. They are glassed over. "I'm moving," she says flatly.

The air is sucked from my lungs.

"*Moving?*" I wheeze.

She nods.

"Where?"

"Connecticut."

I push myself up from the sand. I press the heels of my hands into my eyes and shake my head. Then, glaring down at her, my hands raised above my head, I ask, "And when is this happening?"

"October 1st."

"That's next week."

"I know." She wipes a tear from her cheek.

"Why are you moving to Connecticut?"

She pushes herself up. She cradles her elbows together in her hands. "I was just browsing the internet for building leases and I found this perfect little spot in West Haven."

"Perfect for what?"

"For my dog bakery."

Right, her *dog bakery*.

She says, "I went to the bank, thinking there's no way I would get a loan, but they gave me one."

"Why didn't you tell me about any of this?"

"I didn't think it was really going to happen. Even after I was approved for the loan, I wasn't sure. But then the realtor for the building in West Haven called and said someone else was interested. It was mine if I wanted it, but I had to give him an answer by today."

"And you said yes."

She nods.

My pulse rate has steadily climbed and I can feel it beating wildly in my neck. I bite my lip to stop it from quivering.

How can she do this?

How can she leave me?

What about all those things she said? About how much she loved me?

"Where are you gonna live?" I ask.

"I found a place a mile from the building. A little house on a few acres." Her dimple flashes when she says this.

I can feel tears forming in my eyes.

I can't look at her.

I turn and walk up the beach. With each step, I feel a chunk of my heart fall away. Huge glaciers falling into the icy sea.

A moment later, a hand clasps my arm.

I turn.

Tears dribble off Megan's cheeks. Her bottom lip trembles. "I want you to come with me," she says.

Time stops.

"You what?"

"I love you. I can't imagine life without you. And I want you to come with me."

I try to play it cool. I don't want her to know this is the greatest moment of my life. That this is what I wished for at my birthday dinner.

I ask, "You want me to move to Connecticut with you and live in a little house with you?"

She wipes at her eyes. "Yes, please."

Hugo

I dig my claws into the bark of the tree and climb. I'm a much better climber than I was four weeks ago when I first entered the Mountains. Not only have I grown, but with a few simple tricks learned from Xanthus, I can scoot up any tree in the forest.

I crawl out onto a long branch, then jump to the branch of a nearby tree. I race down the trunk and leap to a rock.

The sky is covered in clouds and it's as dark as I can ever remember it being. I can't see far, maybe a hundred feet or so, but it isn't my eyes I've learned to rely on. It's my ears and my nose.

I cock my head and listen.

Under the light breeze, I hear the hoot of an owl. I'm still small enough that an owl could easily swoop down and grab me. I'll need to stay in the underbrush as much as possible.

I jump from the rocks and scamper to a row of dense brush. Somehow, I don't make a sound. I stop. Listen. All I hear is a light wind. I sniff. There's a scent caught by the breeze.

I turn and head back the way I came. Back upwind. Back to the rocks. Back to the tree. The branch. Jump back to the first tree. I find the lowest branch and I wait. *Stealth and patience, Hugo. Stealth and patience.* I slowly breathe in and out through my nose.

There's a soft rustle.

I hear him pass.

I *let* him pass.

Silently, I creep down the trunk of the tree to the ground. He's standing on the rocks. The rocks I was on. The rocks I led him to. From there, he heads to the brush. The brush I was in. The brush I led him to.

Looping.

That's what it's called.

I hear the hoot of the owl. Hoots always come in pairs and I wait. On the second hoot, I scurry to the rock and fall into its shadow.

I hear a soft rustle.

He's heading back to the second tree. I can no longer smell him, but I can hear every time he sets his paw down.

Paw, paw, paw, paw.

I dart out from the shadows, take three giant leaps, and I pounce.

My mouth is too small to wrap around his neck, so I bite one of his tufted ears.

"You're dead," I tell Xanthus.

21

"THE LAST LEG"

Jerry

"So you're really doing it?" Alex asks. "Moving to friggin' Connecticut?"

"Yep."

We're in Alex's small apartment. Cassie is in Julie's room playing. Alex and I are sitting on his futon. He claps me on the back with one of his meaty paws and says, "And you've known this chick for what, three months?"

Not even three months. "Right around there."

"Well, I'm pretty sure this is gonna blow up in your face in spectacular fashion, but I hope you enjoy the ride."

This is the most encouragement I can expect from Alex. "Thanks, buddy."

"So she's already out there?"

"Yeah, she took over the lease on the 1st, so she drove out last week. I've got a U-Haul trailer with all her stuff in it and I'm gonna drive out in the next couple of days."

"Don't ask me to help you pack."

"I know better." But to be honest, I don't have a whole lot to pack. When I moved from San Francisco, I sold all my furniture and most of my belongings on Craigslist. Everything at my parents' house is, well, my parents'. All I have to pack are clothes and some odds and ends.

Alex asks, "So where is Connecticut anyway?"

"Next to New York. Under Massachusetts."

He cocks his head to the side. "Are you sure? I think it's like an island or something."

A week ago, if he asked me this question, I wouldn't have been sure, but after doing my due diligence on my new home on the internet, I am. "It's not an island, though there is a bunch of coastline."

"What's the name of your town?"

"West Haven."

"Is that where *Dawson's Creek* was set?"

I laugh. "I'm not sure."

"I'm pretty sure it was." He digs out his phone to check.

"Don't go," I hear from the hallway.

Julie and Cassie emerge. Julie's eyes are big and puffy. She sits down on the carpet and Cassie falls into her lap. Julie strokes Cassie's head and repeats, "Don't go."

In the microsecond it took me to decide whether or not to move with Megan to Connecticut, I realized the only things about Tahoe I'm going to miss are Alex and Julie. I'm excited for a fresh start. Excited to begin a new family. But Alex and Julie are family too.

"I'm sorry, kiddo," I say softly. "But you can come and visit whenever you want. And I'll come back once a year; I promise."

"Pinky swear?"

She lifts her pinky and I walk over and intertwine mine with hers.

"Capeside, Massachusetts," Alex shouts. "*Dawson's Creek* was in *Massachusetts!*"

* * *

After saying goodbye to Alex and Julie, Cassie and I walk-jog to the woods. The sky has turned a dark gray and the temperature has plummeted ten degrees since we first left the house an hour earlier.

"One last hole," I say to Cassie as we weave through the fallen pine cones.

I find the shovel hidden in the brush and I wind between the trees for a few minutes. Cassie meanders about, smelling trees and marking spots.

"One last hole," I repeat.

I dip the shovel into the earth in a few different locations but stop short of pushing it down. If not for the drizzle beginning to fall from the sky, I might have walked around for hours.

Cassie comes back, her paws covered in dirt. She cocks her head to the side as if to say, "I've already dug a bunch of holes and marked ten spots. What are you waiting for?"

I smile at her, then I push the shovel into the dirt. It takes me ten minutes to dig down three feet to where it would have been buried.

I don't find our time capsule.

"Sorry, Morgan," I sigh.

As Cassie and I walk back to the house, I glance at the mountains. Thick gray clouds obscure the peaks. I've no doubt the persistent drizzle we're getting at lake level will be the first snowfall of the year in the mountains.

Hugo

I've kept a steady pace for five days, resting for a few hours during the day and again at night. Abandoned dens and hollows are easy to come by and I use all of Xanthus' tricks to hide. To mask my smell. To stay alive.

At night, I hunt.

The first night, I don't catch anything. But on the second night, I pounce onto a small mouse. He's delicious.

I scamper over bramble, through bushes, up and over fallen trees. I climb the steep hills, then scamper down their backs. There are several streams I'm able to swim across, but more often I have to walk for ages until I find a log or rocks I can use to cross.

Once I try to cross a stream and get swept away, but I'm able to swim to a bunch of branches and pull myself out.

One of the streams empties into a lake. For a moment I think it might be my Lake, but it's too small. And there are no houses. No streets. No cars.

On the second day, I have quite the scare.

I'm hopping down the side of a steep mountain, going from rock to rock. Then I hear this rattle, which sounds almost like one of the toys that Sara bought me (which seems like ages ago). I turn around and I see an animal curled up on the rock below me.

It's shaped like a large hose. It's tan and brown. Its head is triangular and it has a thin pink tongue that it darts in and out. Its tail is white and bubbly and I think what is making the rattling noise.

Xanthus spoke of this creature.

A snake.

The snake hisses at me and snaps its head in my direction. I jump to another rock, then another. I turn my head and see the snake slithering over the rocks.

How can it move so fast if it doesn't have legs?

I jump off the rocks to a patch of dirt and I run as fast as my little legs will go. I don't stop and I don't look back. I just run.

Finally, I stop and turn around.

The snake is gone.

The next day, I come to a river. It's wide and it takes me nearly the entire day to find a place to cross. Each hour, the temperature drops. Dark clouds fill the sky and it begins to drizzle. An hour later, it begins to snow.

I'm starving and I want to hunt. To find a mouse or some nuts, but I can feel my body temperature dropping.

I find a small den hidden under a fallen log. After sniffing out that there are no animals in there, I burrow into the deep hole. After only a few minutes, my body heat begins to warm the small space.

And I sleep.

* * *

I pat at the wall of snow with my paw and it falls inward. I shake off the snow and climb out of the hole. The snow would have come up to my ankles when I was a dog, but now it engulfs me up to my neck. I think about heading back into the hole and waiting until the snow melts, but that could be days. Or it could snow even more.

I have to keep moving.

Luckily, the sun is out and it keeps me from freezing. I make my way up and over the top of a mountain and begin down. The farther down I go, the less snow there is. I'm starving; my tiny stomach is screaming for food and I keep a lookout for something to eat. I see a rabbit, but he is the same size as me. Though I wouldn't eat him anyway.

I trudge through the snow all day. When the sun begins to set, I can barely get my legs to move. But I can see the top of the peak I'm climbing. I need to get to the top.

"You can do it, Hugo," I hear Cassie say.

It's the first time I've heard her voice in weeks.

The last time I heard it, I almost died.

Am I about to die?

No.

I force myself to climb through the snow.

Come on, Hugo!

Keep moving.

The sun sets and I keep moving. The moon shines brightly on the white snow and I keep moving. Finally, I make it to the top of the mountain.

That's when I see it.

The tiny yellow lights of a town. And behind them, under the moon, a large lake.

My Lake.

Jerry

I set the trash bag of my clothes next to the other trash bag of my clothes, which is next to a trash bag of my shoes, which is next to a trash bag of my books, which is next to a trash bag of my knick-knacks, which are *all* next to Megan's neatly stacked and labeled boxes. Megan had sent most of her stuff to Connecticut in one of those moving pods, but she had a bunch of extra stuff that wouldn't fit.

I hear a clank and watch as Cassie climbs the metal walkway into the back of the U-Haul trailer. She comes forward and gives my bag of sneakers a few sniffs. Then she sits back on her butt and cocks her head to the side.

She knows something is up. I tried explaining to her that we're moving, but I'm not sure she gets it.

Cassie

Something is up.

Jerry is acting weird.

He keeps putting all his stuff into these big black bags and then carrying them to this huge car.

We're moving.

I know what moving is. We moved *here*. But where are we moving this time? And where are Megan and Wally?

I want answers.

Jerry

Cassie barks.

Once, twice, three times.

I ignore her and jump down out of the U-Haul and go back into the house. I'm half done packing. Turns out I have a lot more stuff than I thought. Mostly *gear* I rarely used: snowboarding gear (used three times), snorkeling gear (used two times), kickboxing gear (used zero times), workout gear (a bunch of dumbbells, an ab-crunch, a yoga mat, and a fit ball, all used exactly one time).

I consider throwing all this stuff out or giving it to Goodwill, but an irrational part of me thinks that one day I might want to really get into snowboarding, snorkeling, kickboxing, and working out. So I toss all this stuff into black garbage bags and lug it out to the U-Haul.

As I'm cleaning out the last of the stuff from my closet, I let out a loud scoff. In the top corner of the closet, hidden behind a memory foam pillow I bought at three in the morning off an infomercial (which was the worst, smelliest pillow ever) is one of Hugo's orange tennis balls.

I remember when I took it from him. He wouldn't go to sleep one night, pounding around on the floor, playing with his ball and I took it from him and hid it behind the pillow to mask its smell. I was always astounded at how Hugo could sniff out one of his balls. Once, we were at Alex's and Hugo kept scratching at a back-

245

pack in Alex's room. Alex and I both yelled at him to knock it off, but he kept at it, pawing at it relentlessly. Finally, after he wouldn't stop, I opened all the compartments of the backpack to show Hugo there was nothing in there, but it turns out one of Hugo's orange tennis balls was in there from when Alex and I went to the beach a year earlier. I handed Hugo the ball with a shake of my head and he scampered into their living room with the ball in his mouth and his head held high.

I grab the ball and I think about tossing it into the bag of trash, but I don't. I add it to my last bag of stuff and carry it to the U-Haul.

Hugo

After I sleep for a few hours, I start down the mountain. The Lake is still a long ways off, but I figure I can get there by the end of the day.

After a few hours, I hear a familiar sound.

Cars.

Not long after, I find the road.

I continue through the brush, trying to keep the road in sight, but the road is windy and it's faster to go directly up and over the remaining Mountains.

Once I crest the next peak, the Lake is even closer.

I can see houses.

They are small, but I can see a few.

The Lake is only a few hours away.

Maybe less.

Cassie

"Alright, girl," Jerry says, giving my head a nuzzle. "It's time to say goodbye."

I don't like goodbyes. Like when Martin came over and said "Goodbye." And when I had to say "Goodbye" to Julie. Goodbyes are sad.

But I have two more goodbyes to say.

I walk out the back door and hop down the porch. I walk to the fence. I look through the small space between two boards and see Storm lying in the dirt on the far side of his yard.

I bark.

Bye, Storm.

He lifts his head slightly and squints in my direction. I wait for him to say something back, but he yawns and rests his head back down on his paws.

I turn around and plod to the swimming pool. Of the seven Almost Frogs, three made it to Frogdom. Hugo didn't make it. (I think he was snatched up by a bird.) But Greenie (Greenie II to be more accurate), Filbert, and Rosie all made it.

Greenie is sitting on the edge of the pool and Filbert and Rosie are both swimming around. (I think they might be making more tadpoles, but I'm not exactly sure how the making of the tadpoles all works.)

I give each of them a sniff.

Goodbye, Frogs.

Good luck out there.

Hugo

A trail.

I find a trail. And then I see two people. They are wearing big backpacks.

Hikers.

I must be close.

Once they pass, I zoom down the trail. It doesn't take long for me to reach the bottom of the mountain and flat land.

Flat land!

I made it over the Mountains.

I scamper to the road. Something about this road seems familiar and I follow it for an hour until houses start to pop up.

"Come here, kitty!" I hear someone yell. It's a she-human. She's chasing me down the street.

I haven't come this far to be captured again. I sprint away from her like she's the snake, then turn onto another street.

I stop.

I've been on this street. This is the street where the Farmers' Market is. Which means the Lake is only a few blocks away. I know how to get home. I know *exactly* how to get home. I can see it in my head: *I go to that street, then turn there, then go down that way, then I'm Home.*

I start running. I see a dog sitting on the porch of another house. I know that dog!

Running.

I know that smell!

Running.

I know that tree!

Running.

I know that mailbox!

Running.

I know that car!

Running.

I know that trash can!

Running.

I know that house.

That's my house!

I'm Home!

* * *

I run to the front door and scratch at it.

Cassie! Jerry!

I claw and meow at the door. No one comes. I run around to the back fence. I know where a small hole is and I scurry under.

I'm in my backyard.

This is my *Backyard*!

I scratch on the back door, but again, no one opens it.

Where are Jerry and Cassie?

They must not be home. And come to think of it, I didn't see Jerry's car.

I jump on a bench on the porch. I used to lie on this bench all the time. I could see Jerry through the window, sitting in front of his computer. I jump to the windowsill. The desk where Jerry would sit at is empty.

I glance around the rest of the room. Everything looks the same except there is no water bowl. The big silver water bowl that is always in the exact same place isn't there.

That's when I realize Cassie and Jerry aren't just not home.

They're *gone*.

Jerry

Cassie has her head out the window. Her golden hair and ears whip in the light breeze.

We're five miles into Nevada, fifteen minutes into our forty-one-hour cross-country drive. My goal is to make the drive in three days. First stop, Cheyenne, which is a good fifteen hours away.

After another few minutes, we pass Zephyr Cove. I remember back to three years earlier when I rode my bike there to watch the 4th of July debauchery.

"Dammit," I shout, slowing down and pulling over to the shoulder. "My *bike*."

I forgot to pack my bicycle.

Megan was insistent I bring it. Apparently, West Haven, much like South Lake Tahoe, is extremely bike-friendly. Megan bought a cruiser bike and she rode it to work every day.

I wait for a break in traffic, then make a U-turn.

Hugo

Gone.

I can't believe they're gone.

Where did they go?

I jump down from the windowsill. Next to the porch is the small blue baby pool. I think back to how Cassie would bark at me whenever I tried to get in. (She was so protective of those dumb little frogs!)

I'm never going to see Cassie again. I'm never going to get to sniff her. Lick her. Wrestle with her. And Jerry. I'm never going to see Jerry again. My human. My Jerry.

I lie down on the porch and put my head on my paws.

Where do I go now?

There's a rumble and I lift my head.

Is that?

Yes.

It's the *garage door.*

I spring up, then dart back toward the hole in the fence. I scurry under, then scamper around to the garage.

Jerry

I grab the bicycle leaning against the wall and begin wheeling it out of the garage.

"Ahh!" I yelp.

A tiny little cat darts into the garage. He's gray and white striped, with darker gray racing stripes on his head, and yellow-green eyes. He rushes toward me and begins clawing at my leg.

I set the bike back against the wall and say, "Hey, little guy. You scared me."

The cat is spinning in circles. It's like he just ate a pound of catnip.

"Take it easy," I say. "You're gonna have a heart attack."

Hugo

It's Jerry!
It's Jerry!
It's Jerry!
It's Jerry!

Jerry

"Where did you come from?" I ask, leaning down and checking the cat for a collar, which is difficult because he's still doing a Tasmanian Devil impression. He doesn't have one, but this doesn't mean much. Not all cats wear collars. I assume he belongs to someone in the area.

He rolls over on his back and exposes a little white belly. I give him a few scratches. "Ah, you like that, don't you?"

My phone chimes in my pocket and I pull it out. It's a text from Megan: **You on the road yet?**

I text back: **I forgot to pack my bike and had to turn around. Headed out now.**

"Well, buddy," I say. "On any other day, I would make sure you get back home safely, but I have to hit the road."

I'm not overly concerned. The next human he saw, he would

attack them, just like he attacked me, and then they would take care of him.

I give the kitten a few last scratches, then say, "See ya later, buddy."

Hugo

I claw at Jerry's leg, but he shakes me off. Then he grabs the bike and wheels it out of the garage.

He doesn't know it's me.

Jerry

I parked my car and the U-Haul trailer on the street in front of the house and I wheel the bike up the ramp. The trailer is only half full and I lean the bike against the wall, then pack a couple of trash bags of my clothes against it to keep it upright.

Something scratches at my leg and I look down.

It's the kitten.

"What are you doing?" I laugh.

I can't believe he followed me into the trailer.

I shoo him away, but he's resilient, he keeps rushing back at me and clawing at my pant leg.

Food.

He must want food.

"Sorry, pal, I don't have any food."

I jump out of the trailer, waiting for the little cat to follow me, but he doesn't. Instead, he turns and begins clawing at one of the many trash bags full of my belongings.

"Dude," I yell, jumping back into the trailer. "Knock that off."

By the time I reach him, he's clawed a hole through one of the bags. He pulls something out through the hole. An orange tennis ball.

I feel my eyebrows raise.

I hadn't seen that ball in over a year, then I decided not to throw it away, and now a tiny little kitten has dug it out from my belongings.

Too weird.

I roll the ball a few feet down the trailer and the little cat bounds after it. The ball is too big for the kitten to hold in its mouth—it's practically the same size as his head—and he bites at the orange fibers, the ball swinging back and forth from his teeth.

He waddles with the ball back to me, drops it at my feet, then sits back on his butt, his tail wagging back and forth.

I lean down and pick him up.

I hold him out in front of me and stare into his chartreuse eyes.

His little black nose and whiskers twitch.

"H—"

No.

It's not possible.

Cassie

I watched the little cat dart into the garage and attack Jerry, then follow him toward the trailer.

What a crazy little cat.

Jerry

I pop the door open to the car and slide into the driver's seat. It took me a long couple of minutes to get the kitten out of the trailer. Once out, I tossed the orange tennis ball into the grass in the Winston's front yard and the kitten darted after it. Then I ran to the car.

I turn the key in the ignition and put the car in drive. I haven't gone two feet when something springs onto the hood of the car, then starfishes itself against the windshield.

Cassie

The little kitten plasters his body to the windshield. It scares me and I let out a loud bark.

Hugo

It's Cassie!
　It's Cassie!
　It's Cassie!
　It's Cassie!

Cassie

The kitten stares at me through the windshield.
　Then he meows.
　It can't be.

Jerry

I turn on my windshield wipers, giving the kitten a scare and he jumps off the windshield.

"Crazy cat," I say, then begin accelerating.

Cassie barks twice.

"What?" I ask. "What's going on? Is it that stupid cat?"

She jumps from the passenger seat and onto my lap and claws at my hands on the steering wheel.

"Ouch! Stop, Cassie! I can't see!" I yell, hitting the brakes and pulling over. I've made it as far as Pete's house.

Cassie is spinning frantically in my lap. She's possessed. I've never seen her like this before. I open the door and she leaps to the ground and begins running down the street.

Hugo

Cassie's ears flap as she runs toward me. I almost forgot how beautiful she is. She's the most beautiful dog in the world.

When she reaches me, she gives me a few long sniffs, then she begins to twirl.

Jerry

I climb out of the car and glance down the street. Cassie has the small kitten pinned to the road and I race forward.

Why is Cassie attacking a kitten?

When I draw closer, I realize Cassie isn't attacking the kitten; well, she is attacking him, but with kisses, her huge tongue slobbering down his little face.

"Cassie!" I shout. "Come on! We don't have time for this."

I grab her by her collar and give her a pull.

She growls at me.

Cassie has never growled at me before.

Not once.

Not *ever*.

I stare at her for a long second. "What has gotten into you?" I say. "It's just a cat. You've seen hundreds of cats."

As if on cue, Cassie leans down and picks the kitten up by the scruff of his neck. Then she turns to me and sets the kitten at my feet. Then she barks five times.

Cassie had done this exactly once before.

When she picked out Hugo.

22

"CONNECTICUT"

Jerry

I throw the small orange tennis ball—which Megan special-ordered from one of her new vendors—five feet into the churning gray-blue water. He races into the surf, swims up and over a small wave, and grabs the ball in his tiny kitten mouth. Then he deftly turns around and swims back.

A small wave carries him the last several feet, then deposits him on the coarse brown sand. He shakes out his fur, then carries the ball to my feet and drops it. Then he sits back on his butt, his tail wagging back and forth. When I don't immediately pick up the ball and throw it back in the ocean, he lets out a loud, "Meow!"

* * *

Two weeks earlier, when Cassie dropped the small kitten at my feet and barked five times, I was in a state of shock. It was clear Cassie *thought* the small kitten was Hugo, but I wasn't convinced. Mostly, because it was *impossible*. Yeah, the kitten attacked me as if he knew me. And yeah, the kitten pulled Hugo's orange tennis ball from a trash bag of my stuff. But those could easily be coincidences.

Regardless, I knew there was zero chance of getting Cassie back in the car without the kitten. So I scooped him up. Even if the kitten wasn't Hugo—which of course he wasn't, like I said, *that would be impossible*—he was still the coolest little cat I'd ever seen.

He rode in my lap for the next four hours. When I stopped for gas in Winnemucca, Nevada, I bought a few tins of cat food, a red collar, and a small retractable leash at the neighboring grocery store. And I bought one other thing: a block of Tillamook Medium Cheddar.

When I returned to the car, I set the kitten on the ground and I conducted my first test.

I pulled the block of cheese from the grocery bag and waved it at him. "Do you know what this is?"

The kitten's tail started whipping back and forth so fast I thought it might break off. After feeding him a few small pieces of cheese and watching him devour them with force, I lifted him up and there it was: a tiny quarter-sized pool of urine.

Happy pee.

We'd been in the car for four hours. Maybe he just had to pee.

Next I put him through a few commands.

Sit. Lie down. Turn around. Play dead.

Each time, he obeyed.

I'm sure lots of kittens know commands. Maybe his past owner trained him well.

Ten hours later, we stopped at a motel in Cheyenne. After giving the kitten a bath (he was a stinky little cat), the kitten slept on the pillow next to my head.

Pillows are soft. Who wouldn't want to sleep on a pillow?

In Davenport, Iowa, I woke up to find the kitten sprawled out on the tile floor in the bathroom.

It was warm in the motel room. Maybe he just wanted to cool down on the tile.

In Youngstown, Ohio, in the middle of the night, I heard scratching. I woke up to the little kitten scratching the front door of the motel. I thought about leashing the kitten up, but I wanted to see what he would do with free rein. The little kitten walked a few feet to a small section of grass in front of the motel, went pee, then came right back inside, where he promptly snuggled up into Cassie's side.

He's well-trained. Undoubtedly, by the same person who taught him all those commands. And who wouldn't want to snuggle up next to Cassie? Cassie is the best.

In White Plains, New York, an hour from West Haven, we stopped at a small park. The kitten chased Cassie around the park, then went off on his own. When he was uncomfortably far away, I yelled, "Hey, kitten, come back!"

He didn't.

"Kitten, come back!"

He continued to ignore me.

I wanted so badly to yell his name—I'd yet to let myself utter it —but I couldn't get myself to do it. I couldn't give myself *hope.*

A few minutes later, he scampered back on his own.

Back in the car, idling in the parking lot, I stared at the little kitten in my lap. Then I glanced at Cassie. She was staring at me with her large amber eyes. I could almost sense her saying, "It is, Jerry. *It is.*"

I pulled out my phone and searched, "Kitten growth chart."

After comparing the kitten in my lap to the pictures and the weights. (I grabbed a five-pound dumbbell from the back of the U-Haul and compared that to the kitten—the dumbbell was heavier), I deduced the kitten was between five or six months old.

I did the math. Today was October 13th. I split the difference and subtracted five and a half months, which meant the kitten was born right around May 1st.

Hugo died on February 24th.

My heart sank.

I turned to Cassie and shook my head. "It isn't him."

I mean, what was Hugo's soul doing? Just hanging around for a little over two months waiting for a kitten to be born? Surely, thousands of kittens were born before this kitten. Wouldn't Hugo's soul have gone into them? And furthermore, dead dogs' souls do not go into kittens, so what did it even matter?

Cassie's ears flattened.

I rubbed her head and said, "Don't worry, girl. We're still gonna keep him."

Even though the kitten wasn't Hugo, I was still in love with him. He was so cute. And he was already potty trained.

I rubbed the kitten's little black nose and said, "Looks like we're gonna have to come up with a name for you."

I put the car in drive and started back on the last leg of our nearly three thousand mile journey. Ten minutes later, I merged onto 1-95 North. A mile later, I crossed into Connecticut. We were three minutes into the Nutmeg State when I pulled over onto the shoulder of the highway with a loud screech.

My heart was beating wildly.

You don't get a soul when you're born. You get a soul when you're *made.*

I fumbled for my phone and searched "Cat pregnancy length."

I clicked on a link and then there it was: Cat / Gestation period, 58 - 67 days.

58 - 67 days.

A little over two months.

It fit.

It *all* fit.

I looked at Cassie and I said, "I don't know how it happened, but you're right. *It is him.*"

Her ears went up and her tail started to helicopter.

I looked down at the little kitten in my lap and whispered, "Hugo?"

The kitten's tail fluttered and his butt wiggled. I picked him up and he gave my nose a soft lick.

"You came back," I cried. *"You came back."*

* * *

Hugo lets out a second impatient, "Meeeooooowww!" and I bend down to pick up his ball. Before I'm able to grab it, a blur that is Wally races in and picks it up in his mouth, then tears down the beach. Hugo gives chase and the two end up in a ferociously adorable wrestling match twenty yards down the shore.

I turn and glance over my shoulder and see Megan and Cassie both watching the pair intently. Megan is sitting in the sand with Cassie between her legs. Both of them have their eyes trained on Wally and Hugo wrestling. Megan's dimple is visible from twenty feet away.

* * *

When I pulled up to our small house twelve days earlier, Megan ran out the front door and tackled me with kisses. It took her a few moments to realize there was a little kitten sniffing Wally's butt.

"Oh, my gosh!" Megan shrieked. "A kitten!"

She plucked him up from the ground and began kissing his little head. After eight to ten kisses, she asked, "Where did you get him?"

"I found him." I paused, then added, "Well, actually, I suppose *he* found me."

"What do you mean?"

I smiled meekly and said, "This might sound crazy, but I'm pretty sure—no, I'm *positive*—that little cat is Hugo."

I expected her to shake her head, to cut her eyes at me, to tell me I was off my rocker. And rightly so. But she didn't.

She simply said, "Wow, that's amazing!" Then she turned to Hugo and said, "Hi, *Hugo*. How are you liking your new body? Probably took some getting used to, huh, buddy?"

And that was that.

A minute later, I was getting the grand tour of my new house.

* * *

I walk over to Megan and Cassie and plop down next to them. I lean over and give Megan a long kiss, then scratch Cassie's ears. Cassie glances up at me for a brief moment, then returns her gaze to Hugo and Wally, who are still wrestling in the sand.

"You don't have to watch him constantly," I say with a laugh. "He's fine."

She ignores me, her head making micro-adjustments as she follows Hugo's every move.

"Guess what?" Megan asks. She doesn't give me time to guess. "My website just went live!" she says, clapping. Then she picks her phone up and passes it to me. "Tell me what you think."

I swipe her phone and the main page of her website comes up. *Treats Pet & Hooman Bakery.*

I thumb through her site for a few minutes, then say, "It's great!" Which is true. Alex designed it, so I knew it would be.

The store is located in a busy shopping area four blocks from the beach—Seabluff Beach—where we are right now. Megan is planning on having a Grand Opening on Black Friday—in a little over a month—and she's clocking tons of hours at the store, over-seeing every last detail.

I couldn't believe the logistics that went into opening a new store: vendors, licenses, store design, signage, hundreds of tiny details. It made writing a book seem easy. On that note, I've been writing five to ten pages a day for the last week and my book is starting to take shape. I'm hoping to get it to Chuck by March or April.

Megan and I spend the next few minutes chatting about the new Netflix series we're currently binging. When she finds out I watched an episode without her, she gives me a soft slap on the leg.

We both laugh and soon we're half wrestling—but mostly kissing—in the sand. Cassie snuggles her way into the fun and a moment later, both Hugo and Wally join in.

I realize in that moment, I'm the happiest I've ever been.

Hugo

The bed is full. Jerry is on one side and Megan is on the other. Sometimes I still sleep on the pillow next to Jerry's head, but Megan always picks me up and moves me. She likes to have her head right next to Jerry's. Wally is in the middle of the bed, curled up in a tight ball. Cassie is at the foot of the bed, her chest rising and falling. A few moments ago, I was asleep next to her, curled into her side.

I jump off the bed and land silently on the carpet. Then I pad out of the bedroom and to the back door. There's a rubber flapping door—similar to the one at the farm—and I push through it and into the backyard.

This backyard is bigger than our old backyard. Much bigger. There are trees—though not as tall as the trees before and shaped different—scattered all over. The trees' leaves have fallen and cover the ground in large piles of gold.

The leaves are the same color as the Big Cat's eyes.

The Big Cat, New Home, Sara, Mom...it all seems so long ago.

A lifetime ago.

I scamper through the yard to one of the large trees. I climb it, then crawl out onto one of the thick branches. I lie down and listen. I'm still getting used to the new sounds. The new chirps. The new rustles. The new barks of nearby dogs.

There's been a lot to get used to here. A new house (it's not as big), a new dog (Wally!), a new human (Megan!), new smells, a new lake.

As for my Lake, I never got to go in. But luckily, there's something here even better than the lake. Something called the Ocean. It's so big that you can't see the other side. The water tastes the same as the lake that wasn't my Lake and if you drink it, it will give you the poops. But it's so much fun. There were only waves on my Lake every once in a while when it was windy, but even when it isn't windy, there are waves in the ocean. (I'm not really sure about all this wave stuff.)

After a few minutes, I jump down, then I climb the fence and make my way to the front yard and the street. I prowl my *territory* for the next couple of hours, following my nose to different smells. I keep watch for raccoons (there are lots of raccoons here) or other Outside cats.

I don't see any tonight.

I hear a dog bark and head in that direction. I climb a fence and find him in *his* backyard, lying next to a doghouse that could easily be Leroy's. He's a big tan dog—nearly as big as I used to be —and half his body extends from the opening of the doghouse. I watch as he licks one of his giant paws with a massive tongue.

That's what I miss the most.

The bigness.

The big paws. The huge tongue. The long stride. And the loudness that came with the bigness.

I think of how easy my journey would have been if I was big. I would have made it back in half the time. Maybe less. Then again, being so big would have made it nearly impossible to hide from the humans. I would have kept getting *found*. And if I was big, I never would have seen Calandia. I wouldn't have been able to even get down into the sewer. So maybe I *wouldn't* have made it. Maybe my smallness is what allowed me to make it back. Maybe I was only able to make it back because I was a cat.

I jump down to the ground and walk a few steps toward the dog. His ears go rigid and he stops licking his paw. He glances up at me.

"Hi," I meow.

He leaps up, growling, and races toward me.

I run back to the fence and climb up. Once at the top, I peer down at the snarling dog reared up against the fence.

I can feel his loud bark against my whiskers.

Is this how I used to be?

The backyard lights flip on and a human walks out and says, "Jerome! Stop barking!" The human squints, then says, "Leave that stupid cat alone."

Stupid cat?

More like, *stupid* dog.

I give Jerome a goodbye hiss, then find my way back to the street. The stars are out in full and I glance up.

All those souls.

I still don't know why the Maker decided not to make me a star. Calandia said that I'll have to ask Him. And I will. (But hopefully, not for a while.)

I told Cassie about my entire journey, but her favorite part was hearing about "souls" and that when a dog dies their soul becomes a star. This made Cassie's tail twirl and then she said something about *still* being able to watch over me, Jerry, Megan, and Wally. (I'm not sure exactly what she meant. She's so smart; sometimes it's hard to understand what she means.)

On my way back to the house, I hear a light rustle in a bush and I go to investigate.

Speaking of souls.

It's a mouse.

I stalk him for a few minutes, then I pounce. Then I swallow him whole. I still prefer a big bowl of kibble or a tin of cat food or best yet, a can of tuna, but I still enjoy the occasional mouse.

A minute later, I push back through the rubber door and stop. Cassie is lying on the floor next to the door. Waiting for me.

Her eyes open and she pushes herself up slowly. She walks over and gives me a few sniffs, then a couple of licks on my head.

Cassie doesn't like it when I go out at night, but I assured her I'm fine. If I could survive living in the Mountains, survive snakes, bears, and owls, then there's nothing here that could hurt me. (Well, except cars. But I learned my lesson there.)

Plus, I told her cats are almost indestructible!

I follow Cassie back to the bed, then jump up. Megan has moved over, and there's plenty of room on Jerry's pillow. I curl up next to his head and give his nose a soft lick.

Cassie

When I wake up to get a drink of water, Hugo is gone. I know he's at it again. Back outside. Doing whatever it is that he does at night. I don't think Jerry knows he goes out. That each night, he sneaks out the little rubber door and heads into the night. I followed him the first night. I watched him scamper up one of the trees, then jump the fence.

From all the stories Hugo told about his long trip home, I know he doesn't need me to watch over him. That he doesn't need me to protect him. I know I shouldn't worry, but I can't help it. (I worry about raccoons and mean dogs and bad humans and all sorts of other things.) I don't want to lose him again.

After a long drink of water, I go and lie down near the small rubber door. My eyes grow heavy and I think back to what Hugo said about how dogs' souls become stars after they die. My tail thumps against the floor as I think about looking down on Jerry from up so high.

What a view it will be.

I know it isn't long until I will be a star. I know from the way my hips hurt and the way I breathe after I run down the beach and how I'm always tired and how sometimes I have to squint to see things. (I know I'm slowly becoming Storm). I'm in no rush, I still have plenty to do here, but like the tadpole headed toward Frogdom, I know I'm headed toward Stardom.

(From what Hugo said, I'm pretty sure all dogs are Chosen Ones, except for a few that become mice. I would like to meet this Calandia, this "two different colored-eyes cat," and ask her a bunch of questions myself. Such as: *what is really happening on Bang Day?* And *where do magical grassy brownies come from?* And *is there such a thing as Super blueberries?* And *what is the number after ten?*)

It's hard to imagine that a few months ago, it was only Jerry and me (and the tadpoles). And now it's Jerry, Me, Hugo, Wally, and Megan.

I love Wally and Megan more each day. Just when I think I can't love them any more, Wally will go and do something so silly (like get stuck in one of Jerry's sweatshirts) or Megan will scratch me in a new spot (how did I not know this spot existed?) or remind me how beautiful and special I am.

As for Hugo, it didn't take long for Hugo and me to get back to our old ways. Wrestling with him is different (I have to be a lot more gentle) and he's much harder to catch (he's so quick), but other than that, I hardly even notice he's a cat.

The biggest difference is with Jerry. Not bad different. Just different. I don't think he needs me to protect him anymore. And it isn't because he's so happy (if Jerry had a tail it would be twirling all day long). I don't think it's my job anymore. It's Megan's job now.

(I'm happy to pass the torch. Protecting is so much work.)

And without having to worry about all this protecting (I still worry about Hugo; I will always worry about Hugo), I can concentrate on loving.

There's a soft thud and I glance up to see Hugo pushing

through the rubber door. I push myself up, a sharp pain shooting through my back leg, then stand. I walk over and give him a few sniffs.

Another mouse, Hugo!

I give him a few licks on the head, then I watch as he jumps on the bed and then curls up in a ball next to Jerry's head. I watch as he falls asleep. Then I walk around the bed and watch Megan sleep. (She hardly makes any noise at all.) Then I watch Wally. (He's on his side and sometimes he makes little huffing noises. I hope he's having a good dream.) Then I pad around the bed and watch Jerry. He's on his stomach and he makes his loud *urnggggggg, urnggggggggg, urnggggggggg.*

Still after all these years—these *ten*—this is my favorite sound in the world.

I listen and watch Jerry for a long time, then I pad into the living room and jump onto the couch. There are big windows in the roof and I can see the black sky.

And all the twinkling souls.

23

"EPILOGUE"

Jerry

My character has just been extradited to the United States and he sees his parents for the first time since six weeks before 9/11. Six weeks before the towers fell and he fled to Mexico, leaving everyone to think he was one of the more than three thousand people who died.

It's a fun chapter to write; the bittersweet reunion of love and shame.

Hugo is fast asleep in my lap. He never misses an opportunity to sit on my lap. Or Megan's. And now that he weighs roughly a hundred pounds less than he used to, it's a tad more comfortable for me.

Over the past couple weeks, I've only noticed one thing about him that's slightly different than before. He doesn't chase squirrels. Or birds. Or even the one rabbit we saw.

I'm not sure why.

And I suppose I'll never know.

Wally and Cassie are both snuggled up next to my legs. Wally is asleep, but Cassie is awake. She gives my shin a lick every once in a while to remind me she's there.

I pop the jar of pickles on the desk open and slink one out. I've been going through a jar of pickles a week for the last three weeks. I crack a big bite off in my teeth. Wally stirs at the sound and I feed him a small bite. Of the three, he's the only one that likes pickles.

I finish the remainder of the pickle, clean my hands with a wet-wipe, then resume writing.

Three hours later, I complete the chapter.

"Who wants a snack?" I ask.

Hugo jumps off my lap and I stand.

All three follow me into the kitchen and I hand-feed each of them a few blueberries and little pieces of turkey.

I make myself a sandwich and a smoothie, then I walk into the living room. It's the second week of November and there are still ten boxes of Megan's stuff that need unpacking.

She's been so busy at the store—it is opening in eleven days—and she promised to unpack the boxes once the "frenzy" was over.

I walk over and open one of the boxes. It's *another* box of cookware. How many different pots, pans, and utensils does someone need?

I carry the box to the kitchen and spend the next fifteen minutes finding homes for the different items, many of which, I've never seen before.

The next box is a bunch of blankets and I stuff most of them into a small utility closet, then drape a woven blanket at the foot of the bed. It's been getting colder and colder each night, and we'll need the extra warmth here soon.

Two hours later and there are only four boxes remaining. I open the top of one and see a bunch of miscellaneous items, including a couple of books. I reach into the box and extract a well-worn novel.

Where the Red Fern Grows.

I shake my head and chuckle; just when you think the two of us can't have more in common.

I set the book on the carpet and reach in and grab the second book.

The Hobbit.

My eyebrows furrow slightly.

I reach into the box and pull out a stuffed animal.

It's brown and tan.

Gizmo.

"What the hell?" I mutter.

I pick up the box and flip it over, emptying the entire contents onto the tan carpet.

I pull items from the pile one-by-one.

A rubber-banded stack of Garbage Pail Kids. (*Barfin Barbara* on the top.)

A G.I. Joe.

A recipe for chocolate chip and Skittles cookies

A crumpled $2 bill.

A Viewfinder with a Scooby Doo disc.

A broken Game Boy cartridge—Skate or Die.

It's all there.

Even my molar.

It's every single item from Morgan's and my time capsule.

* * *

I stuff half the contents into a backpack and then I hop on my bicycle. It's a little over a mile to the shopping district near the beach. My legs pump wildly against the pedals and I screech to a halt in front of Treats less than five minutes later.

I throw the door to the store open.

The sound of a drill fills the small space and a man is on his knees putting the final touches on a large wooden display case. Megan is standing with another man near a long, glassed bakery window that will soon be filled with Pawcakes, Woof Crème Pies and other creations.

Neither one of them hears me enter under the noise of the drill and I stomp forward. When I'm a few feet away, the man glances toward me and Megan's eyes soon follow.

"What's wrong?" Megan asks. "Is everything okay?"

My face must be telling quite the story.

I'm not sure how to answer this question, so I just say, "I need to talk to you."

Megan nods, excuses herself from the man, and follows me to the back of the space and through a door to her office.

"What's going on? Are the pups okay?" Even though Hugo was technically a cat now, we both still referred to the three as the pups.

"Yeah, they're all fine."

She lets out a small sigh, then says, "So what's going on?"

I rip the backpack off my back and set it down on the small desk. A few papers cascade to the floor. My hands are shaking and it takes me a moment to unzip the bag. After two tries, I unzip it, flip it over, and let the contents rain down on the desk.

"This!" I say.

Megan peers at the various items I last saw twenty-five years earlier and shakes her head.

"What about it?" she says.

"Where," I stammer, "did you get this stuff?"

"I found it," she says. "A long time ago. When I was a kid."

"When you say you found it, do you mean you *dug it up*?"

She takes a step back. "How did you know that?"

I shake my head at her, "Don't worry about that. Just tell me how you got it."

She lets out a long breath, then says, "My parents used to fight all the time when I was in middle school. There was a wooded area not far from our house and I would go there whenever they started fighting. I was there one day, just walking around and I tripped on something. It was the handle of an old shovel. I dug it out of the ground and I carried it around for a little while. All of the sudden, I stopped and I dug the shovel into the dirt. I dug a hole and that's when I found this old box covered in duct tape."

"Wait," I say holding up my hand. "What made you dig in that exact spot?"

"I don't know." She shrugs. "I just stopped and started digging."

"Okay," I say, not convinced. "Then what?"

"Wait, why do you care so much?"

"Please, just finish. *Then what?*"

She nods lightly, then says, "I pulled the box out and wiped off the top. Written in black marker on the duct tape, it said, 'To be opened in 2001' or something like that."

"And what year was this?"

"I was fourteen, so it would have been 2006. I figured whoever buried it must have forgotten about it."

They did forget about it, I almost say. At least one of them did. *The other one was dead.*

"I took the box home," Megan says. "I knew the stuff in there was special and so I kept it."

She reaches out her arm and grabs my elbow. "Now tell me why you care so much?"

"Because that's my stuff."

"What?" she says, with a laugh. "That can't be."

I pick up the copy of *Where the Red Fern Grows* and wave it at her. "This, *mine*." I pick up the stack of Garbage Pail Kids. "This, *mine*." I pick up the crumpled $2 bill. "*Mine*." The viewfinder. "*Mine*."

"Holy shit!" Megan cries. "Wait, what about the other stuff?" She picks up the Gremlin stuffed animal and shakes it. "Whose is this?"

I stare at her. I soak up every inch of her holding the stuffed animal.

That's when it hits me: if it was possible for Hugo, then maybe…

Everything comes rushing in at once.

The first time we met, Megan asked, *"You sure we didn't go to school together when we were kids?"*

Megan's nightmare about drowning in the lake.

Sequoia telling Megan, *"You have an old soul."*

How much they both loved to bake.

How they both loved duct tape.

How they both clapped their hands together when they were really happy.

Then the timeline floods in: Morgan died on July, 28th, 1991. Megan was born March 17th, 1992. Megan was born almost *exactly nine months* after Morgan died.

I think back to Megan's question about the stuffed animal. *"Whose is this?"*

"I think," I say, my eyes beginning to water. "That…it was *yours.*"

Megan's face falls.

She blinks her soft brown eyes twice.

"Morgan?" I say softly.

Her bottom lip begins to tremble and then she says it. "Bear?"

* * *

The time capsule opened up a floodgate and over the course of the next several months, little snippets continue to come back to Megan. Montages of her old life. She called them, "Shadows."

"I had another shadow yesterday," she would say. Then she would describe some event from her childhood, from her eleven years on this earth as Morgan. Sometimes I would be in her shadow, like when Megan described in perfect detail camping in her backyard, toasting S'mores, and burnt marshmallow dripping onto her leg. Or when she finally beat my record on Tetris. She even remembered her exact score.

The five of us are in the backyard. Hugo is sitting in one of the trees, little budding leaves just beginning to grow. Wally is sniffing at the trunk of the tree, pawing at the bark, wondering how to get up there.

Cassie is sitting at Megan's and my feet, her head lifting every so often to survey what's going on. It's a rare day off for Megan, which means both she and Cassie are off work. Megan started bringing Cassie to the store when it first opened and she'd become the resident shop dog. It was amazing to see her greet the dogs and humans who came into the store. As for the store, so far it'd been a rousing success. Sales were higher than projected and she was making a killing off dog birthday cakes.

I reach down and rub my hands through the fur above Cassie's nose.

She sighs with pleasure, then lays her head back down. A few moments later, my cell phone rings.

I check the caller ID.

It's Chuck.

I've been anticipating this call and my skin begins to warm.

"Hey, Chuck," I say, answering.

I push myself up and Megan gives me a soft smile.

"Jerry!" Chuck screams.

I take a few steps into the grass, let out a long nervous breath, then ask, "So?"

I sent him my book on May 6th, three days earlier.

"It's amazing!" he screams.

"Seriously?"

"Dude, we're talking bestseller here. Like *number one* bestseller. I already sent it to Alison and she's flipping out. I think she just got to the part where Cassie destroys the wedding."

I laugh, recalling the memory.

I scratched the 9/11 book when another idea struck me.

A magical idea.

"Do you have a title for it yet?" Chuck asks.

As usual, I still didn't have a title when I sent it to him.

I glance over my shoulder at Hugo, lying in the crook of two branches. Then to Megan, sitting on a chair on the back porch.

"I was thinking," I say, grinning. *"The Speed of Souls."*

AUTHOR'S NOTE

First off, thank you for reading. I know there are millions of books out there vying for your time and money and I appreciate you picking this one. I hope you enjoyed Hugo, Cassie, and Jerry half as much as I enjoyed writing them.

A lot of things in this book stem from my real life. I do live in South Lake Tahoe. There is a baby pool in my backyard that fills up with tadpoles each year. There is an old husky named Storm who lives next door. The Farmer's Market is real. Live@Lakeview is real. The 4th of July celebration is pretty accurate. But most importantly, I have two dogs and they are my world!

Here are some pictures of my kiddos! (The first two are Penny and the second two are Potter. Penny is a Shih Tzu-poodle and Potter is a Cavalier-poodle.)

* * *

As for how this story came to be. Well, there's a doozy of a story behind this story. (One I have been dying to tell for almost three years.)

So here it is:

Halloween 2015.

I'd been living in South Lake Tahoe for six months. I had a Buddy the Elf costume and I planned to go to the casinos for the big Halloween bash, but as I was getting ready to go out, I lost all motivation. Instead, I logged onto a dating site called OkCupid.

Within a few minutes, I'd set up my profile and within the hour, I'd matched with a beautiful young lady (who from this point on I will refer to as Susan).

Susan and I spent the next three hours messaging back and forth. She was a huge dork, loved Harry Potter, had two dogs, and suffice it to say, we hit it off.

The next day, I was at the lake with my two dogs and my phone rang. It was Susan. (We'd traded phone numbers the night before, but I was still surprised by her call. Who called anyone anymore?) We ended up talking for a good hour. For the next week, every day we texted, talked, and traded pictures.

I was smitten. A smitten kitten.

I wanted to meet up with her. The problem was: Susan lived on the California coast, seven hours away (near San Luis Obispo).

Before moving to South Lake Tahoe, I lived in San Diego for four years and I desperately missed surfing. So I hatched a plan to drive out to see Susan and to do some surfing.

Susan was all for it.

So the next week, I packed up my two dogs and I drove the seven hours to the coast. Susan and I had been texting throughout my drive and we had plans to meet up that night. I arrived at my hotel around four, went surfing for a couple hours, then puttered around waiting for Susan to text me. (It turns out Susan had to go to some family function, but she only had to pop in, then we would meet up.)

I patiently waited at the hotel for her text.

It never came

She'd totally blown me off.

The next day, I got a text from Susan that she'd gotten food poisoning and ended up having to go to the emergency room. She was still at the hospital. She sent me a picture in her hospital bed with an IV in her arm.

I was bummed, but I understood.

I'd prepared a gift bag for her with a few of my books and some other stupid little things (I think a few of her favorite snacks that she'd told me about) and I asked her if I could drop it off at her house.

She sent me her address and on my way out of town, I swung by and dropped the gift bag on her front steps. As I did this, I could see through her front window and I saw her two dogs. She'd sent several pictures of the two dogs and I already felt like I knew them.

Then I drove back to South Lake Tahoe.

Susan and my relationship continued for the next month. We talked on the phone every day—for hours. But each time I brought up her coming to visit me or my going to visit her again, something always came up. It seemed a little bit fishy (all her excuses), but Susan was very adamant that we were going to get together "soon." She'd bought me a Christmas present and she said would only give it to me in person.

Finally, we made concrete plans. I was going to drive back to Colorado for Christmas, then on my way back from Colorado, I would drive to see her and we'd hang out for a few days. So after spending a week in Colorado for Christmas, I headed out on December 28th.

The drive from Denver to San Luis Obispo is eighteen hours. My plan was to split the drive into two days and I'd booked a hotel in Primm, Nevada, thirty miles outside of Las Vegas.

Eight hours into my trip, headed south through Utah, I got a text from Susan.

Her dog had died.

He was hit by a car.

His name was Hugo.

* * *

I was in the middle of Utah and I'd just started to head south toward Vegas. I easily could have turned around and started back north, toward Salt Lake City, and then driven to South Lake Tahoe. But I'd already paid for my hotel room in Primm and if I'm being honest and I'm trying to be here: I still wanted to go visit Susan. I mean, we'd been talking and texting for two months. I even had a big stocking full of Christmas presents for her.

So selfishly, I texted her: Do you still want me to come?

She never responded.

But of course, she was mourning her dog's death, so I totally understood.

A few hours later, I reached Primm and I pulled into the Golden Nugget Casino where I was staying. We (I had my two dogs with me) headed up to our hotel room. The room wreaked of smoke and it was dingy and dark. And the bathroom was grimy. No wonder it only cost me $49.

As my dogs and I curled up on the cheap, smelly mattress, I decided that I wouldn't drive to see Susan the next day. I would let her grieve. (If one of my dog's died I wouldn't want to see anyone! I would be an absolute mess!) Instead, I would just drive back to Lake Tahoe.

Everything changed two hours later.

My stomach started to gurgle.

The please, I beg you, please don't be what I think this is going to be gurgle.

I ran to the bathroom and I threw up. And I threw up. And I threw up some more.

I'd had the distinct pleasure of having food poisoning on four occasions prior to this, so I knew I would just have to gut out (pun intended) the next six to twelve hours and then I would be fine.

I can't tell you how many times I was sick that night.

Plenty.

But at some point I did fall asleep. On the disgusting bathroom floor, next to the disgusting toilet.

The next day, I called for a late check out.

If it were possible, my stomach hurt worse than it did the previous night. And the pukes had turned into the shits. I couldn't go ten minutes without having to go to the bathroom.

It was obvious there was no way I could drive back to Tahoe. But I couldn't handle staying another night in the same disgusting hotel room. I needed somewhere clean. With a nice bed. And a bathtub.

Between cramping (the worst stomach cramps I've ever had in

my life) and running to the bathroom, I logged onto Hotels.com and I found a room at a three-star hotel in Las Vegas for a hundred and fifty bucks.

But the question was: could I make the thirty minute drive without crapping my pants?

And so began the riskiest drive of my life.

Somehow, I made it. I just remember running into the hotel and tying my dogs' leashes to a random potted plant and then running around frantically (my hands holding my bottom) looking for a bathroom.

Soon the dogs and I were in our room. And it was amazing. It was big and clean and there was this white fluffy bed and this huge bathtub.

I could be sick in luxury.

And sick I was.

All day and all night.

(That's when I realized that I wasn't dealing with food poisoning and it was probably the stomach flu.)

The next day I was still in no shape to drive and I booked the same room. This was December 30th in Las Vegas. The price stayed the same ($150/night), but they warned me the next night, New Year's Eve, it jumped to $350/night.

There's no way I would need to stay another night, so I wasn't worried.

How wrong I would be.

I continued to be sick as a dog. And on that note, I had two dogs with me. Two dogs who needed to go outside five or six times a day. So there I would be, wracked by stomach pains, doubled over, yelling at my dogs in the small grass courtyard to "Please poop! Please, I'm begging you! Pooooop!"

The next day, I was still sick.

It was New Year's Eve and the only hotel room I could find under $200 was thirty minutes away, near Lake Las Vegas.

Luckily it was another three-star hotel. That's where I rang in the New Year.

On the 1st, day four of being sick, I was lying in bed. (I still had terrible cramps, but I could finally eat a little bit. A banana and some crackers a few times a day.) I'd lost eight pounds and you could see all my ribs.

Throughout the past four days, I'd traded text messages with Susan. I couldn't stop thinking about her dog, Hugo. How he got hit by that car. And in my state of delirium, the sickest I've ever been in my life, this crazy thought popped into my head: What if Hugo came back as a cat?

Then I started thinking about how Hugo's soul was on its way up to heaven when it zoomed into this little kitten.

And boom. It just hit me.

The Speed of Souls.

I spent the next hour making a rough outline of the story on my computer.

* * *

I spent two more nights in Vegas. I finally drove home on January 4th. I was sick for seven days. I spent over a thousand dollars on hotel bills.

It would take me a few more months to realize that if Susan wasn't cat-fishing me entirely, that she had no desire to ever meet.

There's no doubt in my mind that if Susan doesn't catfish me, if Hugo isn't hit by a car, and if I don't get the mother of all stomach viruses, than The Speed of Souls never gets written.

So yeah, thanks Susan.

* * *

I want to thank a few people for beta reading and editing the manuscript: my mom, Janell Parque, Kari Biermann, Nadine Villalobos, and Nelda Hirsh.

And lastly, but really, firstly, I want to thank God for giving me this incredible gift. I feel so blessed and thankful each day. I am humbled by His greatness.

If you enjoyed the book, I will ask one thing of you. Please either 1) write a review wherever you bought the book or 2) tell three people about the book. (You don't have to do both, but I implore you to do one.)

If you liked this book, I'm guessing you'll enjoy my *3:00 a.m.* series. There is cat named Lassie who is sure to make you smile :)

You can learn more about me at www.nickpirog.com.

God is love.

-Nick

June 18, 2018
South Lake Tahoe

ALSO BY NICK PIROG

The Henry Bins Series

3:00 a.m.

3:10 a.m.

3:21 a.m

3:34 a.m.

3:46 a.m.

The Thomas Prescott Series

Unforeseen

Gray Matter

The Afrikaans

Show Me

Jungle Up

Other Books

The Speed of Souls: A Novel for Dog Lovers

Arrival

The Lassie Files

Made in the USA
Las Vegas, NV
04 January 2022

39839307R10171